DROWNING LESSONS

DROWNING LESSONS

STORIES BY PETER SELGIN

THE UNIVERSITY OF GEORGIA PRESS

Athens & *London*

Published by the University of Georgia Press

Athens, Georgia 30602

www.ugapress.org

© 2008 by Peter Selgin

All rights reserved

Designed by Walton Harris

Set in Garamond Premier Pro

Printed and bound by Thomson-Shore

Printed in the United States of America

12 11 10 09 08 C 5 4 3 2 1

Library of Congress Cataloging-in-Publication Data

Selgin, Peter.

Drowning lessons : stories / by Peter Selgin.

    p. cm. — (The Flannery O'Connor Award for short fiction)

ISBN-13: 978-0-8203-3210-9 (hardcover : alk. paper)

ISBN-10: 0-8203-3210-0 (hardcover : alk. paper)

I. Title.

PS3619.E463D76 2008

813'.6—dc22   2008020377

British Library Cataloging-in-Publication Data available

for George, my brother

There is nothing but water in the holy pools.
I know, I have been swimming in them.

— KABIR

CONTENTS

DROWNING LESSONS

SWIMMING

HE PLACED THE OARS in their locks and the floating seat cushion on the backseat. He wrapped his goggles in the towel and dropped it between the forward seat and the bow, where the aluminum hull was dry. He pushed against the bow and felt the stern go buoyant as it splashed into the lake. When the prow touched water he gave a last shove, then climbed in and began rowing, eager to get to the float, his private place.

The water, except where he defiled it with the oars (and where insects frayed across its surface, making fern patterns), was smooth as glass. Already the sky had turned a deep, warm blue streaked with white, like chalk marks on a slate board. A single-engine plane grumbled. On the close shore, rings of reflected sunlight thrown up by his wake shimmied like pale silk garters up the trunks of birch trees. As always, he tried not to splash while rowing.

He was seventy-two years old.

Every August for the past twelve years Frank and his wife, Dorothy, had come to the small lake in northern New Jersey, less than an hour's drive from New York City. Theirs was one of a dozen cabins dotting Lake Juliet's wrinkled shore. By planting flowers and a vegetable garden with tomatoes and squash and hanging their daughter's art school watercolors over the couch, they had made the place their own. There was no telephone, no radio, no television. The lake was the only distraction. They liked it that way.

It was not even a lake, really, but an overgrown pond. In fifteen minutes one could row from one end to the other. Still, they preferred to think of it as a lake, "our lake," they called it. It was where they came to escape the pounding heat and headaches of the subway, the black vulgar headlines of the *New York Post*, the noise and soot of traffic, and the tyranny of air-conditioning and closed windows. It was where, before retiring, he had come to escape his job as the supervisor of a four-color printing press, and she hers as a seller of advertisements for a fashionable glossy women's magazine.

Skimming close to the float, Frank pulled both oars out of the water, laid them inside, and glided the rest of the way. Once at the ladder, he grabbed it with one hand while securing a line around it with a clove hitch. Then, taking his towel and goggles, he climbed out of the boat and stood on the float, watching the last wisps of vapor melt off the lake's calm surface.

Back in their cabin, meanwhile, Dorothy prepared breakfast. She fried bacon and mixed pancake batter. For two people who understood each other very little, they had many understandings, one of which was that Frank would swim and she would cook breakfast. It was one of their many routines in a marriage that often seemed to consist of nothing but routines. Sometimes, standing on the float as he did now, Frank smelled, or imagined that he could smell, bacon frying. He could see Dorothy's arms holding the heavy skillet, the flesh of her triceps pillowy and droop-ing. She had been a good-looking woman once, her Irish features square and strong. But she had let herself go. Her once-slim waist was gone, and her arms and legs had lost their tone. Still, she had a lovely smile, her cheeks round and sweet as apricots ripe for picking, and her pale eyes were still bright. It saddened him to look down from those changeless eyes and see the rest of her so changed.

The sun struck the float full. Soon Frank's shoulders baked, and he could feel the day's heat singeing his cheeks and forehead. He stood there, his skin as dark and leathery as a catcher's mitt, scanning the water's surface. He had always prided himself on be-ing fit and trim. Unlike Dorothy, who now dressed modestly in loose-fitting clothes and seldom appeared naked even in private, Frank liked to live close to his skin. He liked the feel of his strong body, enjoyed its nakedness, here at the lake as well as back in their New York apartment — despite large untreated windows staring out into other apartments. His wife was always nagging him either to cover himself or to buy them curtains. But Frank did neither. "Let them look," he said, "if it gives them pleasure. It's the least we can do for our lovely neighbors."

Despite his boastful teasing, Frank understood that, while his wife was fairly typical, he was something of a freak. While Dorothy's body sagged and puffed like those of many women her age, his stood in sharp contrast to the bodies of other men in their seventies. He exercised fanatically, and because of this his belly and limbs were as hard, muscular, and lean as they had been at twenty-five, or even twenty. But his face, that of an ordinary man of seventy-two, with its creased forehead and sagging jaw and large ears sprouting white hairs, no longer went with the body underneath it. It was as though his head and his body belonged to two different people.

He spat into his swimming goggles, smeared saliva onto their lenses, snapped them on, and adjusted them.

Through the goggle lenses he saw something. On the near shore of the lake, some three hundred yards away, parked on the dam, was a small gray car. It had been years since Frank had last seen a car parked there. Near the dam stood a cabin nicknamed the Icehouse, used for that purpose a half century earlier, when the lake had been carved and carted away each winter. The least popular of the cabins, it lacked a septic system because of its proximity to the dam and had an outhouse instead. For as long as he could remember, the cabin had gone unrented and so had been overtaken by scraggly shrubs and weeds. Now, for the first time, a light burned softly inside.

Frank was not fond of change. When things were good, as they had always been at the lake, he liked them to stay just as they were, and so this sudden evidence of someone living in the Icehouse disturbed him, among other reasons because he chose to swim in this part of the lake for its privacy, for the luxury of being alone, all alone with the water and his healthy body. He would swim to shore and back, then lie on the float with his eyes closed, with the float lazily rocking him and the sun painting abstract masterpieces under his eyelids. He would catnap and sometimes even dream. That was his routine. And now it was threatened, shattered.

He rubbed his arms, coughed up some phlegm, spat in the water.

Oh well, he thought. Things change. What can you do?
He plunged.

An arrow-shaped ache pierced his sternum; his mouth filled with cold green liquid. He spluttered and sloshed around ungracefully for a moment, amazed if not slightly alarmed by the audacity of a man his age plunging like a boy of ten or twelve. When his heart had settled a little, he looked toward the point on shore that was his destination. The car was still there, as was that light inside the cabin, its white trim obscured by ragged bushes. And something else too: a dot of bright red. Then the red dot moved. Someone was walking in front of the cabin.

He told himself to ignore whoever it was and swam, beginning with short easy strokes and increasing their length and speed gradually, letting his breath explode underwater, twisting his mouth into the air to refill his lungs, then exploding again, like a piston, his feet scarcely breaking the water's surface behind him as they kicked. As he swam, the lake held him, guided him, stroking his skin and seeming to be in perfect sympathy with every inch of his body, his flesh. He felt himself merging with the water as one merges with another person's body in the act of love. In truth, swimming was as close to lovemaking as Frank got these days, for Dorothy no longer attracted him, nor did she seem to find him attractive anymore, not that way, at any rate. She acknowledged neither his flesh nor her own, as if there were no such thing, only flowers, books, and jigsaw puzzles. Meanwhile, Frank exercised, growing stronger and firmer. Over time, like two rowboats, their bodies drifted further and further apart, with Frank rowing like crazy and Dorothy serenely floating. From this awareness Frank swam away as though swimming from death itself.

When he reached the shore, Frank stopped and treaded water as gently as possible, catching his breath. This was the part he liked best. He barely moved his hands to keep floating. The merest fluttering motion of his fingers sufficed. Aside from his breathing, there was no sound. But as he floated on his back with his goggles collecting fog and the tops of birches swaying, he suddenly heard a series of piercing yelps. Turning, he saw a dark, blurry shape atop the dam. He pulled off his goggles. A dog, a German shepherd pup, stood barking at him.

He heard a woman's voice.

"Stop it, Harry!"

The woman ran up and put the dog on a leash, then stood there holding the dog. "I'm sorry," she said looking down at him from on top of the dam. She had dark eyes and a round, pleasant face framed by hair just beginning to turn gray in places. She looked at him. She wore a red sweater.

"You must be a strong swimmer," she said.

"Thank you," he said, a little embarrassed, as if he'd been caught in some private act of intimacy.

"I sure wish I could swim like that."

"Do you swim?" he asked, still treading water. The bottom could not have been more than inches away. Still, he chose not to touch it.

"Yes, but not half as good as you."

Frank felt himself blush. It was a feeling he hadn't felt in a long time.

"Are you renting one of the cabins?" the woman asked.

"F-Troop," he said, referring to his cabin's nickname. All the cabins at Lake Juliet had nicknames.

The woman smiled down at him, her dog panting gently at her side. She looked about thirty-five, maybe forty.

"This is my first time here," she explained. Her eyebrows were heavy and dark in contrast to her hair. Under the red sweater she wore khaki shorts and sneakers with no socks.

"You here for the whole summer?" she asked.

"Just one month. And you?"

"Weekends only," she said. "My name is Juliet, by the way."

"Juliet? Like the lake."

"Yes, like the lake."

"Mine's Frank."

"Are you here by yourself?" the woman asked.

"With my wife."

"She doesn't swim?"

"No."

"That's a shame."

The air felt colder than the water. Frank began to shiver. "I'd better keep moving," he said.

"Oh, sorry. I didn't mean to interrupt you."

"That's fine."

"Nice to meet you," said the woman. "If you get a chance, maybe sometime you can give me some swimming pointers."

"Be glad to." Frank spit in his goggles again, rubbed the spit around inside them, and snapped them back on. "It's all in the breathing," he said, and then he turned and started back to the float.

"How was your swim?"

Dorothy sat in a wicker chair eating toast and bacon and

reading her mystery novel. She always asked him how his swims were.

"Fine," he always answered.

Breakfast was on the table, with Frank's plate covered by a saucepan lid. Three pancakes, one egg, two strips of bacon, orange juice, coffee. He liked his bacon lean; she liked hers fat.

"Should we go to the farmers' market today?"

"All right," he said, eating his breakfast but with less appetite than usual. They didn't look at each other; they rarely looked at each other. It was part of the routine. Every so often, Frank would glance at Dorothy, but she would not seem to notice, or would pretend not to. Each time he looked at her, Frank felt increasingly disturbed and unhappy. What, after all, did they have to do with each other anymore, he wondered, aside from being husband and wife? Maybe I should have let myself go too, he told himself as he nibbled on a strip of bacon. I should have aged *with* her. Instead, I let her go ahead without me and now look: we've lost each other. Haven't we?

"There's someone renting the Icehouse this year," he said to break his own train of thought.

"Really? That's unusual," said Dorothy.

"Some woman," he said.

"Did you meet her?" she asked, still reading, bringing a coffee mug to her lips but not looking up.

"We exchanged pleasantries."

"What's her name?"

"Juliet."

"Juliet?"

"A coincidence, I'm sure," said Frank.

"Was she in the water?"

"No, no. She was on dry land. With her dog."

"She has a dog?"

"I looked up from my swim and there she was."

They were silent for a while. Frank could not bring himself to eat the second strip of bacon. For some reason it repulsed him.

"That cabin must be in terrible shape."

"I wouldn't know," he said.

"It hasn't been used for so long. It must be full of mildew."

"Maybe. Maybe not."

"Oh come on, Frank, how couldn't it be?"

"Things that haven't been used in a while can still be fixed."

"What?" She lowered her book. "What did you say?"

"You heard me."

"What's that got to do with anything?"

"Just because a thing hasn't been used doesn't mean there's something wrong with it."

"I was just saying it must be *moldy*."

"I know what you were saying," said Frank. "And I'm saying it's no big deal. You clean it up, spray a little Lysol, whatever. Just because a thing is out of shape — "

"For godsake, Frank, what are you getting worked up about?"

"I'm not getting worked up. I just don't hold to the philosophy that things go to pot and that's all there is to it."

"What are you talking about?"

"Nothing," he said, dropping his toast on his plate and carrying it to the sink. "I'm talking about nothing. Let's go to the farmers' market."

For the past twelve years the New Jersey countryside, with its lush, rolling hills and manicured farms, hadn't ceased to impress Frank and Dorothy, conditioned as they were to thinking of New Jersey as Newark and petroleum refineries. Neither spoke as Dorothy drove the hunkering blue rental car. Her mind, he decided, was on tomatoes. And his? It was on the woman who had rented the Icehouse. In thirty-seven years Frank had not thought of another woman. Oh, there had been that one time early in their marriage, but that had been nothing, had gone nowhere. Whereas this distressed him.

"What do you think about corn tonight?" said Dorothy.

"Huh?"

"Corn, what do you think of having corn?"

"Yeah, sure, whatever."

A quarter mile from the farmers' market, a half-acre bed of "pick-your-own" red and orange zinnias grew four feet tall. Once a week his wife picked a dozen to distribute throughout their cabin, putting them in every room. Frank watched through the rental-car windshield as Dorothy waded breast deep in a lake of fiery zinnias.

Before dinner that evening, as usual around four o'clock, Frank set out in the rowboat for his afternoon swim. By then the temperature had peaked. When he reached the float, his forehead and arms dripped sweat from rowing. He wasted no time mooring and putting his goggles on. Soon he was part of the water again, flowing through it as it flowed past him. When he reached the far shore, she stood there, on top of the dam, this time with no dog.

"Hi, there."

She wore a bright red bathing suit. A pair of goggles dangled from her fingers.

"I'll have to put up a no-wake sign here," she said.

"Excuse me?"

"You make such a big wake."

A joke. She was joking with him. He smiled.

"How about those pointers you promised me?"

"Pointers?" Now he was being coy. But things were happening too quickly, and he thought he should slow them down. He took off his goggles, rubbed the irritated skin around his eyes. "Oh, yeah, right," he said. "Sure. Whenever you're ready."

"I'm ready," said the woman from the Icehouse. Her bathing suit fit her snugly. Her calf muscles were strong. She looked fit.

"It's a free lake," he said. "Come on in."

As her body merged with the lake, he felt an odd tingle underwater, as if her bright red bathing suit charged the water with electricity. With her in the water, the lake suddenly felt colder, more quick and alive, while he felt warmer in it. She stood up to her chest in the water next to him. Her breasts were full, and though he tried hard he could not quite keep his eyes from the tawny shadow of her cleavage.

"Let's see you swim freestyle."

She swam a dozen yards, then turned and looked at him.

"Not bad. You've got a good, strong kick. A little hyperextension in the knees, which is good. But you need to work on your arms and breathing."

"I'm all ears," she said.

Frank explained. "Pretend the water's a sideways cliff you're trying to climb. Reach as far as you can, grab hold, and pull yourself along. As you pull your hands back, make sure that they're pushing hard against the water, the harder the better. Maximize that resistance. You follow?" The woman nodded. "And keep your fingers close together. Not touching, but close, like so." He showed her. "That's very important."

"I never knew that."

"Oh, yes," said Frank. "Very important."

She swam again, and he watched her. She had a very strong kick.

"Better," he said. "Now let's talk about your breathing. Now when I breathe —" he demonstrated, "— it's all in the exhale, see? Don't worry about inhaling. Just worry about exhaling. Push it out. Push it out. If you don't exhale hard enough, then you won't have room to get any new air inside your lungs. They're full of carbon dioxide. That's why you get winded."

"I never knew that, either."

"Well," said Frank, "now you know."

Together they swam to the float.

"How did you get to be such a good swimmer?" she asked as they sat catching their breaths.

"The funny thing is," he said, "I didn't start until I was in my forties."

"You're kidding?" Her eyelashes glistened with water. "Really?"

"It's the truth. I hated water. Hated it. Wouldn't go near it. When I was a kid, I wouldn't let my mother give me a bath. I never learned how to swim. Naturally, when I got drafted, they put me in the navy." He pointed with his chin toward the anchor tattooed on his arm.

"That figures," said the woman from the Icehouse.

"I was seventeen, on a Liberty ship. Sick to my stomach every day for thirty-nine days. Then we made the landing at Normandy.

I'll never forget. We had to jump from that big ship into this little LCS down there that looked about the size of a bathtub, and it's going like this and the Liberty ship is going like that, and I stood there, shaking my head, muttering no way, no way, until some son of a bitch kicks me in the rump and down I go. All of a sudden I'm in this tub, crouched on my belly, praying to God Almighty, waves the size of elephants washing over us. Finally we get to the beach and land and there's bullets flying everywhere and all I can think is hallelujah; I made it; I'm on dry land; *the war is over.* And I swore if I survived I would never, ever so much as look at water again." He shook his head.

"What changed your mind?"

"It was the damnedest thing. About thirty years ago I just *wanted* to do it. I wanted to go in the water. It was like shaking hands with a Nazi soldier, you know? I just made up my mind: I'm not going to have this *enemy* in my life. Instead I'm going to embrace it; I'm going to learn to *love it.* So I taught myself how to swim." He shook his head. "It wasn't hard."

"That's an amazing story," said the woman.

"Is it?"

"Yes, amazing."

He had told Dorothy the same story several times, but he did not remember her being amazed. He wondered if she was watching the float now. No, she was reading her best seller or shucking corn for dinner. Dorothy had long since lost any interest in his swimming. He could have drowned, for all she knew.

They swam back to the dam. In the shallow water, Frank gave her a few more pointers, showing her how far out of the water to lift her head and explaining to her again about breathing.

"It's the most important thing," he said. "When you swim

think of yourself as a breathing machine. Breathe, breathe, breathe. Everything else pretty much takes care of itself."

They met several more times. Her swimming improved greatly. One morning after they had swum together, she invited him for coffee. Inside, the Icehouse was cool, even cold, as if ice were still stored there. And it did smell faintly of mildew. Frank watched her open a can of dog food. Her arms were perfectly shaped, gloriously smooth, firm things. He thought of his wife in her baggy robe holding the bacon skillet and felt a sharp, sudden emptiness in his abdomen, as if he'd been gutted.

That same night, with his belly full of corn and zucchini, Frank slept poorly. Several times he awoke from nightmares of which he remembered nothing more than bubbles, black bubbles. He lay there, touching his forehead with a trembling hand. Beside him Dorothy lay fast asleep, breathing deeply, snoring. He shook himself awake. He wanted to make a confession, then and there. He wanted to tell his slumbering wife everything, say to her, *I have reached the bottom of my willpower. I have loved and been faithful to you for thirty-six years, but enough is enough. I have met another woman. The woman in the Icehouse. Juliet. I have fallen in love with her. She swims.*

He had an erection.

He got up and took a cold shower. Afterward, he stood dripping in the doorway of the screened porch where they slept, listening to the electric noise of crickets. Gray dawn seeped in through the rattan shades. Turning, he stood at the foot of their bed.

"Frank, is that you?"

"Swim with me," he said.

"What are you doing?"

"Tomorrow. Today. This afternoon. I want you to swim with me. Will you swim with me?" He stood naked in the dark.

"You know I don't swim, Frank."

"I'll teach you."

"Frank, for goodness — "

"Please," he said, sitting on the edge of the bed. "It's important. I want you to swim with me, Dorothy. I need you to swim with me."

"All right, all right; I'll swim with you, for godsake."

"Thank you," he said, and bent down and kissed her.

"But not this morning. I need to sleep."

"This afternoon will do fine," said Frank.

He went for his morning swim alone. He wasn't surprised to see the woman from the Icehouse waiting for him, already in the water.

"Practice makes perfect," she said, treading.

They swam out to the float. When they reached it, the sun had broken over the tops of the trees to bathe it in yellow light. They rested, drying and breathing together, their bodies touching. Frank lay on his back with his eyes closed, letting the sun paint its Rothkos and Mirós. It took him no time to doze off. He found himself back in the dream he'd had during the night, in which he chased — or was chased by — black bubbles. The bubbles rose from a hideous depth into his face, blinding him. With a gasping start he awoke, startling the woman from the Icehouse, who'd been watching him doze.

"You had a nightmare," she said.

"I know," said Frank.

"You grind your teeth. Did you know that?"

"No, I didn't know that." He smiled. "Please don't tell my dentist. I'll never hear the end of it."

"Your secret is safe with me."

She put a hand on his shoulder, looked at him. Her green irises held tiny flakes of brownish red — like rust. Frank swam in them. A drop of water from her hair landed on his lip. She bent forward to kiss him. Frank broke away. "I've got to go," he said, untying the rowboat.

"I'm sorry," she said. "I thought you'd like it."

"It isn't a question of like," said Frank, climbing in. "I'm old enough to be your grandfather."

"Oh, so it's a question of age, is it?" Before he could say anything, she reached forward and kissed him again, a slow kiss on his lips.

He watched her red bathing suit get smaller and smaller as he rowed, turning into a red dot as he hurried back to his wife.

That afternoon he held Dorothy up in the shallow water. He did the same the next afternoon, helping her practice her breathing, teaching her to reach with her arms and turn her head from side to side. She wore her green one-piece bathing suit. It made her skin look ghostly white.

"Kick," said Frank, buoying her up. "Kick!"

"I'm kicking!"

"Hello, Frank."

The woman from the Icehouse stood there, on the dam, holding her dog on a leash.

"Kick," said Frank, ignoring her.

They spent the rest of the afternoon practicing in the shallows, with Frank teaching Dorothy to kick and tread water. He taught her the freestyle stroke and had her practice it with her feet touching bottom. "Frank, my arms are tired," she kept saying, until finally he relented. "Fine," he said. "You're doing fine. We'll pick up tomorrow." The next day, before lunch and after his morning swim (he had not seen the woman from the Icehouse, which both relieved and disappointed him), he brought his wife with him out to the float.

"Are you sure I'm ready for this?" she asked him.

"Don't worry," he said.

While mooring the boat, Frank saw a red dot in the distance. As they drew closer, the red dot waved. Frank nodded.

"What is it?" said Dorothy.

"What? Nothing," said Frank, turning away. He stepped onto the float. "Come on," he said, taking her hand.

"I'm really not sure if I'm ready."

"You promised."

"I don't want to do this, Frank."

"Please — don't let me down."

She shook her head. "Frank, let me stay in the boat."

"Don't let me down!" He gripped her arm.

"I'm not letting you down! This has nothing to do with *you*! I don't want to swim. I don't *feel* like it. Let *go* of me!"

"Please."

"Let go, Frank!"

"Damn you."

He let go. The boat had drifted away from the float. Instead of falling back onto the seat, his wife fell forward, over the side. She came up thrashing.

"Frank!" she spluttered.

"Swim!" he said.

The woman from the Icehouse stood there, watching, waving. Frank's eyes darted back and forth from his wife thrashing in her one-piece bathing suit to the woman on shore in her bright red bikini. Though only several hundred yards, the distance may as well have been measured in light years. It was the very same distance, he reflected (dimly aware of his wife's spluttered cries), that had stood between him and joy, him and the vigor of his youth, that impossible distance of dark, deep water. No amount of swimming, his own or anyone else's, could broach it.

Frank!

To cross that distance you had to do more than swim.

Frank!

As he watched his wife struggle, an irresistible force gripped and held him frozen — a vibrating electric force that numbed his shoulders and turned his arms and legs to quivering bars of lead. It came from all the way across the water, from where the woman from the Icehouse stood watching him.

Help!

"Jesus!"

He dove in.

The water was cold and dark, dark green. Bubbles smashed into his face. He followed them down and down until his muscles and lungs began to cringe, then surfaced to catch his breath, then followed them down again. In the green darkness he saw nothing, only the pale explosions of his breath as the churning water multiplied the bubbles in all dimensions. He groped blindly, kicking at the darkness until his lungs began to explode. He rushed up into the wavering cone of light, his left leg striking something on the way. Snatching a razor-sharp breath from the surface, he plunged again, found her, and brought her up a dozen yards from the float. With one arm around her wide waist and one for the water, he dog-paddled her to the ladder. Somehow, in a series of movements that cut a wedge out of time, he lifted her out and up onto the float, where he lay her on her back and pinched her nostrils and breathed into her, his warm lips pressed against her cold ones as he massaged her heart. She retched back to life. He rolled her on her side and watched her cough water. Then he sat with his hand on her shoulder, his feet over the edge of the float, his face dripping. His heart pounded in his chest like a wire beater thrashing a dusty old rug.

He looked to shore.

The red dot was gone. There was no gray car, no black barking dog. No light burned in the Icehouse, which looked as weedy, as empty, as abandoned as ever. A blue heron sailed overhead. A breeze swept the lake in a gray parabola. He closed his eyes and sobbed, tears mixed with lake water dripping from his sagging, creased face.

"I'm sorry," he told no one. "So sorry."

With his eyes still closed he felt himself drifting; he felt he could drift like that forever. When he opened them, he saw the clouds shifting high above the trees. He looked down at the water in time to see a creature — a pond skater or a water strider — walking there.

THE WOLF HOUSE

THAT SUNDAY MORNING when I told her, "Mrs. Wolff is dead," my mother groaned, cocked her head, pursed her lips, and said, in a voice barely loud enough to hear, "Che peccato." The next day she lay in her bed, sick, calling to me in her Death Voice, "Alberto? Albert? Sei tu, Alberto?"

Of course it was me; who else would it be? Not Geordie, my twin, who preaches in Vermont. I stood at her bedroom door, like I've always stood there, like I've stood there my whole life, helpless. But this time I did something different. "That's it," I said, marching over, tearing the bedclothes off her. "I'm taking you to the emergency room. They'll do a million useless tests; then we'll go home. Okay?" I felt just like Geordie saying it.

Having piled her into her mint-condition green '68 Rambler American, I drove my mother to the hospital, where they're testing her for meningitis.

She doesn't have meningitis.

So I leave my mother in the hands of experts and go to pick up Lenny Wolff, whose mother is dead. It rains. Lenny's father, wife, and eight-month-old baby boy huddle in a corner of his child-hood living room, surrounded by plastic buckets, Tupperware bowls, and pots catching drops from a leaky roof. Everyone's saying carefully sentimental things like *she's in a better place now.* With his barrel chest, thick neck, and bowed, ruddy head, Mr. Wolff looks like one of the huge red water valves at the reservoir pumping station where he works and where I sometimes visit him. Lenny has a two o'clock appointment with the priest.

"You're late," he says first thing when he sees me.

"Sorry," I say. "It's raining." As if he hasn't noticed.

"I'm on a very tight schedule," says Father Moynahan, a man with thin blue eyes and thinning hair who speaks in a soft, cautious voice. Everything about the man is cautious, grotesquely moderate. He meets us by the confessional. There's a wedding in progress, so he doubts there'll be many "takers." "They don't like to come during weddings," he says.

Lenny stopped believing in God the year we graduated, the same year he quit smoking. Since then he's been waiting for the Catholic Church to collapse, as if his piety had been the main thing supporting it. Only his mom's side of the family remains true to Rome; the rest are lapsed, agnostics, Jews, while most of his friends are atheists like me, Geordie, and Clyde. Though she attended Mass every Sunday, Mrs. Wolff always sat in the last pew, alone, like a shy man in a porno theater. Her mouth would open to sing, Lenny once told me, but no sound ever came out. Father Moynahan, who'll be performing the service, doesn't seem to remember her.

"Was this by any chance the Mrs. Wolff who lived at the Good Samaritan Nursing Home?" he asks Lenny.

"She lived with my father," Lenny answers, his brown eyes narrowing to rusty blades.

"I see," says Father M. "That must be another Mrs. Wolff."

"Yes, it must," says Lenny, stabbing him repeatedly.

Why the hell does Lenny want me here? To keep him from punching the priest? Since the day Geordie and I met Lenny, I've always been slightly afraid of him. It was Clyde Rawlings who brought us together on the rock at Bennington Pond back when we were still in puberty. The DePoli twins were the only first-generation Americans in this small New England factory town, the only atheists, our dead father a scientist and inventor. We'd learned to hate and fear Catholic boys, pimple-faced, plaid-necktied hooligans who'd beat us up at the bus stop for being "Guineas" and not believing in God. We expected no less of Lenny, who loomed barrel chested and fierce on our rock like Samson over the Philistines. Clyde made introductions. "Lenny Wolff, God-fearing Catholic, meet Albert and Geordie, blaspheming atheists." My twin and I froze like headlight deer and remained frozen as Lenny smiled and shook hands with us. Still, there was violence in the guy. You could feel it.

"And you say there are to be Jews at the service?" Father Moderation asks, drawing out the word "Jews," stretching it like taffy.

"My wife among them," says Lenny.

"You didn't want a Jewish service?"

"My mother was Catholic."

"That's right . . . that's right. And your father?"

"What *difference* does it make?"

Father Moderation smiles. "Well, my son, you see, I need to know, if you'll pardon the expression, just what sort of group

I'm 'up against.' Non-Catholics can be, well, impatient with our ways."

"I can imagine," says Lenny.

"At least you won't be preaching to the converted," I say, trying to lighten things up a little. The priest turns hopeful eyes to me. "What about you? Are you Catholic?"

"Lapsed. Apostate."

"Oh." He nods. "I see."

The priest turns back to Lenny to discuss his role in the eulogy.

"My advice would be keep it short and sweet," he suggests. "A requiem mass can seem quite lengthy." Lenny, who played King Arthur in the Immaculate High production of *Camelot* and now earns pin money clowning for kids at birthday parties, looks bugged. "I think you should leave that up to me, shouldn't you, Father?" he says, clenching and unclenching his fists. "She is my mother, after all."

They go over more details, schedules, transportation, parking.

"Well." Father Moderation stands. "I must check the confessional."

He shakes hands with us, giving mine a series of soft, gooey squeezes, like he's milking a cow. As we cross the church parking lot, Lenny's cheeks burn red while his usually red lips go pale. "I'll say whatever the hell I want at my mother's funeral, you Mick pederast son of a bitch," he grumbles.

"What did you expect?" I say, unlocking Mom's antique Rambler.

"A little flexibility would've been nice."

"Oh yeah, right, sure," I say. "A little flexibility. 'We'd like a little flexibility, let's go to the Catholic Church.' Give me a break."

I turn, hoping to see him smile, but he just sits there in the passenger seat, staring out the windshield, kneading his jaw, flexing his fists.

I drive Lenny home, then head back to the house.

Once there were five of us, Lenny, Clyde, Geordie, Stewart, and myself. All summer long we'd dive and swim in the reservoir, also known as Bennington Pond, kicking and thrashing our way to a tiny island at its center with a thirty-foot ornamental lighthouse. Lenny, best fighter of us all but worst swimmer by far, nearly drowned twice. The first time Geordie saved him; the second time Stewie hauled him up onto the rocks. We got along as much out of inertia as anything, though we did share a pessimism about small-town life and trusted everyone else much, much less than we trusted each other. We also did a fair amount of all-American goofing off, with Lenny usually laughing hardest of all, like the time he did his impression of a guy throwing up, using a lukewarm bowl of Campbell's cheddar-cheese soup. (We were stoned.)

Stewie was our second-hardest laugher, also our biggest-hearted goofball. To his lasting credit he turned the whole world into a bathroom joke. Unfortunately, the world included motor vehicles. Three days before graduation, he plowed himself and his dad's Pinto into the town flagpole, which stood at the center of Main Street. We lined up at Stewie's open coffin, paying respects to the powdered jelly doughnut that had been his face, expecting this, too, to be one of his cruder jokes, though no one laughed, not even Lenny. He and Clyde blubbered magnificently, while I envied them, having failed to shed a tear of my own. Nor did Geordie turn on the waterworks. He looked more bored and angry than weepy. The fact is, the DePoli twins have yet to cry at a funeral. Maybe because we don't believe in God. Or maybe we don't believe in *death*.

Having taken Lenny home and garaged my mother's cream-puff Rambler, I walk back to the hospital, to see how she's doing. I've got nothing better to do, and besides, it's only three miles, all under a sky stuffed with clouds. Like many hospitals this one is near a cemetery, and I take a shortcut through it. Death may not impress me, but tombstones do: tiny, tidy stone homes for the dead, so neat in their manicured rows. Some aren't marble or granite, but cast in metal to look like stone. I play a game with myself, guessing from afar which stones are fake, testing for hollowness with my knuckles. A sudden wonder grips me. Is Papa's tombstone fake? What about my grandmother's? And Stewie — do Stewie's bones rest under a phony stone? If so, what of it? Do souls need to live *anywhere*? Do they care less where they live? Such are the thoughts of minds meandering through cemeteries on cloudy days.

I arrive at the hospital midafternoon. It seems hospital beds are scarce this time of year. They've got Mother on a gurney in the hall. She puts down her *Vanity Fair*.

"How are you feeling?"

"Better, tank you."

(The Death Voice, I'm pleased to report, is gone.)

"How was de funeral?"

"Day after tomorrow," I tell her. "The wake is tonight."

She grasps my hand in the busy hospital corridor. "Mi dispiace," she says. I don't know if she's sorry for missing Lenny's mother's wake, or for getting sick, or what. "Poor Lenny, he must be upset."

"Sure," I say. "He's very upset."

"I bet he cry a lot."

What sort of remark is that? "Naturally," I say. "His mom just died."

"Hmmm . . ." I'm supposed to translate this "hmm" into a whole conversation but refuse to do so. Instead I study the manufacturer's label on the gurney rail. Derwood-Kaiser Medical Supplies, Waterbury, Connecticut.

"When is you brother come?"

"Around dinner time, he said."

"Dire lui . . . non preoccuparti. Tell him . . . not to worry." She winces.

I pick up the *Vanity Fair*. Flipping its pages, I come across fat Marlon Brando crying at his son's murder trial. A pretty nurse takes my mother's temperature. One-oh-one.

At suppertime, as promised, from St. Albans, Vermont, where he's a Unitarian minister, Geordie arrives. Unitarians aren't supposed to believe in God, or maybe they just don't have to. Anyway, from what I gather my brother does a good job preaching *around* the Good Lord—like someone eating around the spinach on his plate. He drives an early-model Honda Civic and looks beat up from the trip. He's been divorced two months, and that shows, too.

"How are you?" I say, lugging his garment bag inside.

He takes a look around, shakes his head. I know what he's thinking. A: nothing's changed, and B: what's my jerk-off twin doing still living here? I want his love for me to overwhelm such thoughts. It doesn't. Though I've always looked up to him, Geordie has never liked me. He considers me an embarrassment, a cheap knockoff of his genuine self, a counterfeit coin with his face on it. He especially resents the fact that I've spent the last ten years working at the local bicycle-seat factory. He can't seem to understand that, despite our looking like each other, it's *my* life, that what I do with it is no reflection on him. The reason he's surprised to see me here is because, last he heard, I'd taken an apartment of my own, on the seedy side of town, by the train tracks, next door to Goose Lumber. Until two weeks ago, that arrangement still held. But I couldn't take living alone in that place, in a one-room apartment over a family with something like thirty yapping dogs. When the dogs didn't rattle my brain, the freight trains rattled it. And, to be honest, I didn't like leaving Mother alone in the house. Which I'm sure helps shore up Geordie's impression of me as a *mammone*, which is Italian for "mama's boy."

"Where are you sleeping?" His first words to me.

"In the den." Nonnie's — our grandmother's — old room, where we used to watch *Hogan's Heroes* reruns. "I can move; I don't mind."

He grabs the garment bag from me, drags it upstairs. I consider following him up to our old room, where twin beds and cardboard furniture sag, but it would only annoy him. My following Geordie has always annoyed him. Instead I yell, "Need a hand?"

The sound of unzipping answers. I lean against the balustrade, thinking I'm always at the threshold of things. I want to run up and hug my twin, confide in him about hollow tombstones, ask if he's brought his bathing suit. "They opened a Boston Rotisserie," I call up.

Arms crossed, scowling, Geordie appears in gray underwear

at the top of the stairs. Legs white, belly sagging, hair, at twenty-eight, thinning and gray at the temples. You'd think he was eight years, not eight minutes, older.

We hike in the woods behind the house. Nonnie, my father's mother, was a big believer in wolves. She'd swallowed whole the legend of Romulus and Remus, those twins who, suckled by a she-wolf, went on to found Rome. I've always been fascinated by wolf stories. *White Fang. The Jungle Book. Peter and the Wolf.* Werewolves. I daydreamed that, like Kipling's Mowgli, I'd been raised by wolves. They could have done no worse.

Geordie walks ahead of me, gathering plastic hand-grenades and other relics of childhood warfare, tossing them over his shoulder, hitting me in the face. He pulls branches out of his way and releases them in time to whack my forehead. I don't even say ouch.

In her room, on the folding table next to her portable electric stove, Nonnie kept a bronze miniature statue of Romulus and Remus straddled by the she-wolf. She'd point to the twins one by one saying, "Questo e Alberto; e quello li, Geordie." Tucked away in the rear of the house, Nonnie's room was a museum of smells. Mothballs, soy sauce, lavender, iodine — odors that conjured past lives and dreams of ancient, far-off places, crumbling cities beyond time's greedy grasp. After Papa died (a funeral I hardly remember), Mother treated Nonnie like a prisoner, condemning her to her tiny room and getting furious when she'd step out of her cell to use the bathroom, pasting her with ripe-tomato Italian epithets.

Nonnie's world crawled with wolves. She saw them every-where, in her imagination, in her dreams, slinking across the backyard terrace at night, eyes burning yellow as the petals of the forsythia bush Papa planted just before he died. Their den (Nonnie claimed) was the abandoned guest cottage behind our house. Geordie and I head there now, walking on dirt-and-leaf-covered flagstones through a raspberry patch, prickers clawing at skin and clothes. Nonnie said the wolves lived in the crawl space under the floor and came out only at night. Being six years old and knowing her window faced the woods, Geordie and I believed her. Anyway, who were we to argue with our grandmother, who was ninety, spoke a dozen languages (none English), and made the best fried spaghetti in the world?

At the cottage's empty doorway Geordie kicks through a pile of dead leaves. The floorboards are rotted; the sky pours through a yawning gap in the roof. Kids have been here, punching holes in Homisote walls, scrawling their names in pitch. If a family of wolves ever lived here, they've moved on.

Geordie unzips his fly, pisses into a tangle of venetian blinds. Geordie has always gotten a kick out of me watching him pee. He'd stand at the edge of our driveway, his golden effluence arching into milkweed and bulrushes. I'd stand beside him, hoping to see my own urine arch triumphantly next to his, only to see it trickle away languidly.

"I'm leaving the Barn," he announces, still pissing, his broad back to me. The Barn is the Unitarian Church, only they don't call it a church. I'm stunned — not so much by the news, but because when Geordie speaks to me, it's always a bit stunning.

"Why, Geordie? What happened?"

He shrugs. It's just like Geordie to throw a bomb like that and follow it up with a shrug. I don't press him, knowing if I do he'll just clam up more. He wants the information to work on me, like paint remover. He zips his fly, packing his penis away like a travel accessory. He smiles, pleased that I'm not saying anything. I'm learning. "Poor Mrs. Wolff," he says, smiling.

"Yeah," I say. "Poor Mrs. Wolff."

Nonnie died at ninety-six. I was twelve. And though I didn't cry when told or at her funeral, still, Nonnie's death shook me. I knew she was really gone when Mother reclaimed her room and painted it a resolutely cheerful shade of yellow, the new-paint smell murdering all those other smells I'd loved.

Now it's Mrs. Wolff's turn to be the powdered doughnut. Dressed in sports coats and ties, Geordie and I greet the survivors: Lenny and his wife, Elaine; Mr. Wolff. I've never seen Mr. Wolff in a suit. Until now I've only seen him in the stained T-shirt and green work pants he wears to the pump house. "Good to see ya," he says, hugging me (though built like a bear, Mr. Wolff is not the hugging type). I hug Lenny, then Elaine. Already I'm tired of hugging people. We get in line to look at the corpse, then take our places among the respectful. Next to me sits a girl with long brown eyelashes and cherry lips like Lenny's. I wonder two things: first, is she related to him? and second, is it okay to think about sex with your best friend's relative at his mother's wake? I spend the next few minutes searching for appropriate feelings, but it's like looking for aspirin in a dark medicine chest.

Then Clyde arrives, looking like hell in a seersucker suit. Clyde was always the tallest of us. Now he's the baldest, gauntest, and most successful, with his own video company in Boston. Clyde's latest project: a documentary about the Wright Brothers, narrated by former game-show panelist Orson Bean. When Clyde's done hugging people, I say, "Did you bring your bathing suit?" It's code, our private joke, our secret handshake. Man, he looks awful. "How goes it?" I ask, as if it's not painfully obvious.

"Fine," says Clyde, "thanks to an array of pharmaceutical products. Still working at Corbinger's?" Corbinger's: the bicycle-seat factory. At one point, five of us worked there. I stayed.

"I quit," I tell him. "Last week."

"No shit?" says Clyde.

"Honestly," I say, "ever since they stopped making banana seats my heart hasn't been in it. I just passed my civil service exam. I'm going to work for the P.O." P.O.: that's shorthand for "post office." Somehow it's easier to get out that way.

Like Geordie, Clyde's been through a nasty divorce. The day the papers came through he passed the world's largest kidney stone, his "piece of the rock," he called it. Now he's got a duodenal ulcer, some strange intestinal malady, plus bursitis in both elbows and a bone spur on his left foot. He walks with a cane and wears a special orthopedic shoe: thick, soft, black, a far cry from the brown wing tip on his other foot.

"How's the stiff looking?" he asks.

"Stiff," I say, shrugging. "There are some pretty good-looking nonstiffs here, though." I nod toward the dark-lashed girl. Clyde looks, nods in turn, smiles. All the chronic illnesses in the world wouldn't keep him from admiring a pretty face. When the young lady catches his look, he wiggles his fingers at her.

"So," I ask, "did you bring your bathing suit, or what?"

Clyde closes his eyes and bows his head like he's about to own up to something embarrassing. For a second I'm afraid he's going to say, "Al, those days are over for me," or something heartbreaking. Instead he pops up his head, screws up his face, and says, *"But of course!"*

We gather on a ramp behind the funeral home. Still raining. Water surrounds us, dripping from eaves, gurgling in gutters, splashing into puddles. Lenny lights a cigar. "I can deal with a half hour of just about anything," he says.

Clyde, who never smoked, snatches the cigar, takes a drag. Soon we're all smoking the same cigar. For a second I'm confused, thinking it's Stewie's wake all over again, that the past five years never happened.

"It's all shit and roses." Geordie's ministerial voice upstages the rain.

"Is that what you preach to your congregation?" says Lenny. "'It's all shit and roses, amen'?"

"We don't say, 'Amen.' I did it once; people got upset. We Unitarians are extremely protective of our secularism."

"But," says Lenny, "you don't mind having your noses rubbed in roses and shit?"

"That's right," says Geordie. "Shoot the messenger."

"As for me," says Clyde, changing the subject, "I'm just waiting for life to be perfect so I can go about my business." He breaks into a soft-shoe, but the bone spur waylays him.

Mr. Wolff steps out the back door, sees us all floating in cigar smoke, shakes his big head, and ducks inside.

"Back to the salt mines," says Lenny, flicking the cigar over a dripping hedge and then going back in.

It's strange, but over Bennington Pond and nowhere else there's a break in the clouds. Sunlight spills onto the water, leaving the rest of the world in sullied darkness. A sunbeam singles out the red door of the pumping station on the far shore, beyond the island with the lighthouse. Normally, even on rainy days, the red door is ajar. But Mr. Wolff mourns.

The hike to our rock coats our shoes with mud. We take them off, jam them into a crag, and strip down, except Lenny, who carries his baby son in a papoose sling and thumbs a Bible, searching for a passage to read at his mother's funeral. The joke about bathing suits is we don't wear any. Clyde's dick hangs long and red and is his point of greatest health. Geordie's is shrunken and shriveled, his least healthy part. We have twin dicks.

"Roses and shit!" I cry, tearing a hole in green water. It's late May, and the water is icy still. My testicles retreat into my guts. I feel immortal, twenty-eight years old, but who's counting? My body is twelve, the same age it was when we first started coming here. Freestyle, I head for the lighthouse. I used to be able to swim back and forth two, three, four times. Halfway there I'm winded, treading water. Geordie catches up with me, doing a backstroke, his feet kicking up plumes of sun-spackled water, spouting up into shafts of sunlight, spewing mouthfuls. Then along comes Clyde, doing a scissor kick–sidestroke. Back on the rock Lenny thumbs through Proverbs and bounces his kid, who keeps crying. The cries carry all the way across the lake, to the stone lighthouse, beyond, to the pumping station, reverberating off the red door to begin their journey back as an echo. To our surprise, the island has only been slightly polluted. Cans and bottles wink back the sun's rays; Geordie gathers them up, muttering. Clyde climbs the rusty lighthouse ladder and stands behind the topside railing, sunlight daubing his furry parts. His ailing flesh paints a pink rainbow as he dives. I imagine his symptoms leeching into the reservoir, sending dozens of unwatched pumping-station meter needles flying into the red zone.

"Christ," says Geordie, shaking a banana slug from a Budweiser can. The slug clings to his arm like a hypodermic.

I turn a few somersaults, then surface to inspect the island. More beer cans and bottles, what's left of a campfire, a defunct rubber, and a few hefty turds, origin unknown. My hypothesis: wolf shit. It seems unlikely, I know, but Nonnie's family of wolves had to go *somewhere*. Why not this pleasant little island, where no one can harass them save a few old high school chums who don't even know if they're still friends?

"Albert, Geordie — check this out!"

Clyde points down from the lighthouse. "There — in the shallows!"

The carcass of a dead snapping turtle, tangled in fishing line, its head the size of my foot. Flies spin around it.

"Imagine if that bit your dick off?" observes Clyde.

"Fucking fishermen," says Geordie. "They must've killed it and left it there. Bastards."

I say, "Maybe the wolves got it."

Geordie spins around. "What?"

"The wolves," I say. "Maybe it was the wolves."

Back on the rock, Geordie stacks cans and bottles and wanders off who knows where. Lenny asks me and Clyde to take his kid for a while. He straps the papoose sling on Clyde's back and slips the baby inside. "Get the little bastard out of my sight," he stage-whispers, then forces a laugh, ruining the joke. He needs to concentrate on Bible verses.

Me and Clyde joke about taking the kid "for a ride." We say it like Edward G. Robinson in *Little Caesar*. Meanwhile, the kid — who looks like Eddie G. — makes gooey faces. For a while everything's fine. Then the kid starts crying again. His cries echo across Bennington Pond. He cries like he's being tortured. Clyde tries making gooey faces back at him, but it's no use. "Let him cry," I say. "It'll do him good." His screams fill the woods, bounce off the clouds. Suddenly Lenny comes charging down the path. "Are you out of your *fucking minds*?" he says. "What the fuck's the *matter* with you? Don't you hear him crying? How can you be so goddamn *stupid*?"

"What should we have done?" says Clyde.

"You should have brought him back to me, that's what!" says Lenny, his hands curling into fists. He squeezes them open and shut as if squeezing a pair of rubber balls. For a second I'm afraid. He takes the baby back; the baby stops crying. Clyde looks my way, shrugs.

All the way back to the car Lenny clenches and unclenches his fists. He still hasn't found a Bible passage. Geordie, back from his wandering, has entered one of his monklike silences. For the next hour he won't say a word; he'll just look preoccupied, like St. Augustine on a bad day. Clyde keeps shrugging his all-purpose shrug. The silence nags me. It ages me. I run my fingers along my hairline. We're twenty-eight, all of us, going on middle-aged, going on dead. I swear I can't take this shit anymore, all these funerals and babies. I prefer to live in a war-torn city, in a country where they kill you for talking. I want to crash-land a spy plane somewhere in the Sahara, ride crowded trains full of people burning with dysentery, be nursed by a she-wolf, found Rome. Is that asking too much? Instead I'm coasting along on my last paycheck from Corbinger's, looking forward to twenty years of carting mail through rain, snow, sleet, dark of night, etcetera.

At Boston Rotisserie, Lenny and I stand in line while Clyde waits in the Rambler. Geordie has gone to bring our mother home from the hospital. Why I have no idea, but it's always me Lenny wants with him, whether to bring home chicken or keep him from punching priests. While waiting I notice this item in the local free paper:

WOLF REPORTED AT TOWN RESERVOIR

The Barnum Police Dept. has reported sightings by local residents of a wolf in the woods surrounding the town reservoir, in the area adjacent to the old Bennington property. Authorities have not been able to verify the reports, though Canine Patrol Sergeant Vincent Pomerance believes the animal in question may be a misidentified German shepherd or other wolflike stray dog.

Back at the Wolff home, which seems doomed with Mrs. Wolff gone, Mr. W. has reverted to his T-shirt and green work pants. His asthma is acting up. He makes locomotive-like sounds while shoveling mashed potatoes into his mouth. The rain has stopped. Still, water drips into Tupperware pails, as if a cloud rents space in the attic. Every five minutes or so Mr. Wolff breaks with a choking sound. Though he doesn't say so, I know he wishes we'd all get the hell out of here.

Back home that same evening, I give leftover mashed potatoes to my mother, who claims she hasn't eaten a thing since I brought her to the hospital yesterday. She sits up in bed.

"How was de funeral?" she wants to know.

"Tomorrow," I say. "The funeral's tomorrow. Today was the wake."

Geordie, having excavated his old CO_2 pellet gun, stands in the dusky backyard shooting beer cans, planting his feet and squinting like Clint Eastwood. I wonder how his congregation would feel if they knew their minister was a closet assassin.

"Geordie?" I come up behind him. He turns with the gun propped on his shoulder a la 007. He's got this cold look in his eyes. I swear he saves up all his meanness for trips home. "Did you say hello to Mom?"

He goes on shooting.

"You didn't, did you?"

He feeds another CO_2 cartridge into the gun. "Let me tell you something about our dear old habitually dying mother," he says. "To her way of thinking," he aims at my face, turns me into a beer can, "there are two types of people in this world. Thieves — " he fires into the aluminum siding, " — and Sufferers. You're either one — " he shoots a window, the same window Nonnie used to see wolves through, " — or the other." The window now has a small glass asshole in it. "To be a good person, according to Mom, is to be a Sufferer, since one can hardly imagine a Heaven of Thieves, but one can easily imagine a Heaven of Sufferers. Follow me, little brother?"

I hate it when he calls me that. I'd hate it if I *were* his little brother. I nod.

"To enter the Kingdom of Heaven, one must be pitiable. The more pitiable, the better. The pope honors his most industrious Sufferers with sainthood." He loads the damn gun again. "And so, via mysterious fever and migraine, Mother groans her way to paradise." Another pellet fired; another glass asshole. Geordie takes pot shots: at a downspout, at the barbecue pit, at the bench of a collapsed swing set.

I ask, "Where do the Thieves come in?"

"The Thieves are everywhere," says Geordie. "Take Mrs. Wolff, rest her soul. She turns out to be a Master Thief, stealing the suffering right out from under Mother's nose. Mom doesn't know what hit her. I bet she's been lying in bed for days. Hasn't she? *Hasn't she?*" He looks at me.

"You could still say hello."

He loads bullets. "Have you ever tried to have a sincere conversation with her?" He shakes his head. "It's not possible. Our mother doesn't speak English. Or Italian. She speaks Innuendo."

"So what?" I get up the balls to say. "So what if she's like she is? What *difference* does it make? She's our mother. Get over it, already."

Geordie smiles. It's the first time he's smiled at me during this visit. "Why should I get over it," he says handing me the warm loaded gun, "when I've got my brother to do it for me?"

Families are strange things, especially when they're not really families but just odd mixtures of people living under the same roof. Still, it worries me to think I may never cry over my own mother's death, that at her funeral I might just stand there, dry eyed, not feeling a thing. Already I hadn't cried at my father's funeral, or Nonnie's, or Stewie's. And I'm sure not going to cry at Mrs. Wolff's. When *will* I cry? When do I get to join the great parade of Sufferers?

The day of the funeral it rains. We stand, umbrellas touching (except Geordie, who either forgot his or likes getting soaked). I see Mr. Wolff, a fire hydrant heaving under a yellow sou'wester. I watch Lenny clench and unclench his fists as Elaine holds their baby. I see Clyde leaning on his cane in soggy seersucker. I hear the priest, Father Moynahan, droning under an umbrella that protects him as much from divine inspiration as from bad weather. I try to cry, but it's like trying to pass the world's biggest kidney stone. I want to cry for Mrs. Wolff and her fist-clenching son. I want to cry for Clyde and his various ailments. I want to bawl my brains out for Mr. Wolff and his leaky roof, for bedridden mothers and bitter twin brothers, for Nonnie and fried spaghetti, for hollow tombstones and the rotting corpses of snapping turtles. But mostly I want to cry for the family of wolves that once lived under the guest cottage but never will again.

Suddenly Geordie takes my umbrella, folds it up. Rainwater sluices down my face, tickles my eyelashes. He grabs my hand, gripping it hard, squeezing to crush bone. Soon I'm crying real tears. Finally, he lets go. I look up and see him wet faced, his eyes on the casket going down.

I'd hoped we'd go back to Bennington's for another swim, but it rains. Anyway, it seems we've had enough of water and one another. The four of us say good-bye, hug, and that's that. Later, as I fold his shirts and watch him pack, Geordie doesn't say a word. He packs the CO_2 cartridge gun, tucking it under socks and underwear. Our mother, still in bed, calls to him. We stand at her doorway, just like old times.

"How was de funeral?" The Death Voice is back.

"Fine," says Geordie.

"Wet," I say.

"I should have been there. Ebene, sarebbe stato meglio fossi morta io. Hai capito?" Geordie and I look at each other.

"We understand, Mom," he says, going to and kissing her on the forehead, looking up at me deadpan while doing so. "Don't we?"

Weeks later I'm visiting Mr. Wolff at the pump house.

"C'mere," he says. "Want you to see something."

A hundred yards behind the pumping station is the town dog pound. Mr. Wolff knocks. Canine Patrol Sergeant Pomerance answers. He leads us into the kennel where, in the last cage, a wolf whimpers, a gray female with a white snout. Her teats sag on stained concrete.

"Caught it on the far side of the reservoir," Sergeant Pomerance explains. "Must be sick or dying. Possibly rabid. Didn't even growl."

I gaze into the wolf's eyes — seeping, yellow, cataracted — glowing with primeval forest light. "What are you gonna do with her?" I ask.

"She's endangered, so we can't destroy her," says Pomerance. "I'll find a zoo or someplace. Meanwhile, though, I'm not gonna argue with her."

He and Mr. Wolff repair into Sergeant Pomerance's front office to sip bourbon-laced tea. I wait for them to go, then press my nose through chain links. "Yeah, yeah," I say, getting licked. "It's okay, it's okay . . ."

COLOR
OF THE
SEA

Tell me about loneliness.

At one forty-five in the morning, the sky, the sea, and the horizon were all the same greasy black. Andrew Shields lay stretched out on a life-preserver casing, smoking a Lucky Strike, the diesel-tossed wind curling his hair, the ferry's engines throbbing below him.

When we have arrived, you will tell me, yes?

Other passengers slept indoors, on stiff chairs, on carpet stained by sea salt and cigarette ashes, in sleeping bags, their clothes rolled up into pillows. Andrew felt separate from them all, as if he belonged to another landscape, a world belonging to the stars and the sea.

Promise you will tell me?

The Brazilian woman — Karina was her name — slept below, perched against her backpack. They'd met on the dock. The ferry was late. Like Andrew, she traveled alone. She stood out from the ranks of tourists. In place of cutoffs or baggy shorts, she wore a breezy peasant skirt. A gold Star of David hung in the tip of the mild shadow between her breasts. She had an oval face of pale skin with sharp, boyish features and wore her black hair in a bun. She seemed constantly to lean away from or into things. They'd stood close together scanning the horizon. Andrew lit a cigarette. "Do you mind?" he asked.

"Why? What should I mind?"

"The smoke," he said, waving it away.

"You Americans."

A moment later she said, "Do you get lonely traveling alone?"

Andrew shrugged. "I guess, a little," he said.

"You are lying. I bet you get very lonely."

Andrew was about to reply defensively when suddenly Karina pointed. "Look," she said, clasping her hands together like a seven-year-old. "The ferry!" Seconds later the ship filled the harbor with light and noise. Without warning, Karina grasped Andrew's hand. "I have never been to sea. Only once, when I was little, and then I was sure the boat would go into the water. I fell asleep and dreamed that I woke up underwater and could not breathe. I swore I would never go to sea again."

"What made you change your mind?"

"I was a little girl — it is time to grow up." A crewman tossed a thick hawser that landed with a thump on the dock.

"Look how big it is! It is not a ferry at all; it is an ocean liner!"

Still holding hands, Andrew and Karina pressed forward near the head of the crowd. When their luggage was stowed, Karina stretched out on a bench with a towel for a pillow and said,

"When I wake up, we will be in Crete, and you will tell me about loneliness, yes?"

An old woman in a black shawl, with no upper teeth and a silver crucifix, tugged at Andrew's sleeve. She wanted his section of floor for one of her dozens of grandchildren. The crone fired words, made faces, gestured, implored. At last Andrew gave up his spot, saying, "Okay, okay."

He shivered, pulled out his blue and gray cardigan, which, back in New York, he'd thought would go well with the Aegean. He put it on and, taking his sketchbook, made his way up the brass-railed stairway to the smoking lounge, where he sketched a mother knitting, a crew member filling his pipe, a fat man asleep in a chair with his mouth wide open. He did a dozen portraits. He titled them "The Dormant Ferry Series."

On deck, he sketched a lifeboat silhouetted against the black sky. Not bad, he thought, lighting a cigarette. He noticed a scattering of lights on the horizon, as if a cluster of stars had fallen there. Being the only one outdoors, he felt proprietary toward the night. As he sketched, he reflected on what, if anything, he knew about loneliness. The fact that he had spent so much of his own life alone didn't qualify him. Or did it?

As she opened her eyes, Karina looked dazed and frightened; then she presumably identified the grumble of the ferry's engines, smiled, stretched, and said, "I am so happy!" Andrew believed her.

It was still dark when the ferry docked at Iráklion (Heracleum, home of Hercules), Crete's capital city, though Andrew didn't feel the least bit heroic, crammed into the crowd behind the lowering stern hatch. Amid shouted commands, squawking pelicans, pressing bodies, and thickening diesel fumes, he and Karina held hands again as the hatch crashed down on cracked cement, and they rode the surge of passengers shoving their way toward the taxi lights on shore. When all the taxis had departed, three people stood on the dock in the dim light of dawn: Andrew, Karina, and an overweight middle-aged woman, a pharmacist from Anchorage, Alaska.

"Do you guys know where the youth hostel is?" the pharmacist asked.

Past the ruins of a Venetian fort, down a median strip of coastal highway clogged with morning traffic, they bore their packs, asking directions to the hostel, which they found on a side street. When no one answered their calls at the reception desk, they climbed rickety stairs past rooms littered with strewn luggage and sleeping bodies. They found a room with two empty bunks, but no pillows or sheets. The pharmacist went straight to sleep.

"I don't want to stay here," said Karina. "I want to rent a car."

Back on the street, Karina said, "You still haven't told me about loneliness."

"I will," said Andrew. "I promise." But what could he say of years spent wandering the streets of New York, of insomniac nights writing beneath his own reflection in greasy diner windows, or sitting in dark movie theaters among smells of butter and bubble gum, or watching subway crews pick garbage from between the tracks at Canal Street? What did it all add up to except more of the same wretched solitude? What had it taught him?

The Cretan landscape depressed Andrew, who'd looked forward to pine forests and rugged peaks. Instead he found low shrubs and scruffy dunes, an injured landscape to which insult had been added in the form of poured-concrete architecture, cement-mixer Bauhaus. The whole coast had been razed to erect tourist traps. This feisty little country, thought Andrew, which stood off the Trojans, survived Alexander, defied the Romans and the Turks, and outlasted the Nazis, has failed to fend off the worst barbarians of all: tourists like me. Still, out of the concrete nothingness, if he squinted hard Andrew could see beauty in the parched dunes, in the unbroken reaches of sea and sky.

He sat behind the wheel; Karina had told him she had trouble driving a standard. As he drove, Andrew watched her out of the corner of his eye and sketched her in his mind. Who was she? Was she an artist, a poet? Probably not; she seemed too well adjusted, too childishly happy. For sure she was the type with many friends, though perhaps no intimate ones. He imagined that she scored high on tests and could recite the first stanzas of her country's most famous poems. She was lazy, a quality he knew he could grow to love, especially after the competitive furor of American women. She would spoil her children rotten, but they'd worship her anyway. That smile would always win out. Men would fall for her simply because she'd do nothing to encourage them. Jewish, apparently. Not Orthodox, clearly. No doubt she believed in hell and therefore would never go there.

God would exist and look out for her. No wonder she wondered about loneliness, having never experienced it.

At his last thought, Karina turned and faced Andrew, twirling a finger through her dark hair and smiling as if reading his mind. The little green Fiat shuddered at eighty kilometers per hour along the pockmarked macadam. Every few miles she insisted that Andrew pull over, that they walk hand in hand to the edge of the sea, so she could touch it, taste it, cup it in her hands to see if the water was really yellow blue.

"In Niterói, where I am from, the sea is different," she said. "It is both more beautiful and more sad."

"Why is it more sad?" said Andrew.

"Because it is more beautiful."

With her camera, Andrew photographed Karina facing away from the yellow blue water. She lived in Zurich now, she said, worked at a bank, rarely saw her family, though they spoke constantly, and hadn't been to the sea in over ten years. "I want to hug it," she said, looking out to sea. "I want to kiss it." She closed her eyes and gave the salty air a gentle kiss.

Her father, Andrew learned as they drove on, imported chemical compounds, and her mother was a celebrated literary agent, numbering García Márquez among her clients. The more he learned about her, the more Andrew questioned his musings. Perhaps Karina was more worldly and sophisticated than he suspected. With that thought came another: that he'd been looking for just such a woman, childlike, beautiful, independent, curious, foreign, willing. Andrew had grown heartsick over the hypocritical bearing of many American women, who lulled men by assuring them that they weren't necessary, until the trap was sprung and the burlesque of independence ended. Or maybe he'd just chosen badly.

As they wound up the coastal highway, Andrew heard about George, the lover left behind, the investment banker who'd brought Karina to Zurich and set her up in a high-paying job and a cushy apartment; and Peter, the British lawyer who'd courted her with a box of roses — not six roses, or ten, but a full dozen ("And you know how expensive roses can be!") — and awaited her now in London. The problem with George was that he wasn't Jewish. The problem with Peter — and it was a big problem, a potentially insurmountable problem, a problem that Karina, the paragon of a noninsomniac, had apparently been losing sleep over — was that Peter was *old*. Karina was twenty-nine, and Peter had recently turned forty. Two weeks shy of his thirty-ninth birthday, Andrew had a hard time appreciating the gulf between these two numbers, each of which seemed to him safely removed from death. "Eleven years — that doesn't exactly make him old enough to be your father."

"That is not the problem."

"What's the problem, then?"

"Sex. With someone so old there will be difficulties, no?"

"I beg to differ," said Andrew.

"Well, let me ask you then," said Karina. "Are you as enthusiastic a lover as you were when you were young?"

"I *am* young."

"You know what I mean."

"I don't. And I'm not sure I want to." He floored the gas and shoved the little Fiat into second up the first in a series of steep, green-carpeted hills. Finally, he said, "I'm a much better lover now than I was at thirty, let alone at twenty or twenty-five."

"Really?" This interested her. It interested her greatly.

"I'm a lot more patient. I know what a woman's needs are, and how to satisfy them."

"But what about you?" said Karina. "Are you as . . . you know."

"As *virile*? As *horny*? Can I still *get it up*? I'm thirty-nine; I'm not dead!" But the fact was that even now, alone on a Greek island with this sexy Brazilian, he wanted sex less than he would have at twenty or even at twenty-five. Then he would have wanted it desperately; it would have filled the pit of his thoughts. Now he considered it an interesting possibility among possibilities. He certainly wouldn't push the issue.

"Peter is not like you," Karina concluded. "But I trust him. And he takes care of me."

Andrew began to not like her so much. He turned his attention to the increasingly rugged landscape as they climbed into the clouds and he white-knuckled the steering wheel. Finally, he couldn't resist asking, "Why should some man have to take care of you?"

"He doesn't *have* to. I like to know that he can."

"You fascinate me," said Andrew, lighting a cigarette.

"You don't approve?"

"Approve? No. No, I don't."

"Well, that's your problem, isn't it?" said Karina.

They rode on in silence; Andrew tried to screw up some enthusiasm for sightseeing and considered using an excursion to the palace of Malia — in the town of their destination — as an excuse to dump Karina. But just as he thought so, she pointed to a scruffy side road banking into a field of poppies. "Oh, please, take that road!" she exclaimed with such dire enthusiasm Andrew hit the brakes and fishtailed onto it through a patch of sand. Soon the Fiat, which they had already dubbed "the green frog," twisted up one hairpin turn after another, past Moho and Krassi, towns clustered around Byzantine churches with red-tiled domes like pigeons clustered around a hag with breadcrumbs. They drove through Tzermiado, where women wrapped in shawls ran from their shops, squawking, "Come! Look! Stop! Stay a while! Buy a tablecloth!" waving bottles of homemade wine and baskets of lemons and other fruit. "For your wife!" one woman shouted. "For your daughter!" shouted another. Karina looked at him as if to say, *there, you see?*

From Tzermiado they coasted down through a river valley, between wall-like rows of towering eucalyptus, along hillsides bristling with daisies and arthritic-looking olive trees. Every few kilometers they passed the same old farmer side-mounted on his burro, his mustache as big as his face. Sometimes they pulled over, and Karina took photographs while Andrew sketched. She peered over his shoulder, holding her breath, watching him crosshatch.

"I love watching you draw," she said. "It is like watching a bird build its nest." And suddenly Andrew liked her all over again.

They decided to spend two more days together. "But that is all," said Karina. "No matter what. Even if I like you."

A moment later she said, "Since we are going to know each other for only two more days, and since we are not going to be lovers and will probably never see each other again, we can be totally honest, no?"

"Totally honest," said Andrew. Except for the part about them not becoming lovers, he liked the plan. If good for nothing else, honesty could be diverting. As they rolled from town to town, Andrew did his best to answer her questions sincerely.

"So you are saying," said Karina, "that there is no limit to how many women you would make love to, if you could?"

"Physically?"

"Emotionally. No limits?"

"There are always limits."

"Have you never wanted to be faithful?"

"I don't define faithfulness in terms of monogamy."

"How do you define it?"

"As how you feel about someone. If my love for a woman reduces my desire to make love to others, that's wonderful. But the idea that one's love for another is enhanced by suppressing or, worse, denying the desire to be with others, that's just plain foolish."

"Many of my friends say this, too," said Karina. "You would be happy in Brazil. Especially because you are a man."

Andrew told her of his uncontrollable lusts, of the attacks of desire that had driven him to distraction in his twenties and even later, into his thirties.

"So you have been unfaithful?" she said.

"By your definition, yes."

"And you did not feel guilty?"

"I would have felt just as guilty harboring the desires, even if I didn't act on them. What about you?"

"Never."

"Don't you think about sex?"

"Of course. I think about it with Peter."

"The Rose Giver."

"Do not make fun of him!"

"I wasn't making fun of him. I'm making fun of you. A guy hands you a dozen roses, and you fall in love. If I were to run out and pick a dozen poppies — " the hillside was still covered with them " — would you fall in love with me, then?"

"It's not the same thing."

"True, a poppy's not a rose."

"Do not be presumptuous. You are not my type."

"You're right. I'm not respectable. And I'm not Jewish."

Karina said nothing. She shifted in the passenger seat, offering him as much of her back as possible, while he considered what his "type" might be. Age: between thirty-five and "middle." Lineage: Italian (though he could pass for Greek, he thought). Face: belonging to a country by the sea where thick coffee is sipped from skimpy cups. Profession: drawing storyboards for TV commercials. A Renaissance man. Ads for sneakers and soft drinks. A hack.

"Since you've been here, you haven't wanted a man?" asked Andrew.

"Naturally." She kept looking out the window. "But only to look at. I like to look at men. For me they are part of the scenery."

In Ano Viánnos, a market town high up in the mountains untouched by tourism, they strolled. In a hundred kilometers they'd revealed too much too quickly, and now they were road weary, sick of each other and themselves.

Ice-cream bars in hand, they roamed past battered shops selling fruit and bread, unlit hardware stores where the hardware looked used, cafes with birdlike old men in dark shirts picking at worry beads. Here, at last, was the real Greece: no signs in

English, no discos, no loudspeakers, no mopeds. No cement. No young people either, Andrew noticed, only middle aged and old, all dressed in dark clothes, seeking refuge from the sun. The only signs of activity were the women selling pistachios, baskets of lemons, serving coffee and ouzo to men who seemed neither happy nor sad as they chewed their mustaches, worried their beads, and watched the earth spin. For the first time in Greece, Andrew felt as if he'd arrived somewhere authentic. Karina went for a stroll as he took a seat. Unlike his world, where everything was measured in dollars and convenience, here was a poor, gentle, inconvenient world. He could grow old in a place like this. Everyone else had.

He pulled out his pad and began sketching. The man nearest him, with an oxlike face and missing tooth, turned red, then hauled himself out of his chair, shook his head, and walked away — but only a few steps. Then he stopped and watched as Andrew kept drawing.

The two men at the same table gazed past Andrew as he sketched their contours, outlined long, hairy ears, bristling mustaches, knobby fists gripping cups and canes. Eventually the ox-faced man made his way to where Andrew sat working and sidled up behind him, watching over his shoulder, rubbing his chin, nodding, snorting. After a while he walked past Andrew and retook his seat, where he resumed his former pose.

Finished, Andrew held up the sketch for them to see. The three men nodded solemnly, then, little by little, they smiled and looked at each other. One pointed to the pad, then to his friend, and laughed and slapped the other's back. Soon they were shaking Andrew's hand, slapping *his* back, calling for raki. All three men turned out to be named Yanni, and so Andrew titled his sketch *The Three Yannis of Ano Viánnos*.

"For you," he said, tearing the page from his sketchbook and handing it to them. One of the Yannis hurried across the cobblestones to a small shop from which he emerged with a big jar of honey that he presented to Andrew. More laughter, more backslaps, more toasts. *To the Virgin Mother. To Crete. To the Great Hereafter. To Zeus.* Karina returned, saw them all laughing, and clasped her hands in delight. "To your wife!" one of the Yannis shouted. "Yes," said Andrew, hugging her. "To my wife. We're on our honeymoon."

"He is lying," said Karina, laughing.

"We are going to make many babies."

To procreation! And to your children's children! Stinyássas!

A half hour later, as the Yannis slipped into the advanced philosophical stages of drunkenness, Andrew and Karina got up to leave. They had to fight their way through the shaking of hands and patting of backs and gestures indicating to Andrew that he should sketch them all over again.

"Hold me," said Karina as they stumbled toward the green frog. "I am so drunk."

Andrew drove over washed-out roads, scaring up starlings and seagulls, up sheer cliffs, down windmill-studded valleys, through brown towns huddled like grazing goats around red stone churches. Twice they took wrong turns and had to double back to their junction. By late afternoon they reached the windswept coast town of Áyios Nikólaos, built around one of Crete's two freshwater lakes and linked by canal to the Aegean.

On a small public beach, Andrew dove into the brackish water. But his limbs felt too heavy to swim, so he got back out and lay on a long chair next to Karina, whose purple bathing suit set off the pale contours of her flesh and kept Andrew from concentrating on the scenery or sleeping. After only twenty-four hours, they had reached that stage of a relationship where talk is unnecessary. While she dozed under a shade umbrella, Andrew stared at her full lips and at the gentle dip and curve of her belly. He realized then that he wanted to make love to her and had wanted to all along.

"Loneliness is an adventure," he said, lying there with his eyes closed, the world a vermilion blur behind his eyelids. "Possibly the greatest adventure of all."

It was nearly dark. The sky had turned violet; the waves curled iridescently on the shore. They had driven another fifty kilometers, across the narrowest part of Crete to its opposite coast, to Ierápetra, with its greenhouses and pickling factories, then east along the coast road to Makrigialos, where, as the sun set, they found two rooms in a green wooden house set back from the beach. As the last drop of molten sun dissolved into the sea, they lay dripping like a pair of spent lovers, but (Andrew reflected) instead of making love to each other, they'd been making love to Crete and to the sea.

Andrew asked, "Do you know who Ambrose Bierce was?"

Karina shook her head.

"Ambrose Bierce was an American journalist, a contemporary of Mark Twain, but even more cynical. One day he went to Mexico and was never heard from again. Some say he was kidnapped by Pancho Villa's troops, but no one really knows. Anyway, Bierce wrote a book called *The Devil's Dictionary*, in which he defines 'alone' as meaning 'in bad company.' That's what loneliness is. No longer being able to enjoy being alone with yourself. When you're lonely, the person you really want to be with is yourself."

"That is an interesting theory. And how does one learn to do that?"

Andrew shrugged. "Go for a walk, eat a nice meal by candle-light; romance yourself. Ask yourself, 'What do I feel like doing today?' It sounds strange, but why should it? Why should it be so strange to do with ourselves what we think nothing of doing with others? Why — for example — should I be more courteous to you, whom I barely know, than to myself, whom I'll know for the rest of my life? It doesn't make sense."

"You're right," said Karina. "It doesn't."

"The fact is, most of us are our own worst enemies. Instead of being kind to ourselves, we go out of our way to be cruel, and that leads some to think of suicide."

Karina asked, "Do you ever think of suicide?"

Surprised, Andrew nodded. "Sometimes I think it's why I took this trip." The surf hissed. "I guess I've thought about it at times in my life. Maybe a little too many times, lately." He was going to leave it at that, but then he remembered their vow. "But for no reason in particular, which is the worst of all reasons, since you can't get around it." Now he'd said both too little and too much, and regretted it.

"I, too, have thought of suicide," said Karina. "I don't know why. When I was four, my father was run out of town by the Mafia. They made him take his pants off and run through the vil-lage. Respectability is everything in Brazil. That is why we moved to Niterói." She leaned up, drank her water. "Why do you think of suicide?"

"Because no one has ever bought me roses."

"I wish you would forget about roses. You are an angry man, I think. What has made you so angry?"

"I used to take myself to a barber and get a shave," said Andrew. "I loved the feel of warm shaving cream, the stropping of the blade on leather, the clean, efficient rasps of the razor as the barber stretched my skin, the touch of efficient but caring fingers. Unfortunately, barbers no longer shave people. Matters of insurance. Maybe that's why I'm suicidal." He yawned.

"I'm not ready to sleep," said Karina. "Come, let's go to town."

In the dark, they picked up their towels, rinsed the sand off their feet, and made their way to the green frog. They drove to the center of Makrigialos, a kind of Ocean City, New Jersey, but with pine trees and mountains, where they dined at a seaside taverna to throbbing disco music and Karina looked at Andrew's sketches. Meanwhile, he watched the dark sea lap at the pilings and realized he hadn't felt lonely once since meeting Karina on the dock. Her sparkling, yellow blue openness balanced his brooding, wine-dark depths. He felt as if he'd known her forever.

Back at the house, on a terrace draped with bougainvillea, they shared a bottle of retsina and cookies from the taverna. Andrew sniffled: he was catching a cold. Karina proclaimed that with his sniffles Andrew had eliminated any possibility of their being lovers. "So now we shall never know if what you say is true," she said, smiling.

Just after the moon set, Andrew woke. His cold had gotten worse, and his stomach growled: wine and cookies. He blew his nose, gulped down two aspirin and half a Valium with some water, and tried to go back to sleep. When he couldn't, he pulled on his slacks and walked along the beach. Pelicans and seagulls glided down the cliffs; the shore smeared itself with fog. He walked a long way, past the lighthouse and tied-up fishing skiffs, until dawn stained the eastern sky. Bierce had it right: it was easier to look elsewhere for comfort, even to inanimate things, like paintings or the sea. He walked, sandals in hand, kicking at stones. Now he *was* lonely. And what did loneliness consist of? Dashed hopes? Disappointment? The total absence of passion or pain? The loss of something one never had to begin with? *She thinks I'm angry.* Even in sketching, Andrew looked outside himself, to other objects, other people, as if they were mirrors, showing him who he was, giving him back to himself. The sea is a big mirror, he thought. A vast, nauseating mirror that gives us back to ourselves clean and refreshed, like a box of shirts from the Chinese laundry.

When he returned, he found Karina drinking orange juice on her balcony. She smiled and waved, the morning breeze fluttering her hair. "Where are we going today?" she called.

"We could keep going east," he shouted up at her, "to the tip of the island, or head back through the mountains."

"Let us head back," said Karina. "I am sick of the sea."

Soon the little green frog wrestled the hairpin curves, averaging twenty kilometers an hour through steep bluffs clad in wild oregano, sage, and thyme. The bluffs were home to the horned Cretan ibex, the *kri-kri* so often depicted in Minoan art, a creature so shy and elusive it's been labeled extinct. They saw goats, cows, gulls, swallows, geckos, chameleons. As they rounded a sharp turn, a vulture hung in front of them, motionless, a stuffed trophy suspended in midair, its tail feathers ruffling so close to the driver's window Andrew felt he could reach out and touch them. Then it swooped out of their sight, down toward the distant sea. Karina turned to Andrew with a wild, astonished look. It would have been the perfect time to kiss her, had he not been driving.

They drove past cypress, evergreen oak, sweet chestnut, and Calabrian pine. The old forests (Andrew read in his *Rough Guide*) were gone, consumed to build houses and ships themselves consumed by earthquakes and wars. They drove through a series of dry, dusty villages, places to get gas or food that earned no mention in their guidebooks. They invented a little game. As Andrew drove, Karina would ask him to describe something: an object, a vista, a feeling. Andrew would venture a sentence, which Karina would transcribe into his sketchbook, and which they would each improve upon, with Karina crossing out words and adding new ones. Then she would read the finished product out loud.

"Bravo!" Karina would say. Or, "Not so good."

In Áyios Galinas they found a vacant hotel, with rooms across the hall from each other. On their way to dinner, a blackout extinguished the entire village. They groped down the dark, winding road to the harbor, where they found an open restaurant on the water, sustained by candles and generators. The silence delighted Andrew, no loudspeakers, no disco, only their voices and the tinkling of forks and spoons and the ocean waves lapping against the harbor wall, going *shush, shush*, demanding more silence. Andrew ordered an omelet and wine, and Karina did the same.

Then the power came back; the music blared; the sky broke with light and noise. Andrew laughed — ancient Greece was gone, and so was his trip, almost, and any chance to be with this woman as more than a chauffeur. After dessert, in the dimly lit doorway of a house they happened to walk by, a serious-faced young man tuned his guitar while his girlfriend rolled a cigarette and placed it gingerly between his lips, and this simple gesture made Andrew want to throw Karina on the beach and make furious love to her. Instead, back at the hotel, between both of their opened doors, he said good night.

"Good night, Andrew." She kissed him on the cheek.

"Describe to me the color of the sea."

Andrew tapped his pen against his sketchbook. It wasn't really yellow blue, or aquamarine, or azure, or any color you'd find in a watercolor box.

"Well?" said Karina.

"I'm thinking."

Nor was it the blue of the sky, or robin's eggs, or sapphire, or tourmaline. For too long, poets had been getting away with saying that things were like other things. Andrew would put a stop to it. Here; now.

"I am still waiting," said Karina, combing her fingers through her hair.

Nor should they be allowed to get away with such expedients as "the blue of dreams." The sea is no dream, no sigh, no murmur, no memory. Andrew set his descriptive sights on the far shores of verisimilitude, where, he thought, poetic rendition might meet scientific accuracy. "Impossibly blue" was ridiculous. Homer called it the "wine-dark sea," but that was because the Greeks had no word for the color blue. Then again Homer was blind.

"You have given up?" said Karina.

"I have not! Patience!"

And when you scoop up a handful, what do you get? Clear brine that slips through your fingers, the home of spiny urchins.

What looks so dreamy from a distance turns to salt water. From a great enough distance the whole world turns dreamy blue, absorbing, seducing us. Hence, the Blue of Absorption. The Blue of Arousal. Of Seduction . . . Andrew scribbled frantically.

"I am still waiting," said Karina.

"Got it," he said at last, clearing his throat. "The sea is the color of flirtation, the promise of ecstasy with no guarantee."

Karina rose in disgust to her feet. "I'm going swimming," she said, and ran, dove, and splashed into the sea that Andrew had so eloquently failed to describe.

Rethymnon, a former Venetian port, town of minarets pointed phallically skyward, balconies of hand-hewn oak, intricately carved doorways of cramped shops. The multicolored clay-tiled roofs and ochre walls relieved the parade of sugar-lump and concrete architecture. Rust reds, nut browns, mint greens, and butter yellows melted and shimmered in the oily bay.

They had agreed to part ways here and so spent their last hour in search of a gift for Peter, Karina's lawyer lover awaiting her in London. They passed clear and yellow bottles of raki and ouzo, strings of bright worry beads, finely embroidered linens, glistening olives of all colors and sizes, anchovies, pistachios, stuffed grape leaves . . . Too strong, too small, too homely, too salty.

"Tell me," said Andrew, "just what do respectable lawyers living in London like?"

Karina frowned.

"How about one of these charming paintings?" suggested Andrew, in front of a stall with watercolors for sale at embarrassingly low prices.

"Peter doesn't like paintings."

"No?"

"His tastes are peculiar."

"I'll say. He doesn't eat anchovies, doesn't like olives; he doesn't look at paintings. Has it occurred to you that you may be in love with a dead man?"

"That is not funny."

"He must eat something."

"Steak."

"Perhaps a bottle of Worcestershire sauce?"

"I am not amused."

"I know — how about some roses? A full dozen!"

She turned on him. "I do not like you. Why are you doing this?"

"What? What am I doing?"

"You have been so nice until now. I have so much enjoyed being with you. And now . . ." Tears welled in her eyes.

"I'm sorry." He put his hands on her shoulders. "I must be jealous."

"I think so," she said, wiping her eye.

"Can you blame me? Three days in Greece with a beautiful, charming woman, and now I've got to hand you over to that steak-eating rose-giver."

"I am not yours to hand over," she said.

"I know," said Andrew. "Still, I have to confess, all this time I've been pretending you were mine. I enjoyed our little games."

She nodded. He held her. In the end, she settled for a set of earthenware raki cups. As the proprietor wrapped them in red paper, Andrew stood outside, buffeted by sunlight and shoppers, dragging on a cigarette, wondering about gestures, why he was so bad at them. Flowers, gifts, the appropriate kiss planted at the opportune moment, opening doors, sending cards, saying thank you. Was it laziness, selfishness? Or was he just a regular asshole? He felt a fresh tide of loneliness rising, and there was nowhere for him to turn. It was now or never, he thought, his chance to prevent his loss from being total, to break with the past and make at least a gesture that might change his life. How? Karina, package in hand, skipped out of the store.

"There," she said. "I am sure he will like them. And now you will walk me back to the car, yes?"

As the silence between them thickened, Andrew realized it was too late; he had missed his chance; he had failed. She would forget him soon, but he wouldn't forget her. In his own idiotic way he had loved her. He had to say something. He had to *do* something. But what? They reached the car.

"Are you sure you'll be all right?" he asked. "Driving, I mean?"

"Of course," she said, getting in.

"Wait," he said. "I have something for you." He reached inside his backpack, took out his sketchbook, and riffled the pages, stopping between an olive grove and an old farmer.

"What's your preference? Olive trees or old men?"

"You know how I feel about old men."

He tore out the olive-tree sketch, folded it twice, and handed it to her through the driver's window. She thanked him.

"Wait," he said, tearing out the old man, too, and pressing it into her hands, then a café scene, and a church, and a group of children by a fountain. "What are you *doing*? Don't be *stupid*!" And the fat man snoring on the ferry, and a lifeboat against the black sky. He gave them all to her. He tore out Mount Etna from a distance, and the balcony covered with bougainvillea.

"Stop!" she protested. "You are ruining your notebook!"

"I don't care," he said. And then he bent forward and kissed her on the lips and tossed what was left of the sketchbook into the car. She kissed back, sniffling. It was the first time they'd kissed, yet still she'd managed to catch his cold. Or had she? She pulled away, gathered the sketches off her lap, and put them on the passenger seat, then drove off without looking back.

Andrew watched the green frog stop at a crossing, then continue down the road. She had no trouble with the transmission, none at all. When she'd disappeared around the bend, he turned and started walking. Already the sun was low in the sky. He'd have to seek lodgings. But first he would walk to the harborside to smoke a cigarette and look at the sea.

DRIVING PICASSO

PICASSO CANNOT DRIVE. He finds cars too amusing. I chauffeur him in a lagoon blue open-roofed '37 Fiat Topolino "transformabile" (two passenger, four-cylinder, top speed fifty-five miles per hour). From the sinkholes and mudslides of an unusually wet Hollywood, we make our way south, more or less, toward the Colombian Andes with their terrifying switchbacks (which my boss won't find terrifying; switchbacks amuse him, too).

The year is 1952. I am thirty-two years old and already convinced that I have botched my life. The ad in *Variety* said, "Artist seeks driver for journey of unspecified duration. Should be fresh faced and impressionable. Draftsmanship a plus but not required. Driver's license indispensable. Will provide means." I responded immediately as I'd lost my shoe store to the bank and creditors and groaned at the prospect of going back to work for Morton Cheswick at his Little Red Shoe House. I groaned for the following reasons:

1. I'd worked for Cheswick for eight years, starting in high school at sixteen.
2. The Little Red Shoe House is built to look like a giant saddle shoe, and its clerks wear conical green hats.
3. My father and I lived there, in a small apartment on the upper floor, and I hated the thought of working a flight beneath my home.
4. Cheswick is a cigar-chewing money-grubber who fancies himself royalty because he once sold a pair of white buck oxfords to Jimmy Stewart.

It takes us forever to leave L.A. Every twelve yards we stop and sniff at something. Following six days of rain my hometown is as lush as Rousseau's jungle. Rain drips from palm trees lining the boulevards; the sky is a fuzzy gray blanket. Under my 280-plus pounds the Topolino sags perilously to port.

Under a cloud-stuffed sky Picasso and I set up our easels and paint. One doesn't think of Picasso as a plein air artist. Picasso eats preconceptions for breakfast, and paint outdoors he does, with an amateur's brio and inconspicuous talent, the sort of canvases you'd put your foot through at a flea market. Does it shock me to see the creator of *The Frugal Repast* give rise to Sunday paintings as bad as Winston Churchill's? But I've been with Picasso for three days — long enough not to be too shocked by anything he does.

"Sincerity is not a moral issue but an aesthetic one," he says, putting finishing touches on a view of Hollywood from Griffith Observatory. Having detached the painting from its stretcher, he rolls it still wet (nothing dries in this damp) into a tight tube and shoves it into the Topolino trunk among a dozen other rolls, some mine. Picasso insists that we paint together, though I'd rather just watch. I especially like watching him mix colors. No one mixes colors like Picasso. Excluding my failed-animator father, I haven't known many painters; I grew up in Hollywood. But it's a sure bet most don't mix colors the way Picasso does, the brush a blur as it gathers pigments from light to dark, blending them with a deft twist of his wrist, but never thoroughly.

"The real mixing," Picasso says, tapping his temple, "occurs here. But you know that, don't you, Maestro?"

Picasso calls me "Maestro." At first I assumed that he was calling me Monstro, after the whale in Pinocchio — a crude joke, given my weight. But the real joke is that I am the farthest thing from an artist. I sell shoes for a living, or used to. I had my own store on Gower Street: *Cancellation Shoes, Brands You Can Trust at Prices You Can Afford*. Except for measuring feet, I have no talent (as it is I relied heavily on the Brannock device).

Picasso disagrees. He's seen my napkin sketches and says I have potential. "You have a gift for caricature, Maestro," he told me over a Howard Johnson's breakfast yesterday. "The great ones were all caricaturists. Van Gogh, Daumier, Rembrandt, Da Vinci . . . A good line should carry not only the form but an opinion about the form."

We tear ourselves from the latest swatch of scenery and drive off, my boss singing "My Heart Belongs to Daddy" at the top of his considerable lungs, getting the lyrics all wrong. As a countermeasure I belt Maurice Chevalier songs in my abysmal French, memorized from scratchy albums my dad would play on the Victrola in his bedroom studio while trying mightily to trace Donald Duck's contours to Mr. Disney's specifications.

The sun breaks through clouds. I have only a vague notion where we're going, gained at the top of our journey as we pulled out of the used-car lot on La Brea, where, after days of searching, we discovered our less-than-ideal method of transport under a butter-colored tarp. The Topolino needed only a fresh battery and lubrication. With the top down (it leaks anyway) and the painter of *The Family of Saltimbanques* holding an umbrella over our heads in heavy traffic, I was supplied with the rudiments of our mission, something about an expatriate saint living in a monastery above the equator and below the third parallel, a Sister Maria del Something-or-Other, who once performed on Broadway in her own musical review. This, of course, was before she renounced showbiz, joined the Order of Our Lady of the Andes (a Carmelite order), conceived immaculately, and lost one or both of her legs to a mountain lion — or was it a *Puma concolor*?

Picasso couldn't be sure.

Since then I've been wary of asking questions. Know your place, Son, my father — who could not color or trace within the lines — told me, his only child, always. And I took his advice, genuflecting before my store patrons day by day, applying their knobby, stinking, swollen feet to Mr. Brannock's gauge, squeezing the places where toes should and shouldn't be.

Between song numbers Picasso urges us onward, saying, "Forward, forward! Más allá! Andale!" We leave San Gabriel's mountains behind and make for Joshua Tree National Monument — fine with me, a sucker for deserts, especially one with trees out of the funny pages. Sometimes I think my dad went into animation just to please me, his cartoon-loving son. If not for my love of *Popeye* and the *Toonerville Trolley*, he might have made a fine carpenter or dentist, or unleashed himself completely and gone abstract, or expressionist — or both. But he wished to please me, his fat boy, to make me happy. Is it any wonder I blame myself for his literal downfall, tumbling back-first down the stairs to my storage room under an armload of shoes?

"You should paint a picture," says Picasso. "You could call it 'Father Descending a Staircase.'"

For Picasso the desert is a toy store, burlesque show, and three-ring circus, all in one. He can't get over God's whimsy, his variations on a theme of roots and water. I try to fill him in on some of the cacti's more salient scientific features; how they are capable of holding more than eighty times their weight in water; how, like starfish and octopuses, their limbs not only regenerate when shed, they form whole new root systems where they fall. When threatened, they spew their needles, sometimes at speeds exceeding those of the fastest major-league pitchers, including Satchel Paige, whose fastballs are said to reach ninety miles per hour.

Picasso's interest in science is null. He grasps only form.

"God — the caricaturist!" he muses.

When not sketching with pen in notebook or with fingers in the air (conducting a symphony of line), he uses his body as implement. As we soar past barrel cacti, he hunkers in his seat, arms tucked to his chest, compacting himself into a prickly ball. When the saguaros appear, he stands, throwing his limbs this way and that, seizing their forms. Even rocks and sand aren't exempt. Tumbleweed, jackrabbit, boulder, he apes them all. To ride with Picasso is to ride with all creation in the passenger seat.

From clouds of desert dust the Joshuas leap out at us, puffy branches raised like banditos' arms as Picasso waves pretend six-shooters at them. We park the goat (*Topolino* means "little mouse" in Italian, but Picasso calls it the "goat") and walk, carrying easels, a blanket, and a picnic basket into the park. As deserts are meant to be, it's hot. At 260-plus pounds, even in mild weather I sweat like a sausage. We take off our shirts (Picasso wears his trademark blue-and-white-striped *chemise marinier*; I wear a white button-down, tie dispensed hours ago) and tie them around our waists. We come upon a field of purple sage puddled with yellow flowers.

"Ça va," says Picasso.

We lunch on jug burgundy and spongy slices of Wonder Bread spread to pieces with Skippy. Picasso loves peanut butter, can't get enough of the stuff. "Es un milagro," he says, prying some from his teeth. Though he spices his speech with foreignisms, his English is good — too good, I'd say, having bargained for more idiomatic improvisation, that reckless freedom of syntax only strangers can bring to our tongue.

"The problem with life," he says, his tongue thick with peanut butter, "is that it must be lived in chronological order. That is God's great blunder, one of his great blunders. Imagine if time weren't tunnel visioned, if we could approach our lives from more than one direction, if there might be a flashback here, a flashforward there, as in a good novel. But no: instead we get this one-way journey — as plodding and monotonous as the stretch of road we were just on. To make matters worse, we have to view the road in hideous three-point perspective — as if driving into a tunnel isn't bad enough! It's not even a tunnel; it's a funnel, narrowing as it goes, squeezing us until we turn into a point and die. To hell with perspective, I say! To hell with chronological time! Let us drive backward and sideways; let's go through life inside out and upside down, with our colors reversed, too, while we're at it.

I'm sick of that blue sky; aren't you sick of that blue sky, Maestro? Let's turn it chrome yellow, or purple, or a combination! Stripes! Polka dots! Why not a paisley sky? Or a tartan plaid? As for this gravity business . . . *merde*, don't get me started on gravity!"

Lunch over, the colors of the sky deepening overhead, we stab the sunset with our brushes. But we've had too much wine. "To paint a drunken sky one must be sober," Picasso says, putting away his brushes.

Back at the goat my boss takes out one of his "road maps." These are not maps, really, but drawings he has made in advance of our excursion, bright squiggles, loops, curlicues, and swirls of primary crayon color — red, yellow, blue — on Manila construction paper, the kind used in kindergarten. His "schematics," Picasso calls them. He consults them, brow furrowed, tracing a stubby finger along a rosy contour, nodding, saying, "Comme ça." Meanwhile genuine road maps, courtesy of various trusted oil companies, gather darkness in the Topolino glove compartment, appreciated only as visual poetry.

"So, where to next?" I ask, donning my chauffeur cap — a 1948 Sinclair Championship Baseball Team cap — jamming the car into gear.

"Suivez le piste rouge!"

I lift my snakeskin-topped stubby (I've always favored cowboy boots, since seeing Gary Cooper in *High Noon*) off the clutch, floor the throttle. We spin away in an amber cloud. My boss prefers that we drive through the nights and sleep by day, in the mornings with the air still cool. The Topolino's headlights barely dent the night. No matter, with only desert passing and no cars to either side of us. We drive through outer space. My cargo fires up a Gauloise, thrusts it high into the air, and points to the rearview mirror, where a comet's tail of golden sparks flickers away into darkness.

"You'll set the desert on fire," I warn.

He nods up at the star-dazzle. "Let God play with his own cigarettes!"

We're still headed south: this much I know from the shapes of the constellations overhead. To keep from falling asleep we play Twenty Questions. It's the boss's favorite game, one of his favorites. *Animal, vegetable, or mineral? Does it come in different colors? Can you roll it? Does it have a handle? Is it bigger than a bread box?* Mostly, Picasso dispenses with questions, blurts his guesses into the wind. *Periscope! Aubergine! Platypus!* "Admit it, you *were* thinking of a platypus just now! Don't deny it — I see it in your eyes!"

At dawn's break we search for lodgings. Picasso has a thing for motor inns, the kind with a dozen or so discrete units or "cottages" arranged in a crescent around the parking lot, or a kidney-shaped pool, in which case we avail ourselves of its overly chlorinated waters as both prelude and epilogue to sleep. My employer doesn't say "sleep." He says, "Let's fire up the dream furnaces, eh?" — though I gather this is only a crude approximation of the Andalusian original.

While carrying luggage into Cottage no. 12 of the Yucca Valley Motor Court, I notice something in the car parked in front of the cottage next door. The big, smooth brown car — a Melmoth, a make unknown to me — looks familiar, and I remember it overtaking us on the highway earlier. Its engine purrs; its headlights are on. A radio plays inside. A shadow moves within, and I peer to see a girl in the backseat, her face tinged yellow from the porch light (all the cottages have identical yellow porch lights). She sheds golden tears. As she wipes them with a wrist, she catches me watching her; her face freezes into a wet blur. I consider tapping on the glass, asking, is everything okay? when Picasso nudges me with his suitcase, and we press on to our cabin.

Contrary to folklore, Picasso isn't much of a swimmer. When he does the crawl, his arms flail wildly, slapping the water like beaver tails. His kick is counterproductive. If there are born backstrokers in this world, he's one of them, spewing tall jets at morning clouds. Despite my weight, or thanks to it, I'm good in water — better than on dry land, my body its own raft. Doing a dead man's float, I can read the newspaper without getting it wet. While Picasso spews, I do my twenty lengths, trying to swim a straight line — no mean feat in a pool shaped like an internal organ. Finished, I barely breathe hard. This annoys Picasso.

"How can someone so fat swim so well?" he asks, indignant. I think of all the answers I might give, such as that whales swim very beautifully. But I know my place.

That's when I see her, the girl, the one who'd been crying in the car. Wearing cutoffs and carrying her sneakers, she walks over and sits by the pool's edge, dipping a scarlet toe in the water, watching the ripples flow. There is that pleading, desultory look again on her face. Seeing me look at her, Picasso winks over his newspaper. His hand says, "Go on and talk to her, coward!" My frown answers, "She's scarcely sixteen, pervert!" Our mute argument is cut short by the man who stands in the doorway to cabin no. 13, wearing a suit, calling to the girl, his voice hypercultivated and vaguely European. With the air of a prisoner off to the gallows, the girl picks up her sneakers and joins him.

With a soft click the cabin door closes. The yellow light goes out.

"Mariquita," says Picasso. Translation: "ladybug."

Despite it being daylight outside, Picasso sleeps with the light on and the curtains drawn. He wears silk pajamas, green and gray stripes. Item: Picasso snores. The other night I heard him talking in his sleep. He said, "Proximidad." He gets up five, six times a night. I hear him emptying his bladder and gargling. Newsflash: the inventor of synthetic cubism has an enlarged prostate.

I know all this because my father had an enlarged prostate and because I'm an insomniac, descended from a long line of sleep-deprived antecedents, including my dad. One night, when I was six years old and both of us couldn't sleep, my father whispered in the dark from his bed (his wife, my mother, died in child-birth). He told me the story of a noble Austrian family related somehow or other to the Hapsburgs, whose members one by one contracted and died of familial fatal insomnia, an extremely rare disease resulting from — depending on which authority one appeals to — either exposure to cannibals or to ergot poisoning (ostensibly from a contaminated loaf or loaves of rye). The disease, my father said (his whispers slipping and sliding through the darkness into my ear), took between three and twelve months to claim its victims, during which time they suffered spectacularly: precipitous weight loss, loss of concentration and coordination, nervous twitching, deficits of both short- and long-term memory, difficulty distinguishing between reality and dreams, copious tears, murderous rages, despair, depression, delusions, dementia, and — finally, mercifully — death. In the case of the Austrian

Hapsburgs, the victims all hallucinated that they were being eaten alive by white tigers.

No one could convince them otherwise.

They died of horror and exhaustion.

This was my father's way of comforting me in my sleeplessness.

We lived alone in our cramped cold-water studio above The Little Red Shoe House. The smell of shoe leather, with that of Cheswick's cigars, wafted up through warped floorboards. We were as poor as we were not because my father had too little talent but because he had too much. He could not color between the lines or trace them faithfully. With a bulging portfolio and hat in hand, he went from Disney (whom Dad dubbed the Antichrist) to Warner Brothers to Max Fleischer Studios and back. But every time they gave him a chance, my father blew it by "improving" on the characters he was asked to color or sketch, making them in some little way his own despite his best efforts to honor their originators. He did not know his place, my poor father. Others his age would soon march off to the war and would gladly have taken *his* place (like me, Dad had flat feet, though he was not fat); they would have happily marched in step with Disney or anyone else — provided they didn't have to do so through a field pocked with land mines.

One day I stood by the drafting table watching my father draw a whale. Taped to his light board was the model he was to have followed slavishly, but being my father he enhanced the prototype, transforming Monstro from a sober, lumpy sperm whale to a grinning, jovial baleen. When they saw the result, naturally the people at Disney fired him. But when the movie debuted a year later, in 1940 (I was eleven years old), there was my father's whale brought to Technicolor life on a wide screen: the grinning Monstro children of all ages have come to love.

He could have sued but didn't. He made no effort to claim credit. In the dark, through smells of shoe leather and Cheswick's cigar smoke, my father's whispers found me: *Know your place, Son, know your place...*

Eating any meal with Picasso is a tricky business, with some foods to be avoided at all costs. Breakfast, served twenty-four hours a day at most roadside inns, presents particular challenges. Two eggs fried sunny-side up and served with a crisp strip of bacon will send him into paroxysms of laughter, especially should the bacon be placed in a horizontal line at the plate's leading edge to form a straight face. Cornflakes are okay, but never, *ever* with sliced bananas or fat strawberries (Rice Krispies, it goes without saying, are out of the question). I'm also careful to order foods that won't tempt the sculptor in him — ruling out oatmeal and hominy grits. (At first, silver-dollar pancakes were permissible, until my boss discovered he could make mobiles out of them.)

I've nothing against watching the master work; on the contrary, I wish my dad, who kept a print of *Night Fishing at Antibes* above his drafting table, were here to see it. But Picasso goes too far; he can't leave anything alone; he's an engine in need of a governor. He reminds me of my father, though in my father's case not sketching within the lines did him in, while it has made Picasso a legend. This angers me.

For myself I order the Hungry Man Breakfast Special. I know I'm a glutton; I can't help it; I feel safe within my layers of fat. For Picasso I order an English muffin, resigned to his doing something outlandish to it. Sure enough, with the grape jelly he paints an equestrian Don Quixote into the nooks and crannies.

"Stop playing with your food!" I say.

"Pourquoi pas?"

"Because — restaurants are for eating," I say with a mouthful of pancake.

A smirk breaks over Picasso's bad-boy face, lights up his binocular eyes. He likes getting me angry. Thanks to him, I've broken my code; I have forgotten my place.

"Eating is your métier, Maestro, and one at which, may I say, you are clearly as prolific as you are accomplished!"

Just this side of the border we encounter the Melmoth again, this time at a Texaco service station. Have they been following us, or are we following them? As I pull alongside it the girl plunges a finger deep into her mouth and with its glistening tip writes, "Help!" on the window, the *e* and *p* both backward. I'm now convinced that she is in serious trouble, and just as convinced that I am the one to do something about it. But I am a fat former shoe salesman and know my place. With its tank full and the girl's pleading face pressed to the glass, the Melmoth mumbles off down the highway.

Attracted by colorful serapes flapping in the breeze, Picasso has me pull into one of the countless Mexican tourist shops. He buys us both ponchos and sombreros, the latter doomed to blow off our heads on the highway. From tavern doors music blares into the zocalo, to mix with the dust and wind dancing there. My employer insists that we dance in our ponchos, taking my arm and salsaing me as tourists gather to watch, along with a group of tawny teenaged boys, barefooted and twirling strands of straw in their mouths. The crowd thickens. Choosing a woman from among the spectators, Picasso makes me dance with her. I don't like dancing; I've never liked it. I sweat too much, for one, and even squeezed into pointy, high-arched cowboy boots, my feet are too big and flat. My partner is likewise obese, which I'm sure was planned. She's also drunk and wears great gobs of perfume and jewelry, so many bracelets she rattles. She leads, probably because I can't, making it no less humiliating. She sweats more than I; her breath stinks of garlic and alcohol and something bacterial. Picasso watches, clapping his hands and shouting, "Olé!" like he's at a bullfight, with me the toreador. Why doesn't the SOB dance himself? I wonder, grown dizzy. Must I do this for him, too? Why? So he can laugh at me? So he can find *me* amusing? Dust clouds eddy and swirl, rising to mix with the sweat on my limbs. Every time I step on her toes, my partner cries, "Aeyaaa!" provoking peals of laughter from the crowd and especially from my boss, who throws back his cannonball head and laughs louder than anyone.

As I collapse into the sidelines, Picasso grabs a girl from the crowd, sweet faced in rolled, tight pink pants, brown hair avalanching to an impossibly slim waist. In my dizzy state it takes a moment to realize it's the girl from the Melmoth. For once she's not crying; she's laughing, thrilled to tango with Picasso — though for sure she has no idea who Picasso is. With a metal-bending glare in his eyes the father of *Demoiselles D'Avignon* toggles her back and forth across the dusty square. He's showing me up, proving he's got bigger *sopladores* than I, swinging his bull balls in my sweaty face. When the hypercultivated European reclaims his quarry — thundering across the impromptu ballroom and, with a perfunctory curtsy, snatching her off — I expect the adamantine

Spaniard to put up a fight. But no, he goes on tangoing himself, the stubby prick.

Disgusted, I buy oranges at a stand and head back to the Topolino, where, a few minutes later, Picasso finds me peeling one and offers his assistance.

"Thanks, I can manage."

With a shrug he takes another orange and peels it, all of a piece, the rind spinning away in a bright, leathery zigzag. He spreads the segments like petals, turning his orange into a juicy sunflower. In his hands nothing maintains its integrity. Will I maintain mine? Have I got any to maintain?

I toss what's left of my orange into desert shrubs.

"Are we going to find this saint, or what?" I say.

"You mean Sister —" He says the name again, and again I forget it. "We will get there, Maestro. Patience!"

"I'm in no hurry," I say. "I thought you might be, that's all."

"Why? She is an exiled nun living in an abbey with one or both of her legs missing. She will wait."

"What will you do when you find her?"

"I've been waiting for you to ask just that. I'm going to paint her portrait. She is said to be the most beautiful of all women. She makes the Mona Lisa look like a pig. And yet she has never had her portrait painted. Can you believe it? Only from memory and imagination, since she refuses all requests to sit for her likeness. Many artists have tried; none have succeeded. Picasso will succeed. He has painted the ugliest woman in the world, and now he will paint the most beautiful. It is destined."

Zooming (if forty-five miles per hour qualifies as "zooming") down the Central American coast, blue mountains to our left, blue ocean to our right. I white-knuckle the steering wheel, chewing on my silence, seeing my father's face as he climbs up the stairs of the storage room in my shoe store. His eyes go blurry, then blank. He stares at me, his irises twin polished buttons of lapis lazuli. The stack of shoe boxes teeters. For three months he's been working for me, doing his best while draining the dregs of dignity. He's only fifty-five. The shoe boxes fall, but not before my father, back-first down the stairs. I cry out, *Dad!* At the bottom of the stairs I find him crumpled and covered in shoes, kicked to death, clobbered by brown, size-12 wingtips. Dark blood trickles from his right ear — or is that (I hope against hope) shoe polish? From here on (I don't say or think, but *feel* as I kneel close by him) life will be different. I'll have to take care of him, to dress and feed him, to walk him to the bathroom and back, to change the bedsheets when he soils himself. I'll read to him from books that he may or may not understand; I'll draw pictures, search for signs, see nothing. The shoe store will go on the block. At first I'll try to keep running it, but then I've got to find a nurse for my father, and deal with managers who screw me and can't keep inventory worth shit, and soon it's all too much. I don't sleep. I'm short tempered with customers, who stop coming. The store loses money. My creditors write, telephone, knock. I find that I can no longer tolerate people's feet. I put the store up for sale and get one offer, from Cheswick. I let the bank foreclose: a mistake; Cheswick buys it from the bank, and at tremendous savings. I find work as a counterman at Schwab's Drugstore, the job Lana Turner supposedly held when Mervyn LeRoy discovered her. No one discovers me, the sweatiest soda jerk in Hollywood. My new vocation lasts exactly as long as my father: three and a half months.

"He died in his sleep," I say to no one, Picasso himself having fallen asleep in the passenger seat. He murmurs: "The universe has no edge and no center."

My "other" life recedes, a giant seaborne Brannock device that looks, for all the tea in England, like the deck of a calibrated aircraft carrier. The sky turns the scumbled red of ground beef; the earth below is bruised to grape skins. Fingers entwined over his belly, nostrils flaring, Picasso snores, bull-like in his dreams, though he looks like a baby, that soccer ball head, those over-stuffed eyes. I feel protective of him, a mother pushing her pram. The farther we drive, the younger he looks: the older I feel.

A Panamanian lagoon. Picasso slathers ointment on my burned shoulders. Against my skin his fingers are bear claws. The beach is a frying pan. I'd go indoors and read, but our cottage is too depressing, with the ratty rattan shades, squeaky ceiling fan, and cockroaches skittering. Instead I cool myself in the lagoon, hoping Picasso won't join me.

No such luck. "Attendez!" he cries, splashing after me.

We swim out past the barrier reef, me doing my Aussie crawl, smashing through elephant waves. In his competitive fervor the instigator of *Guernica* and *The Pipes of Pan* swims into my kicking foot; my heel collides with his face. When I look back, he's treading water, holding his nose. Part of me thinks, "Serves him right." Another part is horrified, beside myself.

"You okay?" I say, treading.

He doesn't hear. Or does he? He starts back to shore, doing a sidestroke while holding his nose, a thin ribbon of blood trailing him, reminding me for some reason of my father, who fell for me.

As I wobble out of the surf, he's toweling himself, his back a giant scallop.

"Pablo? Mr. Ruiz?"

With the towel flung over his shoulder he walks up the path to our dreary digs. I shout, "It's your own fault! You swam too close to me!" The cottage door slams. It's painted the same blue as the lagoon, the same blue as the Topolino. I see a brush mixing that color, the bristles picking dabs of lead white, cerulean, and cobalt off the palette. When the mental camera pulls back, the hand belongs not to Picasso but to my father.

I pace in front of the blue door, a swimmer afraid to dive. What else can I do? No prolific master of twentieth-century art has ever been sore at me before.

I knock. The door opens. Picasso wears a white terry-cloth robe. With a nod he motions me into the cool, rattan-shaded space. On the desk: papers spread out under scattered crayons. He's been sketching. On the topmost sheet figures float in a sea of childish waves, blood arrows wheeling like gulls around them. He has mapped our collision, charted its course, latitude, longitude, vector. Annotations filigree the margins, state's evidence: the geometry of disaster. A heavy X marks the point of impact. I recognize my foot. Where it strikes Picasso's Minotaur head the sketch is animated with a series of pulsing slashes. For the rest of me Picasso has drawn not man but whale: precisely, he has drawn Monstro, the grinning leviathan that swallowed Pinocchio and his toy-maker father, Gepetto. He's signed the goddamn thing.

"What's all this about?" I say, picking it up.

He seizes and crumples the sketch into a ball, then lies back in his bed with a wad of tissue pressed to his nose. The ceiling fan squeaks.

The road narrows; the lines of perspective converge. Peripheries are nullified as the geometry of death reasserts itself. We plunge into a funnel. I've grown suspicious of our destination, wondering if we'll ever get where we're going, supposedly.

"Don't you have to be dead to be a saint?" I ask.

"It helps," says Picasso. "But unless one has the goods, one may drop dead forever and it will get one nowhere."

"It would be a shame to drive all this way for nothing," I say.

"You are a skeptic. And anyway can you not simply enjoy the ride? Why does a journey need a purpose anyway?" says Picasso. "For the same reason a picture needs a subject: merely as an excuse for the paint, to have something to hang shapes, colors, and textures on."

"Are you sure you didn't make her up?"

"Who?"

"Sister Whatsherface, the saint."

"The saint, the saint!" Picasso throws his hands in the air. "Is that all you can think about? Such a hopelessly narrow mind for such a broad body! With that sort of mentality how do you expect to get anywhere?"

"She doesn't exist, does she?"

"You will never be an artist, that's for sure!"

"It's all a bunch of bullshit, isn't it?"

"You will be one of the countless poor sods who dream of painting but end up only making pictures of things."

"Does it occur to you, Mr. Picasso, that I don't *want* to be a painter?"

Picasso says nothing. He sits with arms folded, bottom lip pugnaciously pursed, steaming like an espresso pot. We ride in silence for a mile or two. Then he blurts:

"You want a purpose? Fine! Pick one! Whatever strikes your fancy. Say you want to go mushroom hunting, or mountain climbing, or spelunking with those big, fat, flat feet. Maybe you and I will track down Bigfoot or the Abominable Snowman — the South American one! Don't like my suggestions? Come up with your own. Whatever you pick, I will happily accept. And if you can't come up with a purpose, come up with a texture, or a color. Call it a brown journey, or a blue one. Whatever you say, Maestro, Picasso will back you 100 percent!"

We reach the Andes, which shed their cool color and their charm as we transgress them. The Topolino struggles. Now I know why Picasso calls it the goat. Wishful thinking! A goat would chew up these hills! But our little mouse quakes in fear. Halfway up a near-vertical grade, with a gouge of smoke the engine dies. Soon we're side by side, backs to the bumper, pushing.

"Fucking Fiat," I say, forgetting myself.

"It was just so with me and Monsieur Braque," says Picasso. "Two mountaineers roped together, scaling the heights!"

"I told you it was underpowered, but *no*, you had to have it. You and your goddamn *artistic* choices!" It must be the altitude; I can barely breathe.

"That said, were it not for your being more than a little *pasado de peso* . . ."

"Fuck you, you Spanish ape! If you think I'm too fat, then why didn't you pick some pretty little girl to chauffeur you around? Why me? I'll tell you why: because you need someone you can dominate, someone who'll put up with all your Spanish bullcrap, that's why! Well, I'm not taking it anymore. All my life people have pushed me around, making me kiss their fucking feet! Well, I'm goddamn sick of it!"

It's official: I have broken boundaries, infringed, encroached, gone over the line. I have lost my place because I never knew it. Picasso burns me with his Mussolini stare; for a moment I think he might even spit on me, strike me with his draftsman's fist. But then a Disney twinkle lights those Andalusian eyes, and there's that tight little mischievous grin, the same grin that swallows his face when he does something naughty with a brush or pen. All this time we've been pushing the car uphill. Were I to let go now, it would roll backward, flattening the greatest of all living painters.

We reach the crest. Breathless, Picasso bows to me.

"Very well, Maestro." He snatches the chauffeur cap off my head and puts it on his. "What is your wish?"

That's when I see the brown car pulled over to the curve. A man in dress slacks and undershirt works a jack under a rear tire. She's in the backseat. I must act now or forever know my place. This is for you, Father, this breaching of the rules while bowing to them. For once art will serve us.

I sketch out the rough plan; Picasso, with his brain like a brush full of paint, fills in the details. By what we are about to do my boss is so greatly amused he smothers his titters with his hand. Our collaboration has about it all the wit, charm, and spontaneous simplicity of the best animations. Now I see why I love cartoons: they give us the world minus gravity and suffering, a world of primary hues, unambiguous outlines, unbridled possibilities, without weight, subtext, or sophistication. For all his worldly fame I realize now that Picasso is really a cartoonist at heart, a child with his Crayola box, as naive as he is diabolical, prepared to do his bidding for me, his Walt Disney/Antichrist.

"Ready?" I say.

"Rescatar la Virgen de los Andes!" he says, with steely enthusiasm.

Sticking to the plan, I ask the man if he can use some assistance. He seems suspicious and relieved as he hands me the tire iron, wiping his hands on his shirt and saying, as I bend to the task, "I've always marveled at the curious conceit that keeps men floating down freeways on bladders of air." For appearance' sake I give a few turns to a lug before braining him — not quite hard enough to send his gray matter showering down the mountainside, but no love tap, either. He falls into Picasso's arms. As the girl looks on with indolent curiosity, we stuff our scoundrel into the Topolino's passenger seat, but not before relieving Mr. Humbert of his wallet, passport, and other forms of identification. Before sending the blue goat to its final pasture, we grab our luggage — including two dozen tightly rolled canvases — from its trunk. With a series of grunts and our damsel still watching (her sleepy eyes only slightly aroused), we heave the Topolino over the side. When on the sixteenth roll it bursts into flames, Picasso clasps his hands and notes with glee how the colors match perfectly those of the sunset that has meanwhile spread itself, like a knife loaded with Skippy, across the horizon.

You would think our rescued nymph would show some gratitude to her saviors. You'd be wrong. She chomps her chewing gum, her frown as fixed as the stars that begin to appear just then in the sky. We drive through the night with no words from her. In our cut-rate motel room the next morning we force her to sit for us next to a bowl of bananas: the least she can do, the gum-popping twit. Picasso titles his portrait *Still Life with Virgin*. Though I daresay mine is the better likeness, our subject is equally untaken with both our efforts. "They don't look a thing like me!" she squawks.

"Don't worry," Picasso and I chime. "They will."

Touched with an artist's brute fearlessness, I guide our considerably more powerful vehicle to Bogotá, where we drop Dolores off with the proper authorities, who assure us that they know just what to do with her.

From there all roads lead to glory, or close enough. We are a brush loaded with pigment, sweeping across a primed, gessoed landscape, the world our blank canvas. All boundaries have been erased, all outlines eradicated. Wherever we go we spill color; we spew, splatter, and scumble it, improvising subject and form as we please — improvising but also obscuring, demolishing them. Is there a Virgin of the Andes? Who *cares*. If we put her on paper, there she is. If not, not.

From here on, what we say — or paint — goes.

Plaza des Armas, Cuzco, Peru. The fountain sprays as high as the budding trees. We arrived in time for the annual art fair, with Pablo in sunglasses and sombrero, me in a green-visored boating cap. We've nabbed an excellent spot, in the shade of the triumphal arch. Thus we intend to raise gasoline money for our journey back north.

So far, the painter of *Three Musicians*, *The Weeping Woman*, and a thousand etchings of bulls hasn't sold one of what he calls his "Topolino Landscapes." I, on the other hand, former shoe salesman and child of a failed, insomniac cartoonist, have sold twelve.

Picasso's pissed.

"Beginner's luck," he says.

SAWDUST

MR. BULFAMANTE SMELLED like oil of wintergreen. I swear he greased back his gray curls with the stuff. He had a chunky head and cauliflower ears and carried a ball-peen hammer everywhere, as if it were the key to unlock his days. That hammer: a dainty object of brass, so small it disappeared inside his fist. He'd been a boxer in the French navy, he said, and carried his shoulders scrunched high, as if warding off imaginary blows to his ears.

On weekends starting the summer before my junior year of high school and continuing through winter break, I worked for Mr. Bulfamante sanding floors: worst job in the world. Most of the floors we sanded were in new houses, their Sheetrocked walls unpainted, no electricity, no water. We drank and washed our hands from a two-gallon water keg Mr. Bulfamante kept in the back of the van, next to the drums of varnish and sealer.

Mr. Bulfamante liked me to call him Sugar, as in Sugar Ray Leonard or Sugar Ray Robinson, one of those sweetly named boxers. At dawn he would pick me up in his white Ford Econoline van. The van was covered with varnish: dripping down door panels and across windows, staining upholstery, stamping blurry brown thumbprints on the hood, streaking like comets across the windshield. The radio dials were all yellow and sticky. Seeing me standing at the end of the driveway holding my lunch bag, Sugar would flash a gap-toothed smile, nod his big, square head, and mouth the words, *Ya bum!* through the windshield, which had a big crack in it. Sugar called everyone a bum.

Before he'd let me into his van, Sugar would make sure that I'd brought my thermos full of bouillon. Sugar insisted on hot bouillon as the only suitable beverage for floor sanders and boxers, summer and winter. Not lemonade or iced tea or coffee or hot chocolate. Bouillon. And not chicken bouillon, either. Beef. Chicken was for fruitcakes. Also the bouillon couldn't be made from those little cubes, none of that Herb-Ox or Knorr Swiss crap. It had to be real. Homemade. From oxtail or beef brisket bone. Sugar taught me how to make it. He was a widower.

"You make bouillon?" Sugar would ask. He had a thick accent. I couldn't tell if it was French or Italian. Maybe both.

I'd tap the red thermos sticking out from under my arm.

"Good. Bouillon good for you."

I'd sit on the passenger seat, which, like everything else, was sticky with varnish. Over the defroster's useless whir the radio sputtered classical music: *Bolero*. Schubert's Eighth. The *Firebird Suite*. The same music Mr. Quick, my freshman English teacher, had taught me to appreciate on his portable Sony tape recorder.

Sugar would hand me a Kleenex to wipe the fog off the windshield. Then we'd rumble through the morning gloom, the sky still as dark as the roofs of the houses, headlights peering down murky streets, the defroster exhaling lukewarm air, strains of Schubert seeping through static, barrels of varnish and sealer bumping and splashing in the gloom behind us.

I never knew where we were going. It might be an old farmhouse with wide-planked floors thick with paint that would take dozens of sandings to remove, the burnt-paint smell horrible in my nostrils. Or it might be a brand-new house with fresh-laid floors still smelling of oak, caked blobs of plaster forming little bird-guano-like archipelagos all over it. We'd rumble for twenty minutes or so down increasingly narrow roads, Mr. Bulfamante's calloused hands loose on the steering wheel, the sun just burning pink through silhouettes of houses and trees, the van bouncing like a donkey cart. I'd keep my eyes fixed on the windshield crack, watching to see if it grew when we bounced, afraid to speak lest I say the wrong thing and increase Mr. Bulfamante's suspicion that I was a fruitcake.

Sugar suspected I was a fruitcake because of my friendship with Mr. Quick, which began during my freshman year. Sugar had learned about it from my mother. My father was dead. Mr. Quick was skinny and short, with a black mustache, the ends of which he would twist upward, and a rapid, mincing walk to match his name. A lot of kids called him "Mr. Queer," but then they called everyone queer who didn't play sports. I thought he was interesting, like no one else I'd met. I liked it when he read us poems about Grecian urns and assigned stories about the knights of the Round Table.

Jack Quick lived alone in what used to be the caretaker's cottage at Bennington Pond. He wore Frye boots with side buckles and bell-bottoms. He'd been a Rhodes scholar at Oxford and had an English accent, but not really. He didn't drive a car or eat meat or wear ties. His cottage had no electricity. He liked to read and write and play chess by oil-lamp light. He didn't have a family as far as I or anyone knew. His cottage was filled with books on every wall. He didn't drink but liked to sip a certain kind of Chinese tea with a melodic name and a smoky taste and smell. He'd been teaching for less than a year when I started high school.

I began to visit him at his house in early October of freshman year. When the water was warm enough, he and I would swim together in the lake, sometimes with no clothes on, since there were no houses nearby and no one could see us. It shocked me how muscular he was, standing there on a large rock, the sun bouncing off his skin. I never thought you could fit so many muscles in a body so skinny.

At the center of the small lake was an island with a miniature stone lighthouse. I'd swim out there with Jack — I called him Jack — though he always swam faster than I did, his short, skinny legs kicking up sun-speckled plumes of water. Then we'd lie flat on a rock below the lighthouse, looking up through a net of tree branches that seemed to sway and leap out over the water. Sometimes we'd talk. Jack never talked about people or things, only ideas, with every other sentence ending with a question mark. He liked to think, think, think. I said to him once, "Jack, can't you ever stop thinking?"

"Frankly," he said, "no."

Or we'd just lie there silently, eyes closed, the sun warm on our faces, the wind crawling coolly over us, feeling nothing but good. "Doesn't the sun feel great?" I said to him one day.

"As thermonuclear devices go," Jack replied, "it has its charms."

When it got too cold to swim, we'd play chess in his cottage with the stove roaring and mugs of that strong tea that smelled like Wesley Conklin's house after it burned down. Jack would checkmate me, and I'd say, "You bastard!" or, "You slimeball!" or even, "You fucker!" and he'd smile that sneaky, know-it-all smile of his under his black mustache.

Sometimes he'd get me so worked up I'd lunge at him, and we'd wrestle. And though he was no bigger than me, he'd pin me in two seconds flat to the cottage floor, which was wide planked and painted a greenish blue color like the sea. While pinning me he'd grin, and I'd pretend to be mad and call him all kinds of names, though I wouldn't be able to stop smiling.

The van turned up a freshly paved road, bordered by aborted-looking mounds of snow-covered dirt, to a new housing development, some of the houses still without clapboards, sided in tar paper, their yards snowy moonscapes of raw earth littered with shingles and scrap lumber. Sugar stopped the van and checked a house number against the one written on a varnish-stained scrap of paper. He nodded his greasily groomed head, pulled into the driveway, turned the engine off, and yanked the hand brake, hard.

"Ready, ya bum?" he said, punching me in the shoulder.

We went inside and scouted the premises. Using his ball-peen hammer, Sugar tapped the floorboards, *tap, tap, tap*, like a doctor palpating a patient's chest. With the hammer's flat end he chipped away at stubborn plaster deposits, then ran his thick palm across the floor feeling for nail heads and gaps between boards, all the time nodding his wintergreened head, making grunting sounds — the same sounds for approval and disapproval. Then, like someone who'd just sampled a glass of wine, he drew a deep breath, stuck out his lower lip, nodded, and said, "Okay. We work."

First, we dragged in the heavy-duty industrial belt-sander that you pushed like a lawn mower. As I helped Sugar carry it up the steps into the house, its metal edges clawed my palms. Sugar always went up first, walking backward like a scuttling crab. He was powerful — especially for a man in his sixties — and puffed like a steer through his nostrils. He told stories of his days in the French navy, how they persecuted him for being born in Italy, called him "Mussolini" and "Il Duce," gave him all the worst jobs, made him box. Sugar's arms were as thick as my legs. I saw them flex beside the bright red sawdust bag that hung limp, like a deflated punching bag, under the belt sander. An unlit cigarette dangled from his lips. The way he carried that sander you'd have thought he was carrying nothing heavier than that cigarette, while I struggled, afraid I'd lose my grip and tumble back with the sander on top of me, body crushed, blood and bouillon seeping out of me into the snow.

The day Mr. Quick told me we'd have to stop spending so much time together we were hiking the railroad tracks, collecting blue glass insulators that had fallen from telephone and telegraph lines, keeping the best ones and throwing the rest into the weeds like fishermen throwing small fry back into the sea. We were walking by the ruins of an old hat factory when he told me. His voice was quiet, matter-of-fact. I kept saying, "Why?" But I knew; at least, I had some idea. I'd wondered if he might really be queer, and if I might be queer myself, though I didn't think so, not really, since I liked girls. Still, these things had occurred to me. And it had occurred to me too that people were saying and thinking things, even my own mother. But I didn't care. Honestly, I didn't.

Jack said it was for my own good, that someday, when I was old enough, I'd understand. By then we'd both be men, and we could be friends again.

It wasn't fair, I said. What did it matter how old I was? I cursed up at the hat factory smokestack. Jack said, "You're acting like a child." He was right.

I went back to the van for the rotary sander, a smaller machine for sanding corners and against walls. But before using it I had to scrape. I had to go around on my knees with a little scraper scraping inside closets and in corners where even the rotary sander wouldn't reach, scraping gobs of plaster and leveling the uneven spots: you'd be amazed how sloppy new floors can be. I scraped until my fingers turned into claws around the wooden handle and my blisters burst, bleeding pink, until my knees wailed under the flimsy kneepads Sugar gave me to wear.

By then Sugar had the belt sander going, pushing it back and forth, back and forth, his curly hair white with sawdust already, the bright red bag burgeoning, his unlit cigarette dangling (he never actually smoked them), sweat leaking out of his forehead, his breath painting clouds in the sawdusty air. When I'd finished scraping I moved on to running the rotary sander. I wore earplugs and a paper mask to keep the sawdust out of my nostrils, but it got in there anyway.

When you sand floors all your senses turn against you. Noise, dust, heat, smell, pain, hunger, thirst, exhaustion. The sawdust turned to putty in my nose; my ears ached from the noise; my skinny arms turned to rubbery celery stalks as the rotary sander twisted and turned. That rotary sander hated me; we hated each other. Now and then, through the sawdusty corner of my eye, I'd look up at Sugar, hoping to see him switch off his machine and announce lunch, and at the same time hoping he wouldn't catch me looking or see me losing my battle with the rotary sander, being a fruitcake.

I wasn't in school the day they announced that Mr. Quick would no longer be teaching us. I was home sick in bed with a fever. It was late May. A few days earlier I'd gone swimming by myself in Bennington Pond and got hypothermia. The water must have been around sixty-five degrees. When I came out I couldn't stop shivering. The coldness had sunk into my bones. I could hardly walk. I knocked on Mr. Quick's door. He sat me under a blanket in front of his stove and gave me a mug of hot Chinese tea. "I've been meaning to speak with you," he said. "Have you been hearing things, about us? Has anyone said anything to you, asked you anything?" I shook my head no, no, though people had. My teeth were chattering. The next day I woke up with a fever.

I learned about Mr. Quick resigning or getting fired (I never found out which) the day I went back to school, from Clyde Rawlings, on the bus. He told me how Miss Rathbone came into the classroom with Mr. Dillard, the vice principal, and told everyone to hand in the journals they'd been keeping for Mr. Quick, that they wouldn't be needing them anymore, to get out their grammar books.

As soon as the bus pulled up to the school, I jumped off and started running. I ran all the way to Bennington Pond, to Mr. Quick's cottage. The door was open. Aside from a few books everything was gone. The Japanese-style table. The chess set. The blue glass insulators arranged on the kitchen shelf. He'd left behind one oil lamp, its glass chimney darkened with soot, wick burned to a nub. The smell of tea-soaked wood lingered. I rifled through the books scattered across the blue-painted floor, old paperbacks, their brown pages crumbling as I flipped through them in search of a letter, a note, something.

For a long while I stood holding the last book, the light through the windowpanes licking a warm streak down the side of my face, making little rainbows on the floor. I felt the cottage growing smaller and me growing smaller in it, until I thought I would disappear. After a while I sat down. I sat there until the sun rose higher in the sky and the rainbows dissolved and the blue green floor planks grew dusky, like waves in a storm.

I sat in the cottage all morning and deep into the afternoon, until the windowpanes gleamed with ruddy, low-angle sunlight, and my stomach growled. Then I got up and walked out the door.

I was halfway down the flagstone path when a primitive urge took hold of me. I bent down, picked up a stone, and hurled it, smashing a window. It felt good so I did it again. I broke another window, and another. I kept breaking windows until there were no more windows left to break.

A month later I got a letter from Mr. Quick, postmarked Kyoto, Japan. It was a short letter, and there was no return address. He said he hoped I was doing well and that he was very sorry for having left so "abruptly" but that he'd felt it was "for the best." After that I checked the mail every day, hoping there'd be another letter, a postcard, anything. Nothing came.

I never heard from Mr. Quick again.

I stopped giving a damn about things and spent lots of time in my room. That summer my mom got me the job with Mr.

Bulfamante. She did it, she said, to get me out of the house, but I knew she was worried. When school started again, my grades went to hell. I didn't care. My mother spoke to Mr. Bulfamante. I overheard her in our kitchen one afternoon, talking under her breath about Mr. Quick. Sugar said, "Leave him to me. I take care of him."

Sugar didn't stop. He never stopped. He kept pushing the belt sander back and forth, back and forth. I couldn't stop, either. I had to keep going, the sawdust turning to gold nuggets in my nostrils. I was sixteen, thinking this was what my life had come to. I'd blown my grade-point average. I'd never go to college; I'd never do anything. While fighting the rotary sander, I thought about what a disappointment I was to everyone, especially to myself. I wondered what Jack would think if he saw me here, now, and wondered if he'd really been queer, if that was the only reason why we'd been friends, and why he'd left so suddenly. That's when the tears came, mixing with the sawdust. I worried that Sugar would see me. The rotary sander kept whipping and twisting, dragging me along the floor like a parachute in a stiff wind. I'd done only one bedroom. I had five rooms to go and all those closets.

Hours later, after every floor was sanded and we'd applied the first coat of sealer, Sugar said, "Bouillon time!" meaning time for lunch. We stood in the cold air by the back doors of the van sipping the soup from our thermos cups.

During lunch breaks Sugar would give me boxing lessons. It was all part of his plan to defruitcake me. He had two pairs of old boxing gloves, the leather dried and torn. We boxed in our T-shirts. The scratchy gloves pasted my forearms and shoulders with welts. By the end of a sparring session the skin on my arms would be red and raw like a canned tomato.

We'd use the empty new garages as boxing rings, bobbing, jabbing, and feinting on the cold, smelly cement. Sugar never hit me as hard as he could have; he always pulled his punches. Still, even a pulled punch from Sugar could hit pretty hard. After sparring, Sugar would rub down my arms and shoulders with wintergreen oil — he always kept a bottle handy — his thick, calloused fingers kneading away at my ravaged flesh, his breaths breaking like snorts through his nose. The minty liniment stung like fire when Sugar rubbed it into my welts.

I'd gotten good enough to avoid most of Sugar's swift jabs and even get in a few of my own once in a while. Instead of flinching or growing teary eyed like me, Sugar would smile through the bobbing cigarette.

After lunch that day we were dodging and feinting when suddenly Sugar asked me about Mr. Quick. "You ever hear from your fruitcake friend?" he asked.

Something about the way he said it, the glint of a smile in his eyes, the hungry look, made me lose my concentration. I lowered my guard. Sugar's right hook hit my chin, sending me tumbling backward into the garage door, which we'd raised halfway to let out the sealer fumes that leaked in from the house. I banged my head hard into the metal bar running across it and sat myself down on the icy cement, holding my head, colored lights dancing around me like candied fruit in an exploded fruitcake.

Sugar stood in front of me. "Okay?" he said.

I nodded. But I was crying; I couldn't help it. Tears dripped down my face. I didn't care. It wasn't just the pain; it was everything.

Sugar put a thick, sawdusty arm around me. "Ya bum," he said. He said it with affection, which only made me cry even harder.

Then I was gone; I wasn't there anymore, in that cement-smelling garage, on that hard, clammy floor. I was swimming, kicking up white plumes of water, halfway to the island with the miniature stone lighthouse. The water was cold and clean and beautiful. I lay on the flat rock, the breeze caressing me. Then I was sitting with my legs folded in front of your Japanese-style table, smelling that odd fermented-wood smell, lamps burning, stove roaring, sipping smoky Chinese tea, gazing across the chessboard into your eyes and waiting to hear you say, "Checkmate!" We were on the floor then, wrestling, me locked under your arms, looking up at you looking down at me, smiling under your thick black mustache, my shoulders pinned to the wide-planked, blue green floorboards, adrift on that dusky wooden sea. Helpless, happy. Happier than I'd ever been, or would be again.

OUR CUPS ARE BOTTOMLESS

HE ROSE, SHOWERED, SHAVED, put in his bridge.

He dressed in corduroy and plaid. He went into the kitchen. He saw the papers arranged across the kitchen table, in the shadow of the strongbox. He stood at the sink, dampened some rags, and went into the garage.

He heard a rustling sound coming from a pile of dead leaves under some old tires. He imagined a squirrel. He rolled the rags into tubes and shoved them into the crack under the garage door. He took the large red can of gasoline that supplied the lawn mower and topped off the Plymouth's tank. He smelled the rough, pink smell of gasoline.

He went back into the house. He shut off the water, the gas, the electricity. He put on a yellow raincoat. He picked up a bundle of stamped letters bound with a red rubber band and, burying it under his raincoat, stepped into the rain.

Dear less-than-dear Vera:

A quick and final note to tell you no: this had nothing to do with us. In a sense I'd been planning it for years. As Frost said, "I had a lover's quarrel with the world." Only I don't like quarrels. Better to be kind than to be right? How 'bout better to be dead. . . .

He followed the rivers of mud down the steep hill into town. He felt the rain rushing down his face, the sweat gathering under his breathless parka, the tips of his shoes growing wet. He touched the letters close to his breast to see that they were dry. He saw his breath mingle with the fog. He was halfway down the steep hill and could barely see the outlines of sad brick that were the town. He felt the wash of impatient cars dampen his trouser legs. He watched the smokestack of an abandoned hat factory rise up through the fog, a giant, erect brick middle finger stuck into the gray sky. He felt his knees bobbing outward as he tried to slow his descent. He heard, or thought he heard, the roar of muddy rivers colliding under a steel bridge.

Dear Lansing:

Something of a shock, I'm sure, but not much of a shock, not after the gout, the diabetes, the strokes, the arthritis, the tinnitus, the no smoking, the no drinking, the no cholesterol, the no sleep, the inexplicable hard-ons (except on those rare occasions when they might be welcome), the EKGs, the CAT scans, the colonoscopies, the upper and lower GI series, the catheters (ouch!), the jars of Metamucil and Sominex and aspirin. . . . If you own stocks in pharmaceuticals, I suggest now is the time to unload them. . . .

He smelled, or imagined he could smell, coffee brewing.

He arrived soaked from his knees down. He dropped the damp letters into a mailbox. He ran across the street, under the watchful gaze of the steel bridge's girders, into the Café of the Two Rivers, which everyone in the town called the Two Rivers Café.

He took off his parka, hung it, and sat on the far left counter stool. He read on the menu the words:

"Our Cups Are Bottomless."

He ordered eggs over easy, bacon, home fries, white toast, coffee.

. . . Doris:

Probably you think I'm more of a bastard now than ever. So be it. I make no claims for the transformational powers of death: if I make good compost I'll be pleased. What I want from you is not understanding or forgiveness or flowers on my grave, just the opportunity to clear the air on a few matters. But first let me say how touched I was to receive your note after my stroke. . . .

He watched the rain. He considered that the water would be good for the grass in the backyard. Just last week he'd spread new seeds and planted a row of barberry bushes to keep the neighbor's snotty-faced children at bay. The neighbors were not likely to be a problem now; few things were likely to be a problem. Still, he hoped the bushes would thrive . . .

List of jobs:

Radar technician (USN-1944), mill-lathe operator, cardboard-box-factory foreman, landlord, plumber, plasterer, hatband-factory foreman, grease monkey, stock trader, estate planner, pond dredger, gutter repairman, wire-coat-hanger-factory foreman, salvage and antiques dealer, candidate for first selectman, candidate for second selectman, amateur butcher, baker, candlestick maker, leaf raker, driveway plower, bricklayer, floor sander, reciter of off-color limericks —

> *There once was a man from Stanboul*
> *Who soliloquized thus to his tool:*

"First you robbed me of wealth,
Then you took all my health,
And now you won't pee, you old fool!"

. . . emergency-room patient, witness, power-of-attorney holder,
justice of the peace, father, stepfather, grandfather, step-grandfather,
adulterer, uninvited guest, crank, crackpot, curmudgeon, whistler
in the dark, rope pisser-upper, hummer of petrified tunes, quoter of
Ogden Nash:

Any hound a porcupine nudges
Can't be blamed for harboring grudges.

. . . brass-widget-factory assistant foreman . . .

The eggs were delivered to him, one of them running. He took
his knife and sliced down the center of it, letting the yellow yolk
spill into his potatoes. He thought of abscesses, brain surgery.

. . . plunger of toilets, mopper of floors, burner of toast, carver of
turkeys, sealer of driveways, licker of stamps, breaker of circuits . . .

A man sat next to him, smoking. He didn't wish to move, nor
did he wish to inhale the man's smoke. He gave the man as much
of his back as possible.

. . . pumper of sumps, catcher of moles, digger of holes . . .

His coffee was thrust before him, his bottomless cup. He
poured sugar into a spoon and watched it spill over the sides like
sand over the sides of a dump truck.

. . . digger of moles, catcher of holes, smeller of molds . . .

He poured milk from the stainless-steel dispenser, which,
being poorly designed, dribbled as it poured. He redesigned it
swiftly in his head (no spout; small notch at lip) while watching
the milk billow smokelike into the coffee.

. . . breather of carbon monoxide . . .

He compared the color of the coffee in his cup with that of the muddy rivers fulminating beyond the plate-glass window.

. . . Frankly, Vera, I don't see how you can blame me for my few transgressions in light of your more elaborate displays of deceit. But I'm not writing to dispute anything. Everyone wants to be remembered well, and I'm no exception. I could never stand the thought of anyone hating me, even strangers, even the man who gives me stamps at the post office. . . .

He watched the rain. Rainy days are good for the soul, he thought. The rain makes good little defeatists of us all. Only born defeatists do it when the sun shines.

List of wives:

Doris, faithful and dull, cooker of plain meals, maker of even plainer love. A beautiful body largely wasted. Smoked heavily all her life; now dying of lung cancer. What a heart, what a good lady, impossibly good. Couldn't have done better; couldn't have done worse. Did worse. Married Vera. Greek goddess. Greek bitch. Broke me like a dish: you know the Greeks, the way they stomp on dishes when they dance? That was me under her heels. But she could make me laugh. And that beautiful, pear-shaped behind of hers. Could not cook worth a dime. Would bake spaghetti and broil eggs. Nasty to her children. In both marriages I was faithful half the time. Thirty-eight combined years of marriage, four affairs. Not a bad record, or a good one, depending which way you're counting . . .

With a trembling finger he tapped the side of his empty mug. The waitress refilled it.

List of cars:

Ford V8 roadster w/rumble seat. Morris Minor 100 sedan (leaked oil like sieve). Crosly Hot-Shot (could be picked up and carried by two strong men). Studebaker Lark (mint green; white sidewalls). Studebaker Champion (mauve interior; power-assist steering). Simca: nasty clutch. Mercedes 220SL convertible: dream car, should have kept it. Jaguar E-type convertible: nightmare car, never should have bought it. MGB roadster: ditto, electrical harness like a road atlas. No more British cars, please. Peugeot 403: came with a mechanic who looked like Jacques Cousteau; should have come with a lemon-squeezer. Fiat ("Fix It Again, Tony") roadster: wouldn't start in the rain; wouldn't stop in the snow. BMW ("Break My Window"): break my wallet, too (new distributor cap: $65). No more European cars. Used Plymouth Barracuda. Slant-six. That rear window, big enough to sleep under and gaze at the stars. Classic make-out car. Fifty-nine when I bought it . . . Just put in a new battery. Lifetime guarantee . . .

"DieHard."

He had spoken out loud and drew looks. He said it again, laughing this time. They would think him a fool, or worse, a bum (his children wouldn't argue with them). A self-educated man, good with his hands, not so good with money. He'd done everything for himself, just hadn't done much of anything. He enjoyed being right, but it was like cooking meals no one would eat. The things that gave him satisfaction gave him little satisfaction. He sat there, over a third cup of coffee, staring out the window at the brown chaos of tumbling waters. His hands shook. They had been shaking for years, so hard he could scarcely turn a screwdriver. It was like having the DTs, except he didn't drink, never drank. A beer or two in the navy, and those had bloated him. He waved to the waitress. Fill me again, for I am bottomless.

. . . Lonesome? What is the definition of that word? Capable of

*watching birds eternally? Friend of plants? Foe of neighbors? Born
to tinker in solitude? I am a bitter man. No, I'm not; yes, I am . . .*

Beyond the swollen rivers the hills were as raw as his thoughts.
He reminded himself that for three years he had wanted to be with
no one. If he sought companionship, he'd get a haircut, or stop
by the butcher's for meat, or buy brake shoes for the Plymouth at
Sweeny's. For a time he wrote letters to the local newspaper: why
the town didn't need a public pool; why minimum wage was a
lousy idea; why the government should get out of the education
business (this letter copied to his bureaucrat stepson). For a while
he toyed with objectivism, but quickly tired of the ardency of its
practitioners, pants-wearing women and bald, beer-bellied men.
Nasty letters he got after referring to their guru, Ayn Rand, as a
"nut." Opinions were like grass seed: the birds would eat most of
them. If the world could live without his opinions, he could live
without sharing them. Right?

List of friends yet remaining:

_____

_____

_____

Well, no. There were the six to whom he sent letters. His
dying first wife; his very-much-alive second wife; two step-
children, who didn't much care for him and vice versa; and his
own daughter, whom he considered a ditz. (She ran a puppet
theater. Or it ran her. He could never be sure.)

Dear Sharon:

*Well now at least you can cut loose these strings of mine, tangled
up as they were in all kinds of things. I was never sure which of us
was the puppet and which the puppeteer. Were you? . . .*

The final letter was to Lansing, his dearest, oldest friend, former editor of the town newspaper, now surrendering to Alzheimer's in a nursing home. One true friend, dying.

He signaled the waitress again. She appeared with her magic orb. Questioned, nodded, poured. He thought: If only I could stop thinking. If I could just watch the rain, the rivers. He let his thoughts drain out into the floodwaters, joining several uprooted tree stumps and a vaudevillian duo of bobbing bald tires. See what God can make of a little rain? A muddy hell. He finished the fourth cup, then waited, tapping it again with the same quivering finger. The waitress saw him tapping but did not come over. He kept his eyes on her. She wore earrings shaped and painted like colorful birds. Parrots. He thought of his daughter, Sharon, and her moronically grinning puppets. Strings attached.

Oh, see the happy moron
he doesn't give a damn
I wish I were a moron
By God — I think I am!

Come here, silly twit. Bring your magic samovar. Refill my life, what's left of it. Make good your laminated promises. Here, you gum-popping ostrich, over here.

Vile, vile, vile, vile. The whole thing.

Go home. Kill yourself.

No. Sit there. Forever.

. . . Remember T. Roosevelt's dictum: "Do what you can, with what you've got, where you are, while you are there." Or words to that effect . . .

One cup more. The last.

"Waitress? Some more coffee, if you dare, I mean, if you please."

She came; she poured; she conquered.

She burst a pink bubble.

"Will that be all?"

From above her steaming Silex Grail, the young waitress looked down upon him. Before the diner changed owners, he had known its faces well. All were strangers to him now. Day by day the world grows stranger, colder. A furniture-truck driver sloshed in, shaking his rain-wet face, speaking of floods. The old man watched the trucker drip, then swallowed his remaining cupful in a gulp. Will that be all? It occurred to him that the question was a pertinent one. When the waitress spoke again, he answered her by tapping the side of his mug with a trembling finger.

"My cup is bottomless."

"I've filled you five times already."

"You haven't filled *me* once. But let's not quibble."

He tapped the mug again. He didn't have to face the young girl to see her challenging look or hear the fireworks of bubble gum set off in her petulant jaw. He kept his eyes on the streaming plate glass, on the girders of the steel bridge. He had no desire to walk back in this rain. The house would wait; the Plymouth would wait. The keys were in the ignition. The battery was good. A DieHard. Lifetime guarantee. The cuffs of his trousers were still damp. He waited for his refill. And waited.

What's wrong with her?

She had gone on to serve other men. He gazed down the parade of sleepy work faces, some yet unshaven. Once his face had been among theirs. The garbage haulers, the hardware store man, the pharmacist, the milk and the bread and the postmen. The factory workers. None knew him now.

"A bottomless cup," he spoke loudly enough to be heard by all. "What do you suppose that means? In theory at least it means I can drink coffee forever."

Newspapers rustled. No one seemed to pay attention.

He leaned and spoke to the UPS man next to him. "She won't fill my cup." The man ate his eggs.

"Look, here's a tip, see? Worth at least another refill and putting up with an old putz like me."

"Why don't you leave her alone?" said the fuel-oil man two stools down.

"Why don't you mind your own basement? Go clean a furnace." Something else he'd done once or twice in his life. "I'm just sitting here, that's all." His hands trembled at the lukewarm sides of his empty mug. "If I could just get a little more — "

"Pain in the butt," said the fuel-oil man.

The UPS man paid and left.

"Waitress?"

The enigma appeared. She filled his cup.

"Bless you and keep you," he told her.

"That's the last one," she said.

"My cup is bottomless," he reminded her.

"Is there a problem here, April?"

The griddle man had spoken, a man with broad shoulders and a thin voice.

"It's all right, Frank."

"April. Is that your name? How appropriate."

She edged down the counter.

It was your idea to proclaim your cups bottomless, not mine.

I'm only a customer, and the customer is always right. He sipped his coffee. "The thing is," he spoke aloud now, "there are so few things you can count on in this life. You can't even trust your own bones. See this tooth? Chipped it on a chocolate-chip cookie. That tooth was with me sixty-eight years. Then came Chips Ahoy!" A body is a treacherous thing, he thought. Then aloud, "You think it belongs to you, but it's only on loan. Comes a day when you can no longer make the payments. The bank forecloses..."

A young man in a baseball cap took the stool vacated by the UPS driver.

"Their cups are bottomless," the old man pointed out to him.

The griddle man faced him. Thick arms and red hair. He held a griddle scraper.

"This is my diner."

> *A cook named McMurray*
> *Got a raise in a hurry*
> *From his Hindu employer*
> *By favoring curry.*

"Finish your coffee, then go."

> *Consider the case of Mr. Suggs.*
> *he was an eminent entomologist, which is to say*
> *he knew nothing but bugs....*

The griddle man swiped his mug.

"I'm not through."

"Out."

The old man rose slowly, reached for his parka. "You shouldn't make promises you can't keep." He said it quietly.

The griddle man went back to his griddle.

The old man got out his wallet. Then he thought of something. "I'd like to tell you a story."

"April, call the cops," said the griddle man.

"I'd just signed up for the navy. I was eighteen, green as moss, never been to New York." His gaze was held captive by the window. "There were hundreds of us. In Greenpoint they marched us into this huge, long warehouse building by the shipyard. There were showers and bunks and lockers, and there was a latrine. It was like no other latrine in the world. Rather than a series of stalls, there was one long trough running the length of the place, a city block long and tilted so the stuff would, you know, flow down in one direction — " The waitress spoke into the phone. " — into the East River. Anyway — "

"Would you shut up?" said the fuel-oil man.

" — along this thing were these boards, one-by-fours, paired up to be sat upon. You'd hoist yourself up on them and good luck." The waitress hung up. "When my turn came, I must have thought I was mounting a horse; I put a little too much *oomph* in it. Down I crashed, through the boards. And there I sat, at the bottom of this god-awful thing, up to my neck in piss and shit and laughing so hard I forgot to get myself the hell out of there." He laughed just thinking about it. "Talk about up shit creek without a paddle! I haven't thought of it once since then . . ." He wiped a tear from his eye. "Funny." He dropped some change on the counter. "Worst thing you could imagine, and I sat there laughing."

He zipped up his parka and went out the door.

The rain fell harder; the waters roiled, rolled, and churned under the bridge with a relentless, masochistic zeal. More planks of wood, tires, tree limbs, and stumps could be seen, along with what looked like a doghouse, bobbing briefly up and out of the torrent as if trying to be saved. He tasted the last sugary dregs of coffee in his mouth, working them around with his tongue, creating his own muddy pandemonium of fluids.

He started back up the hill, then changed his mind and walked to the center of the bridge. He stood at the railing, peering down at the churning mud, remembering. Here it was, for better or worse, flowing under his knees. He imagined a pair of planks, one-by-fours. Like a rodeo cowboy mounting a bronco, he'd hoist himself onto them. He'd straddle the brown flow of existence and ride it, bucking, until it threw him once and for all. Until it broke his back. Until he couldn't ride anymore.

He walked back up the hill.

THE GIRL IN THE STORY

I'D BEEN AWAY over nine months, in the Pacific Northwest, doing nothing important, nothing you need to know about. When the winter rains began, after a long dry Indian summer, I hurried back home to B——, a small town near Hartford, Connecticut, to reunite myself with Claudette. Too late. I arrived in time to watch her unpack two bags full of groceries, none for me. Among other items, a box of Trix cereal and a deli container of something called ambrosia — made with miniature marshmallows and coconut flakes. I thought, Uh-oh. In the bathroom, Claudette had put away my toothbrush.

"You'll regret it," I said.

Tears welled in her eyes as Claudette apologized. Oh but honey you were gone so long, etc. I took off in the middle of a sentence.

A sunny October day. The hills looked like ... well, like bowls of Trix cereal. I was driving my little red sports car. Datsun 2000. A collector's item. Hard to get parts. A perfect-weather car. Normally, I drove it for fun only. But now I had a mission. The convertible top (as always) was down. In the passenger seat next to me, splayed face down, the little spiral notebook in which I wrote everything. I drove way over the speed limit, with a lump in my throat and a streak of vengeance running from my heart to the gas pedal.

The first person I spoke to that afternoon was Gloria. I'd gone to my alma mater and lain down in the cool campus grass with my hands behind my head, looking up at the flaming tree branches flinging themselves over the central quad. Somehow I knew, if I just lay there like that, things would happen. Sure enough, I'd been lying there for less than a half hour, eyes closed, the sun hot on my cheeks and forehead, when a cool shadow covered my face. She stood over me, clutching a psychology text to her meager chest (Gloria was now a graduate student).

"I had a dream about you recently," she said. Her first words — before I'd even opened my eyes. "In the dream you were vile, sickening, disgusting. You repulsed me."

She said it with a sneer, gritting her teeth. Gloria had coffee-with-milk-colored skin, a so-called Roman nose. Though I'd never seen her smoke, the tips of her long fingers were stained with nicotine. I wasn't sure if I liked her, or even if I found her attractive. With some women it's hard to tell. She was a psychology major, a behaviorist, and we used to argue about her theories. Gloria believed that all investigation of human behavior should be based on objective criteria: hard science. I thought this idea bonkers. What about *feelings*? How do you measure those? What about all the things people think that don't appear to make any goddamn sense, the thousands of impulses that run through our minds every frigging second, like a swarm of gnats? How can you or anyone else begin to understand other people except through the subjective lens of your own impulse-riddled conscience? Psychology can't be a pure science! That's absurd!

You couldn't argue with Gloria. She'd accuse me of having a poet's soul, and if that didn't work she'd hurl some technical phrase out of a clinical psychology textbook at you and shrug her shoulders, like you'd never get it. It used to piss me off. And yet we kept at it every time we ran into each other. The more heatedly we argued, the more we wanted to sleep together. The only thing stopping us was Stephen O'Shan.

Stephen was a little, balding, red-headed Irishman who suffered from an array of mysterious, incurable bone ailments and liked to read *Ulysses* out loud. "Dublin English," he remarked more than once, "is the finest English in the world." Stephen was from Dublin.

"How is Stephen?" I asked Gloria. "Have you seen him?"

"Stephen is fine," said Gloria, looking down at me lying in the grass. The nostrils of her Roman nose looked especially long and dark from below. "Only he's not Stephen anymore."

"No?" I said. "Then who is he?"

"His name is Colin David McDoogle. He's changed it. Legally."

I remembered him telling me that he wanted to do that. I never understood why. "What was wrong with his name?"

"You'll have to ask Colin. I have my theories."

Stephen O'Shan reminded me of a leprechaun. That's a trite thing to say about an Irish person, but in this case it happens to be true. He had that twinkle in his eyes and the walk of someone tip-toeing through a field of very small mushrooms. I'm not up on Irish mythology: I've no idea if there's such a thing as an *unlucky* leprechaun. But if there is, Stephen O'Shan was one. I remember our first meeting. At the annual university poetry jam. Stephen was among the first readers. He did this funny thing about the word "fuck," celebrating its versatility, showing how, for instance, it could be used as a verb ("quit trying *to fuck* with me"), an adjective ("look at that *fucking* idiot!"), a noun ("get away from me, you *fuck*"), an adverb ("that is *fucking* amazing!"), and so on. Me, I read from one of my notebooks. I already had at least fifty of them. I read, "I wasted half my life trying to be Marlon Brando." A voice at the back of the audience shouted, "Don't feel bad! Just think how much time Marlon Brando has wasted!" The voice was Stephen O'Shan's.

In the hallway afterward I went up to him. I told him that I'd really enjoyed his "fuck" piece. "Thanks," he said. He held a handful of pills, different colors and shapes. He tossed them into his mouth, flung his head back, and swallowed. "Health issues," he said. He pointed to the notebook under my arm. "Fascinating stuff," he said, in a choked voice (a pill had lodged in his throat).

"You liked it?"

"I did; I did indeed. How many notebooks did you say?"

"About fifty. I've lost count."

"Fascinating."

The next time I saw him was just before Christmas break. He wore a down fisherman's vest with many pockets and a dark green kilt. I called to him across the green. "Stephen!" He looked up at me and smiled a forced smile. He looked bad. He had deep, dark wedges under his watery blue eyes and the beginnings of a not very impressive mustache. He looked confused, distraught. I asked him where he was going. "I dunno," he said. I invited him to my parents' home, where I was living. We got into my sports car. The kilt gave off a smell of cloves. "Spice wine," he said. He'd been out drinking the night before.

My room was in the basement. It smelled of mold and washing-machine lint. Two cheap bookcases made of particleboard sagged under the weight of past notebooks.

"Fascinating," said Stephen, picking one notebook off the shelf, riffling through it. "May I make a suggestion?"

"Please."

He swallowed a pill. "Why don't you throw them all in a lake?"

"Pardon me?"

"Your notebooks. Why don't you throw them in a lake?"

"A lake?" I said.

"Yes: a lake."

He said it with that twinkle in his eyes. Stephen was one of those people who could smile without smiling, thanks to that twinkle. His lips were pale and dry. His forehead skin had a greenish, coppery tinge to it. You can't blame me for suspecting that he was a leprechaun.

He asked about the pile of paper next to my typewriter, and I told him I was working on a novel. "Really?" he said. "What's it about?" I told him. "Fascinating," he said. Then: "Might I give you another piece of advice?" I didn't say anything. "You must do away with the melodramatics of the past. Give your hero a middle-class background. Where does he work? What does he do? Get some dirt and grease on his hands, under his fingernails. I want to see those dirty fingernails. Show me the town where he lives, the already-tired faces lined up at the greasy-spoon counter, eating their breakfast." Detail by detail, chapter by chapter, Stephen went over every aspect of my novel, which I had not written and he had not read. "Yes, yes — exactly!" he would interject every now and then, responding to some idea of his. Or: "No, no, that won't do; that won't do at all." He insisted that I write down everything in my notebook. In two hours I had thirty pages of notes. "Ah, the irony of it," he said. "If I could only do the same for my novel."

"You're writing a novel?"

"Aye," he said. "Trying. I sit myself in front of the machine and draw a blank. Nothing. Nada. Funny, isn't it?"

He swallowed another pill.

"What are the pills for?" I asked.

"Pain."

Two weeks passed before I saw him again.

"Bastard," he said, and walked right past me.

"Stephen? What's up?"

"Bloody bastard. Dirty fucker. Son of a bitch." There was no stardust in his eyes.

"Where are you going?"

"I'm late for class," he said. "Fucker."

He kept walking. I tagged along.

"What's the matter? Why are you mad at me?"

"You were supposed to meet me last night, remember?"

"I *was*?" I had no such memory.

"We had an appointment."

"We *did*?"

"I got robbed, thanks to you."

"*Robbed?*"

"Five hundred fucking dollars. My life savings. I left it on the bar when I went to phone you." His pale blue eyes shined wetly. By the pitch of his voice I could tell he was loaded with pain-killers or tranquilizers or whatever they were. He sounded like a tuba.

"I'm sorry," I said. "I completely forgot."

"Ah, ya bastard."

He walked faster.

"What the hell were you doing with five hundred dollars, anyway?"

"I just borrowed it from the bloody bank, shithead. I was using it to pay the rent on my cottage."

"Why are you walking so fast?"

"I'm late for bloody class. Don't ask me so many bloody questions."

"Look, Stephen, I — "

But instead of walking to his class, he walked off campus, to a nearby bar. I followed him.

"You have no idea," he said, twisting past crowded tables, "what it's like to live in constant pain."

He sat down at a table. A waitress came. I ordered us both soups and salad. Stephen ordered a double scotch on the rocks. I ordered a martini.

"Do you know what John Fowles says in *The French Lieutenant's Woman*?"

I said, "No, what does John Fowles say in *The French Lieutenant's Woman*?"

"In *The French Lieutenant's Woman* John Fowles says that tragedy is all very well on stage, but in real life it comes closer to perversity."

He told me to write that in my notebook. I did.

"Do you know what I intend to do?" he said when his drink had come, the sparkle coming back into his eyes, his brogue thickening. "First off, I intend to swallow a massive overdose of these bloody pills — " He showed me the pills; they were wrapped in a napkin. "Then I'm gonna set fire to the bleeding cottage that those bloody bastards are overcharging me for anyway." The cottage was a dozen miles from campus, on Lake Candlewood. "Then I'll walk across the frozen lake in my underwear while the damn thing burns to the ground. I'll leave nothing; not a trace. The police will walk among the remains saying, 'What's this? Is this his typewriter? Is this his arm? Is this his dick?' There won't be nothing left, I swear. If I could figure out a way to get my car in there, I'd burn it, too. They won't even find my name. I didn't tell you, did I? I'm changing my name. From now on it's Colin. Colin David McDoogle. Colin David McDoogle . . ." He said it a few more times, then fell asleep with his balding red head next to his soup.

That same night, in my basement bed, I dreamed that Stephen was being interrogated by an officer of the British army. In the dream, when the officer said to Stephen, "Describe your pain to me," Stephen said, "It's like I swallowed a fucking elephant."

Before the school year ended, we saw each other once more. We were walking down a budding trail through the woods near the lake.

"She's got me so damned confused," Stephen said. He still went by Stephen then.

"Who?"

"Gloria?"

He'd never mentioned her before. "Isn't she married?" I said.

"Separated," he said. "That's what's got me so damn confused. She keeps saying she's going to get a divorce."

"She's a psychology major," I said. "A behaviorist."

"She's bloody smart, is what she is. Can't resist a smart woman."

"You like her?"

"That's an understatement. I'd say I'm in love with her." He turned to me. "She came to my cottage, you know. All by herself." He said this with a wink as if it were proof that she loved him, too. "She let me cook her dinner. Don't tell me she's married." He skipped a stone into the lake, then winced from the pain. "Dammit," he said.

"You all right?"

"Ach, when will I learn?"

He took off his shoes.

"What are you doing?"

"Taking off my clothes; what's it look like?" He stood naked, facing the water. "Coming?" he said.

"It's November."

"You'll never be the same if you don't."

I put my notebook down and took off my clothes. We dove simultaneously. The water was like frozen razor blades. We jumped right back out and stood shivering with our balls turning blue, penises shrunken to the size of pitted olives, giggling like five-year-olds.

"There, you see?" he said.

"It feels good," I had to admit.

"Tell me, when did you start keeping those notebooks of yours?"

"In eighth grade. My English teacher, Mr. Fesh, suggested that we keep a journal. I never stopped."

"I see you took his advice. What about mine?" He nodded toward the lake.

"What purpose would it serve?"

"It's like this," said Stephen. "Once upon a time there was a very wise man. A brilliant scholar. He taught in many schools and universities and traveled around the world. He was quite well re-garded. By the time he was fifty he had collected all his extensive knowledge into one great, thick notebook, and this thick note-book he carried with him at all times. And those he visited in his travels would reach out to touch the notebook, to admire it and the great man who had filled it. (He was, without question, a great and learned man.) Well. One day he was walking through a village, surrounded by admirers, when suddenly a beggar in rags ran up to him, yanked the notebook out from under his arm, and tossed it down a well. Needless to say, the famous scholar was shocked, as were all the townspeople. The beggar turned to him then and said, 'If you want it back, I can get it for you, and it will be as clean and dry as before.' Can you guess what the great man's reply was?"

I shook my head.

"There was none. He kept walking. And then the great man went on to become a *truly* great man. What you need, if I may say so, is for someone to yank the notebook from under your arm."

I handed him my notebook. I pointed to the lake.

He shook his head. "Nah, it's not that simple. You may find, my good friend, that you've got to tear the pages out yourself, one by one."

I didn't tear out any pages. I kept on filling them. I filled them all the way to Oregon and back. I filled them with pipe dreams, and when the pipe dreams failed to materialize, I filled then with regret and self-pity. I knew Claudette would dump me. I knew it the night I announced to her, in a winter field lit by stars and by the eyes of deer frozen into statues, my intention to leave. "It's something I have to do," I said. Claudette said she understood. She said it in a voice choked with tears. Did she also understand that, three months into my absence, she would not only take up with some other guy but let him move into her apartment? Still — it wasn't her fault. I should have known better. I could have predicted it; I could have *planned* it. I might as well have begged for it.

Now here I am, back, lying under a chilly sun, looking up into Gloria's dark nostrils, past the pale hairs growing there, straight up into her behaviorist's brain. She says, "Would you like to see him?" referring to Stephen, aka Colin. "He'd love to see you; he'd be thrilled, I'm sure."

She tells me she's living with him at his cottage, by the lake.

"It's strictly a roommate situation," she says. "Nothing serious."

"He's crazy about you."

"Oh," she says. "He's gotten over that."

"Are you sure?"

"Yes. And his name is Colin. He's very sensitive about it."

We rode in Gloria's car — an old Saab with a leaky muffler — up Route 7 to Sherman. The car rumbled and spluttered. Only psychologists, I thought, drive ratty Saabs. Psychologists and middle school algebra teachers. Bourgeoisphobes. On the dashboard was a postcard with an embossed sand dollar.

"Colin sent me that. From St. Croix. He has relatives down there."

"Really? I didn't know that." I held the postcard in my lap.

"You can read it, if you like."

I read the card. *Having a wonderful time, though physical condition appears to be getting worse. Wish you were here. Love, Colin.*

"What exactly is wrong with him, anyway?"

"No one knows. Something to do with a missing vertebra. I think he was born that way. Sometimes it keeps him up all night. He's almost always in pain."

Gloria's car smells like a ham sandwich. Also on the dashboard: one of those plastic nose-and-eyeglass masks, the kind with big, bushy eyebrows.

"I use that to freak out truck drivers who stare at me," says Gloria.

I put it on.

"Think Stephen will recognize me?"

"Of course *Colin* will recognize you; you have such a distinctive face."

By the time we pulled into the driveway it was late afternoon. The cottage was smaller than I remembered, no bigger than a one-car garage. Two big willow trees leaned over it, one on either side. Out back, I could see the lake gleaming. I heard a powerboat go by.

Colin stepped out and stood in the doorway. Wearing the

mask, whistling "When Johnny Comes Marching Home," I walked right past him, into the cottage.

"Jaysus!" said Stephen/Colin. "Jaysus!" He threw his arms around me. "How the hell are you?" I still had the weird mask on. He seemed different, frailer. He'd gone balder and grown a beard. The beard was full of gray hairs. "Jaysus!"

The cottage seemed larger inside. One room, with a loft and a kitchen. The temperature fell. Colin lit the kerosene stove, and we sat together, by its ghostly yellow glow, having drinks and exchanging summer tales of woe and glory. I told them how I'd hooked up with a jazz band out in Oregon, but me and Lester, the bassist, kept fighting, and then — having done his best to keep the peace for months — the drummer quit, and then everything turned to shit. Gloria had gotten her divorce. And Colin — well, except for having legally changed his name, he didn't have much to report.

"Ah, it's still the same me," he said. "A few more gray hairs, a few more aches and pains, a few more pills. Now you, on the other hand — you've changed."

"You seem more relaxed," said Gloria.

"That's it. More at peace with yourself," said Colin. "More open and honest. Wouldn't you say, Glo — " His face suddenly contorted with pain. He took a vial of pills from his pocket — he still owned the fisherman's vest full of pockets — and swallowed three with his wine. Gloria and I looked at each other. She shrugged as if to say that this was routine, nothing to be alarmed over. Having emerged from the pain, Colin saw my notebook lying next to me on the floor. "Still lugging that thing around?" he said. "Jaysus! Some things never change!"

"It's only been nine months," I said.

"That's where you're mistaken," said Colin. "Half a year can make all the difference in the world. It can change everything. A day can change everything! Right, Gloria?"

Gloria ran a thin, nicotine-stained fingertip around the rim of her wineglass, making it sing. We laughed. Colin ordered pizza by phone and asked me to go with him to pick it up. He took Gloria's car. He drove terribly; he couldn't shift. I asked him what had happened to his car. "Aye, the fuckin' bank got it, that's what."

On the way home, with the pizza scalding my lap, Colin reached over to open the glove compartment. He took a stapled sheaf of paper from it and put it on the pizza box. "It just came spilling out of me," he said. The story was three pages long, typed single spaced on stained, buckled yellow paper. It looked as if it had been used repeatedly as a saucer. "It's the story of my life, so to speak," said Colin. "Go on," he said. "Read it!"

I started reading. The title of the story was "The Story of My Life."

"It's a love story," said Colin, grinding gears.

"Are you in love again?"

"Am I in love again? Jaysus! Was I ever not in love?"

"Who's the lucky girl this time?"

"The most beautiful girl in the world. A living miracle. Read, read."

The story takes place at a table in the university snack bar. In it, the "most beautiful, sophisticated, intelligent woman in the world," who is an organic chemistry major and whose name is Andrea Laestrygones, tells Coleman Winston McGuinness, the protagonist, that she has had a dream about him. "I had a dream," she says to him, "and in the dream there was this little red-headed leprechaun, and the little red-headed leprechaun was you." The protagonist, who is seated, slumps back in his chair, the words "little red-headed leprechaun" "echoing in his brain." The second single-spaced page of the story is devoted to describing the protagonist's multiple, incurable, and mysterious physical ailments and how he is haunted and tortured by them. "Suicide," Coleman explains gamely to the others at the table, "is not always an unreasonable solution." The others seated around the table disagree vehemently, saying there's no excuse for suicide. Only one other student agrees with Coleman, a guy named Henry, who wears a beret and plays the saxophone. This, I recognize, is supposed to be me. "What do you know of constant pain, of eternal torment?" Coleman, on his feet, clutching a plastic fork and shaking it in the air, challenges the others. "What do you know of being an invisible cripple, suffering invisible torture? They have wheelchairs for the visibly handicapped, crutches for the lame, white canes for the blind, padded rooms for the insane. But what have they got for the likes of me? Cortisone! Tylenol! Codeine! Who are you all to tell me suicide's a cop-out, you who have no reason to try it!" When one of the others laughs at this remark, Coleman lunges, attacking him with the plastic fork. Henry pulls them apart. But in the end it's the pain of a broken heart that finally defeats the protagonist, who, one night, sets fire to his lakeside cottage and, in his underwear, "with the flames painting the eastern sky orange behind him" walks across the frozen lake, never to be seen or heard from again.

I lay the story down on the still-hot pizza box.

"Sound familiar?" said Colin.

By midnight the temperature had fallen well below freezing. We huddled in blankets around the kerosene stove. Gloria was the first to yawn. We all started yawning. "Time for bed," said Colin. They argued then over who should sleep where. Colin said we should all sleep in the loft. "It'll be warmer," he said. There was only one bed. "You sleep in the bed," said Gloria. "Nonsense," said Colin. "I prefer the floor; it's better for my back. You take the bed." I wondered why they hadn't worked all this out before. I sat downstairs, by the stove, with a felt-tipped pen, drawing dislocated hands and faces in my notebook, between the pages of which I had tucked the sand-dollar postcard from Gloria's dashboard. When they had stopped arguing, I switched off the lamp, put my notebook away, and climbed up the ladder to the loft, where they were both lying — Gloria in the bed and Colin in a sleeping bag next to it. On the other side of the bed was another sleeping bag. I undressed quietly and got into it. After a while Colin spoke, whispering, describing the bubbles in ginger ale. "You're making me thirsty," said Gloria. "No problem," said Colin, who got up and went downstairs. As we heard the sound of ice cracking, Gloria slipped her arm out from under the covers; her nicotine-stained fingers hovered in the air over my chest. I reached out and held the longest finger, stroking it, squeezing it in my fist, milking it. Colin climbed up the ladder with three glasses of ginger ale. When we'd finished drinking, he took the glasses from us and put them aside. And then all of us went to sleep, or pretended to.

In the dark, later, I reached up and found Gloria's hand still there, her fingers wavering like sea-anemone tentacles. I stroked them, then reached up and found her shoulder. From the sound of his breathing, I assumed Stephen — Colin — was fast asleep. I had an erection and was dying for Gloria to touch it. The night went on with us exploring each other silently with our hands. I felt Gloria's breasts, the moist insides of her thighs. She stroked my chest. My fingers found her clitoris and rubbed it, and she let out an almost but not entirely imperceptible sigh. I brought my wet fingers to her lips for her to suck on, then raised my midsection off the floor so she could reach my cock with her fingers. Then she bent over and used her mouth, and I came. She played with the stuff, drawing little ringlets around my navel, taking her dripping, nicotine-stained fingers to her lips as I settled back down, trying not to breathe. I heard Colin roll over. He gave a little groan, unzipped his sleeping bag, and flipped the top back. *He's getting up!* I closed my eyes, rolled over, pretended to be asleep. I felt my stuff leaking and melting into my sleeping bag. I heard Gloria say,

"Colin, are you all right?"

He started down the ladder.

"Colin?"

I pretended to be asleep.

"Colin?"

I kept pretending.

A door slammed. Gloria shook me.

"Wake up!"

We dressed and climbed down the ladder. Gloria looked inside the kitchen. "He's out there," she said. With blankets over our shoulders, we went outside and stood by the lake. The lake was frozen. We heard loud *thwunks* and looked out and saw the silhouette receding on the ice. As it kept receding more *thwunking* sounds swept across the lake. The ice couldn't possibly be thick enough to hold anyone.

"My God," said Gloria.

I took a step onto the ice; she held me back. "Don't," she said. "It's too dangerous." I took another step, broke through, and plunged in up to my knees. "Jesus!" I said, getting out.

"I warned you," said Gloria.

"What about him?"

"Colin doesn't need ice."

Except for "the flames painting the eastern sky orange," it was just like in the story. The word "destiny" popped into my mind. I tried to convince myself that it was all meant to be, that it was somehow necessary, that we were all acting out parts that had been written for us, and so we weren't responsible, really — it was God's will, or the devil's, or the will of an unlucky leprechaun.

"It's my fault," I said, sitting in front of the stove.

"Don't blame yourself," said Gloria. "We're all to blame. Colin, too. He doesn't understand lust. It's not a part of him. He only understands love. That doesn't make him good, and it doesn't make us evil."

"But I made it happen."

"You responded to a stimulus. We both did."

I had to ask her: "That story Colin wrote, the one in your glove compartment? The girl in it, is that supposed to be you?"

Gloria nodded.

In the morning Gloria wrote a phone number down on the sand-dollar postcard. "It's the number of some people who own a cottage on the far side of the lake," said Gloria. "He goes there sometimes when he's upset."

I hitchhiked back to the university. I didn't want Gloria to take me. The German smoke-alarm salesman who picked me up said that unless America returned to its old way of educating the young it was headed for trouble. "Zee abbrennezhip zystem is ze only vey to go." I agreed with him all the way to campus. At the snack bar I found a pay phone and dialed the number on the sand-dollar card. With the number ringing I imagined several possible exchanges taking place.

Phone Conversation no. 1:

Seven rings. A groggy voice answers.

"Stephen?"

"The name is Colin David McDoogle."

Click.

Phone Conversation no. 2:

Four rings. An old Irish woman's wheedling voice answers.

"Is Colin there?"

"Nope. Dead. Fished him frozen out of the lake early this morning. Poor fellow. Say it was a broken heart did him in."

Phone Conversation no. 3:

Eleven rings.

"Is Colin there?"

"This is he."

"Colin, it's me."

Silence.

"Colin, I'm very sorry."

"Sure."

"I want to see you."

"I'm in bed. I'm sleeping."

"I just want to — "

The line goes dead. This last exchange is real. As I hang up, I can feel Colin's hatred seeping into my bones. I can't stand being hated; it drives me crazy. I look around; I don't know what to do; I have no idea. The snack bar is crowded. Why did I come here? I don't belong here. God, get me out.

I find my sports car. The top is still down. The leather seats are moist with dew. There's a parking ticket tucked under the windshield wiper. I'm not sure this life has anything to do with me, or me with it. I put the ticket in my pocket and get in the car. I don't bother wiping the seat. There's frost on the windshield. I pull out into traffic, cut off another car. The driver blasts his horn. I blast mine back. I get on the highway, headed north, past hills looking like bowls of Trix cereal, thinking: Claudette. I've lost her this time; I've really lost her; I've lost her for good.

THE SEA CURE

SHE WAS THE LAST PERSON off the bus.
Clarke stood across the street in the zocalo, watching it unload
its cargo of brown-skinned passengers, when she appeared, wearing a flowing dress of pale parchment-colored fabric. Except for
the tops of her feet, suntanned between the straps of her white
sandals, and her shoulders (visible through a scrim of blonde hair
and likewise suntanned), her skin was very pale, as pale as her
dress: as pale as the sand Clarke had slept on during the night.

She opened a small parasol that also matched her dress and
stepped into the pall of dust raised by the bus, oblivious to it and
to the screams of children begging their mothers to buy them
ice-cream bars from the stand a dozen yards away. Standing in
the oval shadow cast by her parasol, she spoke with the bus driver,
who leaned against the bus's front fender smiling and worrying
his set of rosary beads. Though she obviously spoke Spanish,
Clarke refused to believe that she was a local.

She's not from around here, he told himself. No way.

Clarke hadn't wanted to vacation in Mexico. He hated Mexico.

He couldn't decide what he hated more: the crass commercialism, the package tours, the inauthentic strip hotels, or the authentic poverty. He hated the food, the monotony of rice and beans doctored with powerful spices. He had never been a beer lover, but he reserved an especially dark place in his heart for that which went by the name cerveza. And how could any nation that offered but one generic kind of cheese call itself civilized? The sun was too hot, the music too loud, the streets too dusty. As for what the Fodor guide touted as Mexico's "ancient cultural heritage," Clarke had seen enough jungle-spangled ziggurats to last him a lifetime. He ached for civilization in the present tense. So far, only the country's beaches had survived his condemning scrutiny.

The trip had been Lewis's idea. Lewis, Clarke's adopted brother and traveling companion. Lewis, whose recent success — a series of documentary films on the westward expansion and the routing of Native Americans ("a milestone in documentary filmmaking" — *USA Today*) — had made it possible for him to pay for both their trips, while Clarke's earnings as a freelance graphic designer barely covered his overhead. Since sixth grade, when Mrs. Decker, their social studies teacher, pointed out the historical significance of their joined names, fate had united them like an ampersand. They summered together at Lake Winnipesauke, where Lewis's family had a cabin. When both of Clarke's parents died in the MGM hotel fire in Las Vegas, the Bigelows adopted Clarke. Since then they'd been like brothers, odd ones, with Clarke six feet two to Lewis's five feet six and weighing fifty pounds more. Still the ampersand held.

Done talking to the bus driver, the woman turned and, walking in the shadow of her parasol, made her way to the ice-cream stand, a wooden lean-to festooned with Christmas lights. Clarke watched her stand at the end of a line of mothers and noisy children, a marble pillar of serenity amid their hysteria. Flicking a strand of seaweed from his clothes, Clarke crossed the street and joined them, standing behind her in line, imagining the molecules of his foul breath reverberating off the delicate bones of her vertebrae. He hadn't brushed his teeth; his clothes, hair, and skin were full of sand. He'd elected to sleep on the beach as opposed to staying in the increasingly smelly room at the Blue Parrot, where Lewis lay sick in bed. Lewis had been lying there for four days, since their arrival in Playa del Carmen, where they'd come to catch the ferry to Cozumel. He had been running with his backpack toward the dock when he suddenly collapsed.

"I think I've just had an incident," he told Clarke, his face yellow and coated in sweat. A local doctor diagnosed *la tourista*, travelers' diarrhea, and prescribed bottled water, bismuth, and bed rest.

"You don't have to stay here," Lewis told Clarke in their hotel room. "Go on to Cozumel, enjoy yourself. I'll be fine."

"Right. And leave you here."

"I would if I were you." (Not true; Lewis wouldn't have left Clarke, and Clarke knew it.)

Four days later Lewis's condition hadn't improved. Clarke suggested he see another doctor, an American one, preferably.

"There you go again with your bigotry," said Lewis. "You think all Mexican doctors are shamans and voodoo priests."

"I think you should get a second opinion, that's all."

"I'll be fine."

That night Clarke found a smooth, flat patch of sand by an

overturned fishing boat, spread out a hotel blanket, and lay there, looking up at the stars, wondering why people read significance into a spattering of cosmic debris, however lovely. He saw odd lights combing the shore, biologists with flashlights looking for turtle hatchlings. Volunteers (he'd read) came from all over to rescue the hatchlings. To the firefly-like dancing of flashlights Clarke drifted to sleep.

From the frosty display case the woman chose an ice-cream bar that matched her dress and her parasol, then returned to the sidewalk, where she stood licking it with a tongue as pale as the rest of her. Clarke was overcome by a sudden, urgent need to speak with her, as if he were a parched plant only her voice could water. Still he kept his distance, the shipwrecked feeling enforcing his silence. A drop of ice cream fell on his shirtfront. What would he say to her, anyway? *How do you like your ice cream? What flavor did you get? Really, me too!* He wondered if she'd purposely chosen her ice cream to go with her outfit. *What a charming parasol, by the way. Where did you get it? You don't say? Excuse me, but I couldn't help noticing, I couldn't help but notice . . .*

The woman tossed away what was left of her ice cream, folded her parasol, and got back on the bus, which grumbled off in a cloud of purplish dust.

On the way back to the Blue Parrot, Clarke stopped at a grocery store and picked up a bottle of Seven-Up. In their room Lewis shivered under a flimsy sheet. The ceiling fan squeaked. The room smelled like an outhouse in bad need of cleaning on a hot summer day. Clarke filled the foggy bathroom cup with warm soda.

"I asked for ginger ale," Lewis said.

"You're in a primitive society. No ginger ale."

The morning sun splashed palm-frond shadows across the rattan shades, which were lowered. The floor's ceramic tiles, where visible under scattered clothes, guidebooks, and backpacks, looked like they had been grouted with shit. Clarke pressed the cup to Lewis's lips.

"You look like hell."

"Bless you and keep you for saying so."

Clarke put a hand to Lewis's forehead. "You're feverish."

"I want you to do me a favor," said Lewis.

"And I want you to see another doctor."

"Get me a stone from Tulum."

"A what? From *where*?"

"From the ruins down there. A stone. For my collection."

Back in New York, Lewis kept a ceramic planter in the living room filled with crumbled bits of ruins from the world: from the Pyramids, the Parthenon, the Forum, from Stonehenge, from the Temple of the Winged Lions at Petra, from the Berlin Wall and the Great Wall of China, from archeological digs where he had volunteered in Turkey, Egypt, and Spain, the crumbs of civilization. The planter weighed over a hundred pounds.

"You want me to travel seventy miles through a swamp for a stone?"

"Tulum is one of the most beautiful of the ancient cities," said Lewis. "It sits on a cliff overlooking the sea, with temples dedicated to the honeybee god."

"Christ," Clarke said.

"The bus leaves at noon. Take your bathing suit. I hear the beach is lovely down there."

Clarke wore his sunglasses and the last of his clean shirts, a yellow madras. Locals filled the bus: shoeless teenagers, toothless old men, and mothers bouncing babies in their laps. Clarke was the only gringo. The driver's rosary hung from his mirror. He fingered the beads, crossed himself, and jammed the bus into gear.

The trip took two hours. The sun burned Clarke's face through the opened window; the wind whipped his hair. He thought of the woman with the parasol, pictured her walking alone along the parched, barren highway. The image stayed with him for most of the trip. By the time the bus pulled up to Tulum, Clarke was hot and sticky. He longed for a dip in the sea. A second bus arrived and unloaded its cargo of tourists, who, armed with cameras and guidebooks, swarmed the ruins. To save his life he couldn't imagine what they all saw in a bunch of rocks. He headed for the beach. He'd get the damn stone later.

The sun shone brutally. Clarke put on his sunglasses. Close up the sea was a pale green color, like the verdigris on bronze. To get away from the tourists, he walked nearly a mile, shedding his shoes, inviting the wet sand between his toes. Isolated at last, he stripped down to his Speedo, slathered sunscreen over his wintry skin, then stood there, the surf's tongue licking his feet, thinking maybe Mexico wasn't such a bad place after all. He dove in, came up splashing, and looked around, amazed to have such a place all to himself.

While drying himself he noticed, in the jungle growth just

beyond the beach, the remains of a seaside taverna. Sections of thatched umbrella lay scattered like the tails of huge, rotting fish. Mixed with the bones and wood scraps were strings of colored lights like the ones decorating the ice-cream stand.

Before heading back to the bus stop, Clarke stopped for lunch. Chicken "ala Venezuela": tomatoes, onions, chili sauce, and the requisite rice and beans. At four o'clock the place was deserted. An indigenous organ-grinder serenaded him with an up-tempo version of "Moon River." At the table next to him a monkey — a smelly creature with flamboyant genitals — made faces at him. Clarke had the waiter remove it.

He was about to catch the next bus when he remembered Lewis's stone. He bent down and picked up the first stone he saw, a blue gray specimen that fit neatly into his palm. He pocketed it just as the bus arrived in its dust cloud.

As the bus growled through orange, low-angled sunlight, he saw the woman with the parasol again, walking alone down the highway, her parasol high, its shadow forming a cool puddle at her feet, her bleached colors in sharp contrast to the vivid greens and ripe browns of the surrounding swamp. Clarke's memory of her felt ancient, like he'd known her from somewhere before, in a past life or in a dream. With his eyes closed, he saw her more clearly, an ivory odalisque emerging from an endless sea of sapodilla and mangrove as he drifted off to sleep, and dreamed a series of dreams. In one dream he and the woman walked side by side down a sandy strip of beach. As they walked, the woman's pale skin took on the colors of the surrounding landscape. In the last dream she sat beside him, holding a small notebook open in her lap. Using a red ballpoint pen she sketched a series of figures that, for all their strangeness, looked familiar. In the dream Clarke asked, "What are you sketching?"

"Time," the woman answered. "I'm sketching time."

The angle of the sun had sharpened considerably, coming in straight and bloodred through the bus window from the horizon as the bus grumbled on. Then Clarke realized — with the sluggishness of a patient coming out of anesthesia — that he hadn't been dreaming. The woman with the parasol was there, sitting next to him, having boarded the bus (apparently) while he slept. With her red pen she sketched what looked like a cross between an eye and a lemon.

"And that?" asked Clarke pointing, his voice still groggy with sleep.

"This is kim, the sun," said the woman.

She had a deeply feminine voice that she kept to a whisper. "It stands for one of twenty-four hours," she explained, her English delicately accented. "Twenty kims equal one uinal. Eighteen uinals — or three hundred and sixty kims — equal one tum."

"A tum — that's a year?" said Clarke, still half in a dream.

"Perhaps. However," said the woman, "when dealing with the Maya one can never be sure of anything."

She smiled. She had large, healthy teeth. Clarke pointed to another drawing in her notebook: a fat, recumbent figure balancing a saucer-shaped disc on his belly.

"That is Chacmool, the god of sacrifice."

"What's that thing he's holding?"

"A plate — for the heart." She smiled. "Human sacrifice was important to the Maya. Four village elders known as *chacs* would hold the arms and legs while the chest was opened by the *nacom* using an obsidian knife."

"Charming," said Clarke.

"Civilizations are strange. One moment they astonish you with their beauty; the next they astonish you with their cruelty. Like people, yes?"

She snapped the little notebook shut. Despite her efforts to shield herself from the sun, her skin had been ravaged by it, turned leathery where it had been most exposed. She had to be thirty-five, maybe forty. Her skimpy nose was at odds with her sensuous lips and large, deep-set eyes (the same verdigris shade as the sea Clarke had bathed in that afternoon). She spoke more of the Maya, about how while Europe slept through the Middle Ages the Maya charted the heavens, mastered mathematics, evolved one of the earliest forms of handwriting, invented the calendar, and built vast, beautiful, and elaborate cities without metal tools or wheels. "And the most amazing thing of all is that their ancestors are still with us today, riding on this bus as we speak." She nodded toward a teenager asleep across the aisle, his feet propped on the seat in front of him. Clark was less impressed by the history of the Maya than by the woman, by her beauty and sophistication.

"Where are you from?" he asked.

"From Mexico. Why?"

"You don't look like a local."

"I'm not sure what you mean."

"I mean you could almost pass for an American," Clarke said and instantly realized his mistake.

"You mean a gringo?" she said, smiling. "I was born in Mérida, two hundred miles away. But yes, I suppose I could pass for a *nordamericano*. I once lived in your country, in fact."

"Did you?"

"I did. I was a student at the University of Arizona. I studied theater there. But I had to come back," she said, looking suddenly sad. "The man I married hates *nordamericanos*. He is suspicious and prejudiced, my husband." She smiled. "But I was also in love back then, and he insisted that I come home. He lives in Mexico City. He does not like it here, by the sea. Where are you from in America?"

"New York," said Clarke.

"New York!" She clapped her hands. "It must be so marvelous! How I'd love to go back to the States, but my husband will never let me. He is a builder. He hates your country as much as he hates the sea, and he hates the sea. I have never known a man to hate the sea as much as my husband does. What is your purpose here?"

"I'm vacationing — with a friend."

"Your girlfriend?"

"A guy. Lewis. He's my adopted brother."

"And where is he?"

"At our hotel. He hasn't been feeling good. *La tourista*."

"Has he seen a doctor?"

"We saw one at this clinic."

"There is a very good doctor near where I am living. You should bring your friend to see him. Dr. Torres. They say he is very good. Where is your hotel?"

"In Playa."

"It is not so far. Here." She opened her notebook. With her red pen she sketched a map showing the highway and the bus stop and an *X* indicating the apartment complex where she lived. Next to the *X* she wrote *Puerto Bienvenido*. "The bus from Playa arrives every day at three o'clock. From the bus stop it is only a short walk. Here I am now."

The bus arrived at her stop. She tore the page from her notebook, folded it once, and handed it to him, her fingers grazing his. "Theresa María Sánchez de Bernat," she said. "In the U.S. they call me Terry."

She extended her hand. The bus began to move. With an alarmingly shrill cry, she commanded the driver to a halt. Holding the closed parasol, she took a moment to compose herself and took her sweet time getting off the bus. Clarke watched her through the window as the bus pulled away. He saw her walking; then suddenly she disappeared. With no houses or other roads in sight, it was as if she had walked directly into the swamp.

As soon as he opened the door to their hotel room, the stench of Lewis's sickness wedged itself into Clarke's nostrils. Lewis lay curled up on top of the covers. The ceiling fan squeaked.

"How was Tulum?" Lewis asked, his voice thin.

"It had its moments."

"Did you get my stone?"

Clarke produced the stone from his pocket and handed it to Lewis.

"This is a fucking pebble," said Lewis.

"It's not a pebble; it's a stone."

"It's an ugly pebble. Where did you get it?"

"From the ruins."

"The ruins are made of sandstone. This isn't from the ruins."

"You asked me to get you a stone from the ruins. I went to the ruins and got you a goddamn stone. What do you want from me?"

"Were you even down there?"

"Yes!" said Clarke. "It took me all fucking day. Where the fuck else do you think I've been? And for your information there's nothing down there. Nothing but a bunch of old carved-up rocks and a beach. And a smelly monkey. Christ, I hate this country."

Lewis's intestines growled. He reached for and took a slug of bismuth from the amber bottle on the nightstand. His cheeks were hollow, and all the color had drained from his face.

"You need to see a doctor," said Clarke.

"I saw one," said Lewis.

"You need to see another." Clarke explained about the woman and the doctor she had recommended.

"How the hell did you manage to hook up with the only rich white bitch in Yucatán?"

"Who says she's rich?"

"She's white, with a fat husband in Mexico City and a condo by the beach with a fleet of mestizos waiting on her hand in glove, being exploited."

"So why does she ride public transport?"

"Because her chauvinistic husband won't let her drive." There were times when Clarke deeply resented Lewis's reverse snobbery, and this was one of them. On the nightstand next to the empty Seven-Up bottle a cockroach worked the air semaphore-like with its antennae. Using *The Lonely Planet Guide to Mexico*, Clarke crushed it.

"Was that called for?" Lewis said.

"I thought he was exploiting you."

"Switch off that fan, would you? It's freezing in here."

Even with the sun down, the temperature outside was still in the nineties, with the room only slightly cooler. Clarke switched off the fan. He felt Lewis's forehead again and gave him two aspirin.

"Here's the deal," Clarke said. "Tomorrow you and I are going to see that doctor. Don't fight me on this, Lewis. I did you a favor; I got you your stupid stone. Tomorrow you'll do this favor for me."

Riding the two-thirty bus with Lewis the next day, Clarke couldn't help feeling guilty — not about the stone (which Lewis gripped in a feverish hand like the talisman he held it to be) but because he knew he was as eager to see the woman in white as he was to get Lewis to the doctor, maybe more. Clarke had wanted them to take a taxi, but Lewis wouldn't countenance such ostentatious displays of imperialist opulence. Lewis sat in the aisle seat, away from the blazing, breezy window, his sweaty head resting on Clarke's shoulder. In the netted luggage rack over their heads, a farmer's bag of seed corn bounced. Clarke studied the map that Theresa — Terry — had drawn for him, her handwriting as jagged and clumsy as a child's.

At three o'clock, on schedule, the bus pulled over. No one else got off. As they wavered on the empty roadside, the driver gave Clarke a curious smile, crossed himself, and closed the door. The bus left them in a cloud of mauve dust.

"It should be just a short walk. Think you'll make it?" asked Clarke.

"If the alternative is dying here, yes."

They walked about a hundred yards, Clarke helping Lewis

with an arm around his waist, to a small road buried in the tall weeds. Walking hip to hip Clarke felt something sharp in Lewis's pants pocket: the stone, the ersatz good-luck charm. They'd walked another hundred yards when he started to worry. What if the map was wrong? What if there was no Puerto Bienvenido, no condo by the beach? What if he'd dreamed the whole thing? They kept walking, Lewis's body growing heavier, his forehead dripping. They stopped to drink water, Clarke giving Lewis the last sips from their only bottle. Lewis coughed. Clarke tossed the empty into the swamp, where it floated in the tea-colored water. They had walked at least half a mile.

Down the road Clarke saw something: a white rectangle rising like a Goliath refrigerator from the jungle verdure. Closer, there was a sign. *Puerto Bienvenido.* As they neared the tall, featureless building, Clarke's head burst with images of running water, of ice trays and glasses gray with condensation. He yearned for air-conditioning. "We're here," he said.

"Strike up the band."

A fallen palm tree blocked the road, uprooted (Clarke guessed) by the last hurricane two years before. It had been that long since a vehicle had passed beyond it. Clarke all but carried Lewis the rest of the way to the building, which, he saw as they drew closer, was still under construction, or (he realized with even more dismay) it had been left unfinished, abandoned. Its empty windows yawned in great gulps of sea air. The plastered walls of its exposed units were buckled and stained with salt. Electrical lines and copper pipes dangled; concrete slabs gave way to raw armatures. Behind the building a yellow backhoe crouched, frozen like an iron dinosaur, its rusty maw still bearing a payload. Only the building's upper-floor windows had been glazed.

"I'll be right back," Clarke said, depositing Lewis in the marble foyer. He went to the intercom panel to find it dangling from a matrix of colored wires. He tried the elevator; it didn't work. He bounded up the stairs to the top floor, which held three apartments. A wreath of mangrove roots, spray-painted white, hung from one of the doors. He knocked lightly at first, then less lightly, and then he pounded. He tried the other two doors. He bounded back down the stairs.

"I can't find her," said Clarke. "She must be around here somewhere."

Lewis said nothing.

Clarke went around to the side of the building facing the sea. He saw nothing, no people, no children, no toys, no laundry, no signs of human life, just the surf and the wind carrying sand into his eyes from the beach. The beach! Maybe she'd gone for a walk along it. He ran to the water, his sneakers slipping in sand. A horseshoe crab inched its way along a deposit of sea scum. Far down the shore, about a mile away, Clarke saw a cluster of buildings, nothing more. With his fingers vaguely touching his lower lip, he looked up at the building's top-floor windows. In one set of windows white curtains fluttered. He turned and gazed out to sea again, wondering why so many went so far out of their way to coexist with this vast desert of salt water. As he wondered, a parchment-colored dot appeared down the shore.

"Theresa!" Clarke shouted and ran toward her.

Seeing him approach Terry smiled. "Ah, so it's you!" she said. "I am so glad that you have come," she said, twirling her parasol. "Isn't it beautiful?" She looked out to sea. "According to the Popol Vuh, before the surface of the earth existed there was only the calm sea and the great expanse of sky, alone and tranquil, nothing more. How beautiful it must have been! I can't understand why my husband hates it so. Can you?" She failed to notice the distress on Clarke's face.

"I brought my friend with me. Look," Clarke said. "You said you knew a good doctor. Dr. Torres, I think you said. Remember?"

"Oh, yes, Dr. Torres. He is very, very good."

"Can we phone him? Do you have his number?"

Terry shook her head. "There is no telephone. My husband, he built this place for me. At least he says that it was for me. He has built many places." They had started toward the building. "It was almost finished when the hurricane came. *Mala suerte.* Now he has no intention to finish it. Still, I'm happy here. 'Here is the sky, all alone,'" she recited. "'*Here is the sea, all alone. There is nothing more — no sound, no movement. Only the sky and the sea. Only Heart-of-Sky, alone. And these are his names: Maker and Modeler, Kukulkan, and Hurricane.*' Ah, this must be your friend. So good to meet you!"

"The pleasure is all mine," said Lewis, not looking up. A sharp odor of diarrhea filled the vestibule.

"The doctor," said Clarke, "how far is he from here?"

"Dr. Torres," said Terry. "Not very far. A few kilometers."

"I don't suppose you have a car, by any chance?"

"Oh, no," said Terry, laughing. "My husband won't let me drive. But you can walk. It's just down the beach. It is faster that way anyway. But you must hurry before the tide comes in."

"When will that happen?"

"Oh, there's time."

Lewis moaned. Clarke knelt to feel his forehead. He asked Terry if she had any aspirin. She wasn't sure. "You're welcome to look," she said.

"What's going on?" Lewis asked.

"I'm going to see if Terry has some aspirin for you," Clarke said a little more distinctly than necessary. "We're going to get you some aspirin, okay? And then we're going to get you to a good doctor. Okay?"

Except for a white sofa facing the large open window and an antique malacca chest, the apartment was bare. Empty white-plastered walls. No electricity, no telephone, no refrigerator, no air conditioner, no running water. "A man who works with my husband comes once a week with water and other supplies," Terry explained. "He has to leave the truck on the road and then bring everything on a cart because of the fallen tree, which my dear husband has neglected to remove, nor will he fix the road, which, as I'm sure you saw, is very badly rutted." While speaking she searched everywhere for a bottle of aspirin, finding none. "No aspirin," she said. "I'm sorry."

Clarke wondered how annoyed he should be, if he should be annoyed at all, since it was all a dream, the same dream he'd had on the bus. He was still on that bus, asleep and dreaming this as it rumbled through the swamp, a dream of pure whiteness in which shadows and reason did not exist. A soft breeze from the sea parted the pale curtains, toying with strands of Terry's blonde hair as Clarke looked at her, thinking if she was crazy he didn't want to know it, not now. Under any other circumstances he would have wanted to make love to her, to take her there in her shell of an apartment on her ghostly white sofa, to run his hand up under her pale dress, to feel those lips against his.

But these were not other circumstances.

"Look," he said with what he hoped was enough sharpness.

"My friend is very sick. He needs help. Have you at least got some water in this place?"

Terry looked perplexed. "Water? Yes, yes, I think so."

She produced a gallon jug with less than a few cups of water in it. "The man hasn't come yet this week, and I'm afraid this is all I have left." She found a desiccated orange in her refrigerator. "And here is an orange, if you like." Clarke took the jug and the orange and stood there. For a moment he felt as if he could not move.

"Would you care to see a photo of my husband?" said Terry.

From inside the malacca chest she produced a photograph of a Cesar Romero clone with a crown of rich white hair. Clarke heard a liquid growl somewhere that sounded like running water, but he couldn't be sure.

Terry stood by the window. "Here is where I spend my time, most of it, by this window looking out. Doctor's orders. The doctor is my husband." She spun around and faced Clarke, her hands gripping the windowsill behind her. "Rest and being alone by the sea. That is the best remedy, he tells me. The only remedy. He calls it the 'Sea Cure.' Tell me," said Terry. "Do I look cured to you?"

Clarke hurried down the stairs.

"That is the hotel there," said Terry, pointing down the shore to a distant group of buildings. "I had a drink at the bar there once. That's when I saw Dr. Torres. He was sitting all alone in the cabana, wearing a pink suit with a white handkerchief in its pocket. I asked the hotel manager, 'Who is that distinguished-looking gentleman sitting over there?' 'That is Dr. Torres,' the hotel manager said. 'He is a very, very capable man.'"

With Lewis slung over his shoulder, Clarke started down the beach, leaving Terry behind. He did not even say good-bye to her.

He never wished to see or even think of her again, ever, not even in his dreams. When she called after him one last time he did not respond or look back.

Even without the extra weight, the sand would have made walking hard. Every dozen or so yards Clarke stopped to shift his burden from shoulder to shoulder. Within a quarter mile the beach gave way to a fringe of pebbles that in turn gave way to jagged rocks. Though from their starting point the shore had resembled a single smooth beach curving off toward the horizon, in fact it consisted of a series of inlets compacting a distance of several kilometers into its folds. Before long the setting sun absorbed every trace of color, leaving only the crescent moon nestled against a sky punctuated with bright stars. With sundown came cool air and swarms of mosquitoes. Ahead of them burned the lights of the hotel complex that was their destination.

Clarke slapped at a mosquito on his neck. He wiped the sweat from his brow. The smell of Lewis's shit clung to his fingers. Clouds rushed in to cover the moon briefly before drifting off again. The hotel lights seemed as distant as ever. As he struggled over the rocks, Clarke pictured Terry watching him, twirling her parasol, her pale dress glowing under the light of the moon. He stopped for a moment, waiting for the dream to dissipate, but when reality took its place it was no better. Meanwhile, the tide rose; the fringe of rocks grew steeper and less navigable. Finally there was only water.

"We're getting there," said Clarke, trudging in black waves up to his knees, the distinction between sea and sky lost to the darkness. Every so often he looked toward the shore to see Terry's ghostly figure standing there, glowing atop the steep rocks, a pair of white sandals dangling from her hand. In the opposite direction the moon shone, bright and big as the sun, but in an unambiguously black sky, painting bright, bold streaks across the surface of the sea. It, too, was a dream, thought Clarke. He refused to believe it; he refused to believe any of this, refused to believe that he and Lewis would perish on this miserable stretch of Yucatán coastline, that any god, however malevolent, would engineer such an absurd end for anyone.

Something sharp dug into his shoulder.

He swore.

That's when he saw the group of lights down the shore, not the hotel lights but smaller, dimmer ones, moving like the ones he had seen on the beach two nights before. More biologists in search of turtle hatchlings. Clarke had read in some nature magazine that the hatchlings instinctively made their way toward the brightest available light source. Under natural circumstances that source would come from the sea, from the moonlight reflected there. But under unnatural conditions, deceived by man-made lights, the hatchlings would often head inland instead, becoming food for lizards and snakes, drawn to their dooms by the deceitful brightness.

In a strained voice Clarke cried out: "Hello? Hello! *Help!*"

But the lights were too far; his voice was too weak. Sounds of surf and insects overpowered it. There was nothing to do but keep moving, through the rising surf toward the tempting lights. He heard a sound in his head, a humming sound mixed with the surf and insect sounds. The humming sound rose in volume and pitch until it sounded like someone screaming. He switched Lewis to his other shoulder and the sharp object dug into him again. Then something in the water — a skate or a stingray — stabbed the bottom of Clarke's foot and he toppled.

"I'm sorry," he said, hoisting Lewis's inert body up from the mounting waves. "I'm sorry." Tears and salt water stung his eyes. The stars were out. "Jesus," he said. "Holy Jesus."

With the last of his strength, hobbling on his throbbing foot, he carried his brother to the nearest rock and sat there, holding him, catching his breath. They wouldn't die like this. No one dies like this, in a dream. As Clarke held him, he felt something sharp in Lewis's pocket: the stone, the good-luck charm, the lie from Tulum. That's what had been digging into his shoulder. He pried it out of the drenched pocket and held it, weighing it, considering whether he should toss it into the sea. Then he changed his mind and put it in his mouth instead. It tasted like salt. He sucked on it thinking, *we will not die like this; we will not die like this.*

He sucked on the stone and stroked Lewis's head as the tide continued to rise.

WEDNESDAY AT THE BAGEL SHOP

IT'S NOT LIKE ME to wait for people. Ten minutes, okay maybe fifteen. A half hour tops. Any person more unreliable than that isn't worth waiting for. But for you I'm willing to make an exception.

One reason, of course, is that I realize it takes you at lot longer to get from one place to another than, you know, the average person. The four blocks from your apartment building to the bagel shop, which would take, you know, a healthy person maybe five, six minutes, would take you at least twenty-five. At least . . .

Not that you're not healthy. I'm not saying . . . that is . . . well, you *know*. What do you call yourself? *Disabled*, is that okay? (Christ, I'm not good at this stuff.) I mean, I wouldn't want to *offend* you. I don't exactly have much experience in these matters. Who does?

It's not even like we've known each other all that long. We met — when was it? — two months ago? Not here, in the bagel shop, but there, right across the street, 105th and Broadway, that lousy corner where the creeps play video games in the cigar store, and they're always setting off firecrackers on the sidewalk, those rotten kids. I was waiting for the light to change when suddenly you pulled up alongside me with your crutches. I mean, the thing is, normally, this being New York City and all, I wouldn't have noticed. That is, I wouldn't have paid any *attention*. But you were . . . well, hell, you were like really beautiful, you know? Okay, pretty. You were real pretty. I'd never seen such a pretty . . . oh, Christ. Do you believe that? I was about to say *cripple*. I meant a pretty . . . well, you know what I mean.

Then you did something really unusual. You *talked* to me. Right there, on the street, to a perfect stranger, in broad daylight. "Good morning," you said, like you knew me, which, of course, you didn't. You said it with this big smile. At first I figured, okay, now she's gonna want something. I mean, this is New York, right? She's gonna hit me up for some change, or maybe a cigarette, or ask me to help her cross the street, something. But you didn't ask for anything. The light changed, and you just kept right on going. It was like really weird.

Now when I say you were pretty, I'm talking about . . . well, your eyes. They're like really blue, like the sky. That's dumb. Eyes aren't like the sky — or like diamonds or stars or any of the other dumb things writers are always saying they're like. Eyes are like *eyes*. To be honest, yours were kind of small, *are* kind of small (they're still in your head, right?), but really shiny. And the way they looked straight at you, like really *direct*, through the bangs of your short, almost black hair. And those really full lips, you know, what's the word? — sensual, like, with teeth showing lots of gums, but in a nice sort of way, making your smile look extra big and, I don't know, *juicy*. I guess that's what I'd call it. A *juicy* smile. If that's not, you know, pushing things.

As for your clothes, all I can say regarding them is no one is ever gonna give you an award for fashion. We're talking yellow Danskins the color of Gulden's spicy brown mustard with tear holes in them the size of my fist from falling, which I know you do a lot of in your condition. And a sweatshirt the color of green mold with the hell stretched out of it so it's like hanging off your shoulder, you couldn't even give it to Goodwill without getting dirty looks. Then you had this big, floppy shoulder bag, the kind with all the fancy colored stitching, like a Ukrainian egg. Not exactly *Women's Wear Daily* material. But still, I mean, take it as a compliment, the fact that you managed to look pretty damn decent, you know, for a girl on crutches. Or should I say a lady? These things confuse me.

So anyway there we were with the light already turned green and you starting to cross when some spitooey-faced jerk sets a firecracker off practically right under your legs — or should I say your crutches? Anyway, it shook *me* up, but you, you went right down. I mean, one minute you're standing, walking, or whatever you call it, and then *boom!* You're down — flat on your face, your crutches all over the street. You said as I was helping you up it was because you were spastic. At first I thought you had to be joking. I mean, give me a break, how many people go around saying, "I'm spastic," to complete strangers? But you meant it. You have what's called an adverse reaction to sudden loud noises. Your brain gets screwed up and all your muscles go haywire and if you just happen to be standing, down you go. I mean, it must be awful around the Fourth of July.

So then I help you get up and we cross the street and sure enough, we're both going to the bagel shop. You tell me it's your favorite place, which I find hard to believe, I mean, the way it smells and all. Actually, I was just gonna pick up my usual coffee (dark, two sugars) and buttered raisin to go but you asked me if I'd join you, and I thought: what the hell. So we're sitting there in the bagel shop with coffee. That's when I first really notice your eyes, the way they sparkle, shine, whatever. Tell you the truth, I'm not that used to women looking at me. Not that I'm ugly, but I'm just not used to it. And the way you did was so *direct*, so like looking inside me, like almost right through me, just about.

What the hell did we talk about? Bagels? I was afraid to ask about the crutches, you know, to come right out and say, "Hey, what's wrong with your legs?" like a jerk, though that's exactly what was on my mind. I mean, you can't expect a person to just *ignore* a thing like that. So I say, you know, real subtle, "How long have you been on those *things*?" — those "things" being crutches, not wanting to say the word, figuring it might make you sensitive or something.

Again you surprised me; you were full of surprises. "I was born this way," you said. Not nasty, just matter-of-fact, with a shrug, like it was some kind of freak ability you didn't want to boast about, like those people who can drop a whole box of matches and shout out the number. What do they call them? Idiot somethings.

Not that you were an idiot. As a matter of fact you seemed very intelligent. Just from the look of your eyes I could tell. To be honest, something about them made me feel pretty dumb. I mean, for some reason I felt *intimidated*, don't ask me why. I mean, I've never been shy with girls. I'm usually pretty cool. The people in my building, the ladies in particular, they *know*. They think I'm like a ladies man, a real *maneuverer*. They even tease me about it. I mean, some of these ladies are as rich as they are beautiful. Still, they don't intimidate me. But *you*. I don't know, maybe it was the black and blue marks on your forearms, the ones from falling all the time. I kept on looking at them, I couldn't stop. It's unusual to see so many bruises on a girl (lady?). I mean, it's interesting. Also I was noticing your muscles. I mean, they were like *big*. You must get pretty strong, going around on those crutches. I have to admit, for a second I wondered if your arms were stronger than mine.

It's ten after nine now. I figure I'll wait another ten minutes.

So we talked. Blah, blah, blah this and that. You told me you did social work, reading books out loud to people. I still don't get it. I mean, if they can't read, what good's being read to gonna do them? I mean, I personally don't read, not that often, catalogs and shit, a newspaper now and then, maybe the *Racing Form* if I'm in the mood. But getting paid to read to people, is that really a job? I mean, isn't it more like babysitting or volunteer work?

Then you drop the big one on me. You tell me you're a writer. Holy shit. A *writer*?! Oh, sure, I figure, shit, like she writes poetry like my sister in her diary. But no, you say you've had a novel published, and you got a contract for a second one you haven't started yet. Imagine, getting paid for something you haven't even started!

Me, I know what I'm paid for. I stand by the door. That's it: I'm a doorman. I see what comes and what goes. All kinds of weather. Got to have an eye for trouble. I know this other crip —, this lady like yourself, only she's in her seventies, walks, you know, with one of those things like a backward chair, back and forth to the grocery store. Takes her forever. I guess she's not really a . . . I mean, she's not like you, she's just *old*. I used to feel sorry for her, but then I found out she does just fine. It's why she tips me like she does, every Christmas.

But you're a totally different story. I mean, you really *do* things. It's amazing all the things that you do, considering . . . The thing is, you've got spirit. I guess you know that.

Quarter after . . .

Like when we decided to go to the movies together. I figured: what the hell, give her a nice time. At first I didn't know how you'd get on the subway. I mean, would I have to carry you down the stairs, or what? Yeah, it was slow going. But you made it down the stairs all by yourself. Me, I just stood there. Mostly I didn't know what to do with my eyes. I mean, do I watch her legs, her feet, do I stand there smiling like an idiot, or do I just look around, you know, nonchalant, like there's nothing special going on? It took some getting used to.

And the crack between the subway and the platform; that must be scary. I mean, what if one of your things got caught, and then the train started moving, with you stuck there, and you'd get dragged? I hated to even think about it.

Or what, God forbid, if some creep should decide to push you, like some of those creeps do, in front of a train? What then (God forbid)?

Then you told me something truly amazing: that people actually *spit* on you. That you'll be going down the street or just standing somewhere minding your own business and suddenly someone passes by and lays one down right at your feet, or worse, right *on* your feet, *splat*. When you told me that, I swear I got so mad I was like shaking inside. I wanted to get my hands on one of those spitters, to grab him (or her) by the neck and choke them and spit in their eye and see how they like it. I almost wished it would happen right then. But it didn't.

From the moment you told me about the spitting, I felt different about you. It was almost like I started to feel, I don't know, *possessive* or something. Standing next to you on the subway platform, with all those strange people, I felt like (wow, this is weird) *proud*, like I was privileged to be with someone special like you. Or maybe I just felt, you know, like the good guy, the hero, the guy who comes to the rescue of the lady in distress . . . you know, not that you're helpless or anything but . . . I mean, shit, I can't get over the way you *move* on those things. I mean, it's not like you *need* any help from anybody. Me included.

But listen (and this is the big point I'm leading up to here): when we got to the theater and were in our seats, and the lights went down, and it was dark and we were both quiet, staring at the screen, eating popcorn out of a big bucket in my lap . . . it was at that moment I started feeling certain, well, I guess you could say typical male feelings. Maybe it was the darkness, or the quiet, or the smell of the popcorn, or your hand reaching across through the dark over my lap, or just the way your face, and those eyes, looked in the light reflected off the screen as the credits started rolling . . . but I started to get, well, excited. And I thought to myself, holy shit! This can't be happening to me! I'm actually getting excited over a . . . with a . . . I mean, she's a . . . you're a . . . Christ, I said to myself: what the hell is *wrong* with you, Dominick? Didn't your parents teach you *anything* growing up? Huh? Didn't they teach you not to take advantage of crippled girls? I mean, shit, what an ape.

Okay, so I used the word "cripple." So what? Disabled. Same difference. Call a spade a spade.

Twenty-five past. Hey, are you gonna show up, or what? What's happening? Christ, I hope you didn't fall or something. Another ten minutes, that's it. Then I'm out of here.

So afterward, after the movie that is, I escort you back to your place. I mean, it's dark and God knows what could happen to somebody like you, you know, with so many creeps around. I mean, I'm not about to let you go home by yourself.

So we get there, this big old hotel on Broadway at 105th. By that time I'm hardly even noticing anything. I mean, I guess people are looking at us coming down the street, wondering, you know, what's he doing with her, and vice versa. I feel like I'm in a scene in some gritty movie, with newspapers blowing at my feet and steam coming out of the sewer, that sort of movie, what they call film noir, which is French for black and white, not the kind of picture you take your family to. Not for mass circulation, or whatever.

The hotel is sort of run down. There's a doorman there, but really he's more like a security guard, no gold braid, no cape coat, not even a uniform: just a white shirt with big, round perspiration stains under the arms. I mean, this guy wouldn't last *ten seconds* at my building. At least he calls you by your last name. Me, I try to know all the first *and* the last names of everyone in my building; I even try to know their dogs' names, though that isn't always possible. But at least this guy's that much on the ball, even if he does look like shit. Or else he just remembers certain people, you know, with things that stand out.

"Good evening, Miss Daltrey."

He smiles a big, greasy smile, then looks at me. I'm not sure I like the look on his face, which to me seems to be implying something like, "It takes all kinds." Something like that. Or it may be just the fact that he hasn't shaved, which is pretty inexcusable.

Then he says, "Package arrived for you."

He hands it to you. It's a big envelope, about as big as I've ever seen. You look at the return address, nod, and shove it in your shoulder bag. I ask you what it is. I can't help it; I'm curious.

"Galleys," you say.

I don't know what that means. I figure it has something to do with the fact that you're a writer. But if you plan to keep me in the dark, I say to myself, go right ahead, be my guest.

Then you look up at me and say (another surprise!), "Coming up?"

I'd feel really rude saying no, so up we go. I have to say they've got that whole place well figured out. No stairs. Elevators all over the place. And where there aren't any elevators, there's ramps. Obviously there are a lot of people like you living there.

When we get to your room, the door's unlocked. I can't believe you just leave it like that. Can't believe, that is, until I take my first look inside. Jesus, what a (pardon my language) shit hole. I mean, not to be offensive, but I've seen seventh-graders with neater rooms. For starters there's kitty litter all over the floor. It kind of irks me, the idea of someone like you having a cat to take care of, like you don't have enough problems of your own. Plus there's clothes, papers, and books scattered everywhere, like a hurricane just blew through the place. Even if the place was straightened up, it wouldn't be any palace. It's only one room, first of all, with a tiny kitchen stuck in the corner and shelves made out of bricks and scrap wood. Plus it smells sort of like fried cat pee, if you know what I mean. No wonder you leave the door open. Worst thing a burglar could do is leave the place cleaner than he found it. There sure isn't anything worth stealing, except maybe the computer, which kind of shocks me at first. I mean, it doesn't look like the kind of place you'd see a computer. I mean, you'd think the kind of person that lives in a mess like that wouldn't know what a computer was.

Then I remind myself: hey, she's *different*. She can't take care of herself like other people. It's a miracle she's even *alive*.

"Would you like some tea?" you ask me then.

Tea, shit, I need a drink. I ask, "Do you by any chance keep any bourbon around?"

You don't drink, you say. "The strongest thing I can offer you is Constant Comment."

Constant Comment: sounds like something you use to permanently clean your toilet. But it isn't; it's funny-tasting tea, with spices and shit. I wonder, is it something all cripples drink?

So we sit there, me on your unmade bed and you in your wheelchair, which is the only chair in the place. At this point I'm starting to get really nervous. Somehow seeing you in that wheelchair makes everything . . . I don't know, more *intense*. I mean, you're sitting right up close to me, and there I am on your bed with the sheets all rumpled up behind me, and naturally the thought crosses my mind, you know what I mean. And meanwhile I'm sipping this weird-tasting tea, asking myself: Can I be *doing* this? Am I for *real*?

Nine forty-five.

And you, you just keep looking at me with those eyelike eyes. I get so nervous I spill half my tea.

It was a summer night, the temperature just about ninety. Your place had no air conditioner, not even a fan. So I was sweating, wiping the stuff off my forehead, looking around. You were there, in front of me. I'm not sure if I noticed them before, I guess I did, but your breasts . . . they're . . . how do I say? Impressive.

Pillowlike. The kind of breasts that make you want to put your head down between them and go to sleep for about a hundred years.

Your cat was in your lap; you were stroking it. Archimedes, you said its name was. It kept purring and rubbing its whiskers against the black and blue marks on your forearms. Something hit me then: it stuck there inside my brain. Then it broke loose and came to me. You lived a cripple's life, with a cripple's wheelchair and a cripple's cat and a cripple's smells, in a building full of cripples. And I'm sitting there, staring at your breasts, getting all excited and thinking, *I'm about to get it on with a cripple*.

"Well," I say. "This is nice."

"Yes," you say. Your voice is soft, whispery, like a feather duster. "It is."

Suddenly the cat jumps off your lap. You bend down and start massaging your leg, going up and down with both hands; you say it helps the circulation. I can see that the muscles in your legs are gone, melted away. All the same, they don't look so bad. "Here," I say. "Let me do that for you."

"Oh, would you please?"

Sure, why not. Sure.

So there I am massaging your legs, you making tiny little moany-groany sounds with your eyes closed; it's all so very quiet except for the moany-groany sounds. Before I know it I can't smell the colors, I can't feel the light, I can't see the sounds, I don't taste a thing. It's all happening in my hands, at the tips of my fingers, there in the dark with our eyes closed, both of us falling down all over the place, into softer and softer layers, with the sheets falling off the bed and me holding onto your bony legs for dear life, your face, your lips, under your arms, everything wet, drying the sweat off my forehead in the sheets, kissing you there, there, all over, all over our faces, all over each other, me prying, trying to get your legs undone, not thinking anymore, not even knowing what's what, which way is up, unable to stop. God. We just went at it, like wild. Like two *animals*. Slipping and sliding, back and forth, in and out, hearts smacking together, sweat oozing down our cheeks, tongues like whips, hands like grappling hooks, clothes and arms all over the place, rolling down a hill ten miles long and covered with moss, then lying there, dead.

Jeez, are all cripples *that good*?

(I'm waiting five more minutes. Then I swear I'm getting up and leaving.)

We were frozen there then, perfectly still, afraid to even breathe, me looking into your eyes, beautiful. God, you were beautiful then. Really.

Then it hits me, the sadness. Shit, I thought. She must feel really good right now. I mean, I could tell we both felt really good. But then I thought; I can get up now. I can get up and walk away on my own two feet, no crutches, no wheelchair, no nothing. She'll never get up, not *completely*. She'll never be free, like me. This is her life; I'm just a visitor. Sure, she can write a few books. That's about it. The rest is daydreaming.

Man, did I feel sad then — for your sake. And guilty as hell, you know, for taking advantage. I mean, I could see it meant a lot to you. I mean, I'm sure you didn't take it lightly. I mean, I couldn't just leave it at that, could I?

That's when I decided: Dominick, you've got to follow this thing through. At least see her a few more times. At least get to know *the kid* a little. (The kid: that's what I called you to myself.) Nothing permanent. Taper it off little by little. Beyond that, you can't be responsible. I mean, no contract signed, right?

I said, "I better go now."

You didn't say anything. You just kept stroking the back of my head, smiling. At the door I said, "How about the bagel shop? I could meet you there — sometime?"

You said that would be nice.

"Fine," I said. "How about Wednesday? I'll meet you for breakfast."

"Sounds good," you said.

"Fine," I said. "9:00 a.m.?"

"Sounds good."

"Fine."

And that's how we left it. As a matter of fact, I left feeling pretty good about myself. Like, you know, I'd done a good deed. Something like that.

So here it is. Wednesday. The bagel shop. Nine ... fifty-seven ... Nine ... fifty-eight. So why aren't you here? I mean, there's got to be some *explanation*. I mean, you wouldn't stand me up, right? I mean, no way would you stand me up, right?

Right?

Why would you stand me up?

I'll give it another five minutes.

Another five minutes.

Only.

EL MALECÓN

malecón: an embankment, levy, dike, seawall, cliff, or coastal highway.

THE CAR VIVA COLÓN "borrowed" was a late-model Cadillac convertible, the paint of which had faded to a blue paler than that of the sky. He had been walking to his brother-in-law's *yuga de cana* stand where he worked, when, stopping to rest against the trunk of a date palm, he noticed the car parked in its shade, and the set of keys gleaming on its red-leather-upholstered driver's seat. The car was parked about a mile from the bank of the river where Viva lived in a rusty tin shack. His brother-in-law's red and yellow sugar-cane-juice stand was another two miles away.

He had been walking slowly, using a piece of dried-out sugar cane as his walking stick. Though Viva prided himself on his fitness, lately his legs had been giving him trouble. Most of the pain was in his ankles, but today the knees were starting to hurt as well, and he found himself walking more and more slowly and stopping to rest more often, leaning against things whenever he could.

Viva was in his seventies — where exactly in his seventies no one knew, including Viva. Most of his teeth were gone. It was the sugar cane that had done it, all the years of gnawing on raw cane. Viva's missing teeth were — more than the soreness in his ankles and the stiffness in his knees (and the stomachaches and hemorrhoids and hearing loss in one ear) — to him signifiers of old age. The realization that he was old had come to him one day not long ago when, after a long, unprofitable day of selling peanuts to motorists, he boarded a crowded bus on its way back from the public beach. The bus had been filled with rowdy young people, and Viva had been forced to stand, squeezed in among them on his tired legs, his bags of unsold peanuts suspended from wire clothes hangers, as they pointed and laughed at him.

"Where are your teeth, old man?" one of the youths jeered.

"Yes, old man, tell us all: where have you hidden them?"

They all laughed, and Viva, having little choice, laughed with them, showing his full set of missing teeth.

He had to smile now, remembering their laughter and how it had exhausted them and made them hungry so that, by the time the bus reached its destination, every one of the little plastic bags of peanuts that had hung from the wire coat hangers was gone, and Viva's shirt pocket exploded with pesos. And so it was Viva who had had the last, silent laugh as he walked home in the dark.

It's not so bad to be old, he had thought then, and realized it was the first time he had ever thought of himself that way.

Now, leaning against the date palm, sucking a piece of sugar cane, Viva noticed several things about the Cadillac, including two large dents, both as big as mangoes, one on the driver's-side door and one on the right side of the trunk. The car was, Viva concluded, most likely not the car of an extremely wealthy person. Still, its owner must have been well-to-do, since a car, any car, was expensive to import, let alone a convertible with so much chrome. All that chrome alone, Viva hypothesized, had to be worth its weight in gold.

Cruising along the *malecón*, Viva rested his left elbow on the door and sank back into the red upholstery. While driving, he made several other observations regarding the car. He noticed, for example, the fair quantities of blue white smoke that billowed from its exhaust and deduced that the car was in need of a tune-up, if not engine work. Still, this did not undermine Viva's faith in its owner, who was perhaps not mechanically inclined or too busy to attend to such matters. Perhaps the car belonged to a well-to-do woman, or to the son or daughter of a rich man, a tycoon who could buy and sell all the sugar cane and peanuts in the world. At the very least its owner was the proprietor of a fine restaurant, or a travel agency, or one of those big, fine stores along El Condé, with huge plastic signs lit up from within.

Whoever it was enjoyed the elements: the sun, the wind, the spindrift that blew into Viva's face from the surf dashing against the seaside cliffs. That the car was a convertible pleased Viva more than anything. He shifted into cruise and adjusted the rearview mirror, so he could see not only what was behind him but also a good portion of his own face, which looked suddenly young and strong to him, with the midday sun carving a bold shadow under the brim of his straw hat.

It had been many years since Viva had driven a car. Only

now, after driving a distance of several kilometers, did he gain a feel for its various controls, while becoming familiar with the effects of motion on its mass and shedding his fear of becoming a little white cross at the side of the road. He looked at the dashboard clock. According to his calculations, he would reach his destination, a coastal village forty kilometers to the north, just before sundown.

Something occurred to Viva then, and he pulled over. Opening the car's hood, he checked the oil and water; he even checked the water in the battery compartments and the level of windshield-washing solution. For a man who had never owned a car, Viva knew a great deal about them, and he was proud of his knowledge. He had known others with cars, mostly old Fords and Japanese makes, most of them so rusted through one could see the passing roadway between one's feet. Viva had helped many a friend change a tire or a spark plug, do tune-ups, adjust carburetors, replace windshield wipers and shock absorbers, install radios and antennas. He had even replaced one fuel pump and one generator. All these things he had done without the aid of a manual, working by sheer instinct, consulting, if he had to consult anything, a book for boys called (in translation) *The Lore of the Motor Car*, containing many colorful and detailed illustrations.

Yet in spite of being as at home with a screwdriver as with a machete, Viva's hands were most comfortable with natural things. He preferred to make his living by way of God's creations: peanuts, coconuts, and sugar cane.

As he sped along the coastal highway again, with the white-sand beach in plain view through the palm trees to his right, Viva's imagination expanded, as did his fantasies. He fantasized about all the places, wonderful places, that this fine car could take him to, countries and cities, some oceans away, others on no map at all aside from the one in Viva's head. The endless possibilities, combined with the brightness of the sun striking him square on the cheek, had a dizzying effect upon him, such that at the next curve there came a squeal of rubber against pavement. Viva's body leaned hard to the left before bolting upright. Having made several swift adjustments, Viva wrested control back from the car again and proceeded a little more slowly, with both hands gripping the steering wheel.

His destination, the only real one, was the village of his childhood and most of his young manhood, when he had worked the sugar-cane fields. His plan, once he arrived there, was simple: he would drive twice up and down the village's main street, past those walking and standing in front of their brightly colored shacks. At each end of the strip he would honk the horn, and then they would turn their heads and see just who it was who had come down the street in such a marvelous vehicle. At which point Viva would smile (with his mouth closed, so as not to display his nonexistent teeth) and wave. If they failed to turn their heads in time, he could always blow the horn again. But unless absolutely necessary he would resist doing so.

Then he would drive off, leaving this image of himself — a proud, smiling, youthful elderly man in a straw hat waving from the red seat of a sky blue Cadillac — etched permanently in their memories.

Then he thought: perhaps someone in the tiny village would recognize him. But the odds were against it. Years had passed since he had spoken to any of what remained of his family there. They were second and third cousins and nephews once removed, most of whose faces he would not have recognized, let alone their names. Why would they remember his name or his face? How would they remember it? The years had changed him. He had grown older, lost most of his hair and all of his teeth. No, to them he would appear to be a well-off, mysterious stranger. A friendly, mysterious stranger.

Still, there was always the slim chance that someone would recognize him, and this someone would report to others, who would in turn report to others, until eventually all the once-removed nephews and second and third cousins would learn that their uncle or distant cousin had been observed smiling and waving from the driver's seat of a sky blue Cadillac convertible.

But there was no point dwelling further on all of this. For now Viva's main concern was to arrive safely. The highway opened up and dipped down. Soon he was gliding past the long beach at Boca Chica. It was a Saturday, and though late in the day the crowds were still thick. In an hour they would be packing themselves into buses for the tiresome ride back to the city. Toward sundown, with traffic clogged by those returning from the beach, business at his brother-in-law's stand normally peaked. Cars and buses full of thirsty people — all craving something cold, sweet, and wet and more than willing to part with twenty-five centavos — would pull up to the traffic light near the stand. Viva imagined the look on his brother-in-law's face when he arrived during what might have been the stand's busiest hour, only to find no one attending it. Viva smiled. Of course, he would be let go. So be it. He could always go back to working the beach, parading up and down its length with a wheelbarrow full of green coconuts and a machete. Three chops and he could prepare a coconut: two chops to split the nut in two and a third to slice away a wedge with which the soft, gooey inside could be scraped and eaten. True, it had been a long time since he had worked the beach with his machete. Perhaps he would not be up to it. Perhaps his legs were too far gone. The dry stalk of sugar cane sitting in the passenger seat beside him was a bitter reminder. Perhaps he would have to go back to selling peanuts. Perhaps he would beg his brother-in-law to let him keep his job. Perhaps he would get down on his knees and cry and beg.

But what was he thinking? He would not have to beg for anything! He would complete his mission and arrive safely home, give the car a good, quick hosing down, look it over to see that it was in good condition, then walk, with the keys in his pocket, to the police station, where he would explain to the officer in charge that he had (the truth!) discovered the car with its keys on the seat and — being a good and honest citizen — had taken it upon himself to remove the car temporarily from the proximity of thieves. Having done so and having spent the greater part of the day searching for its owner (not quite the truth, but close enough), he was now turning the matter over to the city's capable and dedicated police.

Of course, they would question him. Why had he not notified the police immediately? The answer was simple enough. He saw no reason to burden the police with a matter that might very easily resolve itself without their intervention. Why had he taken the car for a ride? Well, gentle officer, the answer to that is again quite simple. I am an old and defenseless man. Had I merely stood guard at the car's side, I would have left myself open to attack, and for the car's sake, you see (and for it's owner's sake!), it was better for me to . . . Also, I have bad legs. True, but then why had he not —

But they would not ask so many questions! On the contrary; they would see him clearly and immediately for what he was: an honest citizen doing a good deed. The car's owner would be contacted; he (or she?) having claimed his/her keys, would then inquire as to the identity of the noble citizen who had performed the good deed. In the next day's paper there would be an advertisement informing Viva of his reward. The amount of cash would be considerable. Viva would never have to work again. He would buy an apartment in the heart of Santo Domingo, with a ceiling fan and an air conditioner. Once and for all he would tell his brother-in-law to go to hell.

He drove on.

But he did not wish to think of any of this for the present. For the present he wished to think of nothing but the sun and the wind on his face and the vibrating power of the engine in front of him. His entire past, along with the polluted river and the rusted shack on its western bank, faded in puffs of bluish white smoke behind him. To his right he saw squat wooden huts and grasslands, to his left the sugar-cane fields in which he'd toiled in his youth, with the railroad running alongside them. This part of the *malecón* he knew by heart, every shack and tree, having walked it so many times and having once, long, long ago, ridden it by burro all the way from his home village to Santo Domingo, with his father in front of him, a journey that had taken nearly a whole day.

Still, watching the scenery pass from the driver's side of the convertible, Viva could not get over how different it now looked, how the sky seemed to stretch further out to sea and the ground appeared closer to his eyes. He looked at the gas gauge again, then at the speedometer. One by one he examined all of the instruments with needles pointed in different directions, instruments that now seemed more familiar to him than the landscape itself. The Cadillac — this conveyance of leather and steel — was suddenly more a part of him than the soil that he had worked as a youth and that had nourished him all these years. He felt his body merging with its parts, his foot melting into the accelerator, his hands blending with the steering wheel, his flesh merging with its steel. He felt powerful. Perhaps his teeth were missing; perhaps he was old. But his mind was as clear and sharp as ever, and the wind racing by made it feel even more so. Even his eyesight and his hearing seemed to have improved. The tires hummed along the pavement. He turned the radio on — he had been saving it until now — turned its volume high, and tapped his fingers on the steering wheel to the rhythm of the salsa music that played. With each tenth of a mile added to the odometer, he felt more of his past being left behind, until nostalgia, sweet and brown as the smoke bubbling up from the stacks of the sugar mill, bubbled up in him as well, filling him with happy sadness, and his heart did a little fluttering dance in the wind. All who had ever laughed at him, all who had ever ignored or not spoken to him for years except to insult or poke fun at him, all would see his photograph in the newspaper and read about his good deed, and their already small hearts would shrivel with regret and remorse. Here, they would have to admit, was a man of virtue, a man who, having been neglected by so many for so long, was owed a lifetime of admiration and respect. Now, now was the —

In the heat-undulating distance ahead of him something shimmered. A glint of silver. Closer, and Viva saw the black head rising out of its dull gray uniform. The police officer stood in the center of the two-land blacktop, his badge catching and tossing back the sun, a rifle suspended from his shoulder strap. His arm stretched high in the air, signaling for Viva to pull over.

What is this? Viva wondered. A roadblock? On a Saturday afternoon? Perhaps the police officer was simply waving him by. But no: as he drew closer it became clear; he wanted Viva to pull over. Why? A routine check. Viva would be asked for his driver's permit, which he did not have. The officer would then lean close and smile and await his bribe. But Viva had nothing to give, only a few centavos left over from the day before, enough to make the officer laugh. And then what? Viva's pulse quickened in his throat.

Now he was within yards of the officer and continued forward at a snail's pace. He wondered: Did the officer know? Could the police have learned about the missing car in such a short time? In that case, a good deal of explaining would need to be done. But no: the look on the officer's face clearly indicated a routine of some sort. In fact, he looked bored. He gestured for Viva to pull off the road so as not to block traffic. Viva complied.

"Good day, sir," Viva greeted him, keeping his smile intact as the officer approached. "A routine check?"

The officer nodded. He did not seem to be in an especially good humor. As predicted he asked to see Viva's driver's license.

"Of course, my good man, no bother at all," said Viva, reaching for the wallet he did not own. He patted his empty pocket. "*Ay coño*, do you believe it? I have forgotten my damned billfold! I'm old; I'm losing my memory. My children are always angry at me because I keep forgetting things. You understand, I'm sure. After all, I wasn't breaking any laws, was I?"

"To drive without a license is breaking a law."

"Ah, yes, my man, but I forgot, you see? I forget everything these days. I shouldn't drive anymore. After today, I will stop driving. I promise. May I please go now?"

He had broken into a sweat. The officer's eyes hardened.

"Please, I am just a toothless old man who could be your grandfather."

The officer leaned close and smiled. "Is that so?" he said. "Well, then, Grandfather, now is a good time to show your fosterage, understand?"

Standing erect, the officer shifted his glance to Viva's pants pocket.

Now Viva became truly panic stricken. It was one thing to be caught driving without a driver's license, another, far worse thing to be caught driving without at least one peso in one's pocket. Viva's eyes darted helplessly, catching a glimpse of the officer's powerful-looking motorcycle parked, just as the Cadillac had been, in the shade of a roadside palm. His previously calm demeanor began to melt away in the late afternoon sun. He licked his lips.

"Sir," Viva trembled in his seat. "I have no money."

The officer's smile vanished. "Get out," he said.

"Please, sir, I am old — "

The officer pointed his rifle. "Out."

"Please, please — listen — I want to tell you something." Viva was crying. "I confess; I did it. I have — "

"Out!"

"Please." Viva buried his face in his hands. "Please, sir, please — "

The officer lowered the rifle. He pulled the door open, reached forward and, by Viva's left arm, started to drag him out of the car. In a panic Viva grabbed hold of his sugar-cane walking stick. Using all his strength, he brought the cane down on top of the officer's head.

The officer's cries sounded distant as Viva tried to slam the car door again and again, unaware that it was the officer's hand that prevented it from closing. He put the transmission into drive and squeezed his foot down hard on the accelerator. The Cadillac's tires spun up a wall of sand as it sped off, dragging the officer a dozen yards before depositing him in a whirl of dust. The officer rose slowly to his feet. It took him several moments to find his rifle, to aim, to fire. Viva saw the windshield shatter to his right. He ducked his head and pressed his foot down harder on the gas pedal. As though gripping life itself, his hands gripped the steering wheel.

The Cadillac veered off the edge of the *malecón*. It scraped between the trunks of two palm trees and went over the side of the cliff.

Still, Viva felt he was in control, though it was the control of a person dreaming. He saw, flashed in rapid succession, a series of picture postcards: of surf, of palm trees, of white-sand beaches, the dazzling chromium grills of expensive cars . . . The Cadillac did a three-quarter turn in midair and seemed to hold itself in suspension for a moment before bouncing off the jagged, balsamic cliff face and landing in the ocean, which proceeded to lick it, like a lioness licking the fur of her young, with a harsh, salty tongue.

Boy B

MY TWIN BROTHER does not look like some-
one who recently attempted suicide. He stands by the nurse's station, trim, suntanned, smiling, the muscles of his cyclist's arms
bulging from the sleeves of his canary madras shirt. With his sandals and his gym bag slung by a strap from his shoulder, he looks
as if he's just wrapped up a two-week stint at Club Med.

"How are you?" he asks shaking my hand, his grip strong and
assured as ever, the grip of a college dean greeting freshmen on
orientation day. As always, Lloyd's handsome face comes as a bit
of a surprise to me, since I happen to own an identical face, with
a little less flesh on mine and a scarred chin (courtesy of Lloyd's
practicing his baseball swing in the living room when we were
nine). Otherwise we look pretty much the same, except that I'm
a few pounds thinner. And while Lloyd's good looks seem to me
solid and durable, mine blur and waver like a photograph in a
developing bath or a reflection in water. At least to me they do.

"Fine," I say to him. "How are *you*?"

"Great," he says. "Just great."

I believe it. Yet ten days ago he lay sprawled across the Duncan Phyfe bed he and his wife had shared until the month before last, his belly full of Château de la Chaise and diazepam, the empty wine bottle and prescription vial on his nightstand. Had Lisa, who'd moved into a neighbor's house, not come by to borrow a casserole dish, he would be dead, probably.

"Well, I'll bet anything this must be your brother, Edward," says the young, attractive duty nurse. Red hair, freckles. His type.

"Amazing deductive powers these psychiatric nurses have, don't they? This is Dana," says my brother, introducing her like she's his date.

"Your brother is something else," says Dana with a sly look.

"Bet you're glad to be getting rid of him," I say.

"Now why would you say that? I'm going to miss him. Your brother's a sweetheart," says Dana. "And I bet you're every bit as sweet."

"He's not," says Lloyd. "I'm much sweeter. There's no comparison. Come on," says Lloyd to me. "Let's get the hell out of here."

"You all take care," says Dana, watching us go.

We float through the bay of gleaming paint and chrome that is the visitor's parking lot, where I have lost the rental car. It's hot as hell in Alabama. As we comb the lanes in search of a white sedan (I'm not even sure if it's a Ford or a Chevy), already Lloyd's impatience starts to flare. "The spaces are numbered," he reminds me. "Didn't you make a note of the number?"

"No, Lloyd," I say. "I didn't take note of the number. If I had taken note of the number, we'd be in the car by now."

We locate the car. A Honda. Lloyd stows his bag in the trunk. The upholstery is hot as a griddle. As we fasten our seat belts, my brother says, "Is there air conditioning in this thing?" I — who asked for the very cheapest subcompact and can scarcely afford *it* — shake my head.

"Great," says Lloyd.

With that "great" I realize several things. First, that near-death experiences notwithstanding, my brother is still as much of an asshole as ever, and second, that in coming here I have made a big mistake. It was not my idea. It was our mother who phoned me in tears, begging me to drop everything, as if I had anything worth dropping, and hop on a plane. "He is your *brother*, Edward." She would have dropped everything herself had "everything" not included a kidney dialysis machine. So I'm dispatched. Heck, I've got nothing better to do than fling paint at canvas.

Lloyd directs me through a series of increasingly posh neighborhoods, into one of quaint Victorians with gabled roofs — some made of tin — with wraparound porches out of a southern-fried fairy tale. I hardly recognize his home, Lloyd, who's quite handy, has done so much with it. There's the new picket fence, white to go with the trim, the house itself yellow like his madras shirt, with cantaloupe and nutmeg accents to complete the gingerbread effect. He's added a porch swing and a red mailbox and wicker furniture. The roof of the porch is painted blue to match the sky. I swing the car past the pachysandra that swoops up to but stops just short of the edge of the house, like a well-trained dog. As we creep up the drive ("Slowly," says Lloyd, "or you'll displace the gravel"), my brother fills me in on the latest improvements to his neighborhood, the new cupola on the Episcopal church (the old one struck by lightning), the first Starbucks in town, the Salvation Army store, which, after years of petitions to the zoning board and letters to editors, he and his neighbors have finally succeeded in shutting down.

"When you buy a house, you buy the neighborhood. That's one thing I'm grateful for," says Lloyd. "I've got the best neighbors. We've cleaned up most of the riffraff, with one exception." He thumbs the house behind his: the neighbor Lisa has moved in with, a woman with a passion for sparrows and motorcycles. "I've offered her twice what that house is worth, but she won't move. There's something wrong with her."

I nod. I live in a rental in Marble Hill, the Bronx.

As we carry our bags to the door, Lloyd tells me all the trouble he went through to get his new patio bricks. "You'd be surprised how hard it is to find bricks like these. The ones they make today are either too big or they're too perfectly shaped. They have no character. They don't make bricks like these any more." We stand in the sliced shade of my brother's pergola.

"How's your place?" Lloyd says as we step into what he calls the mudroom. "Still got that crazy lady living next door?"

He refers to a woman with nine cats and at least one dog that never sees daylight; I hear it barking through the thin wall that separates my bedroom from her kitchen. I also smell its shit, along with the shit of all those cats, whose litter box or boxes are emptied all too infrequently. The stench leaks into the hallway, so bad at times I have to hold my nose while turning the key in my lock.

"Yeah," I say. "She's still there."

"Jesus. How can you stand it?"

"It's gotten better," I lie.

In the mudroom two bicycles hang on racks along with spare

tires, a bicycle pump, caps, gloves, helmets, and a collection of jerseys in bright acidic colors, like flags on steroids.

"Tomorrow we ride," says Lloyd.

When we were kids, Lloyd and I had this running vaudevillian shtick. One of us is a millionaire, the other a pauper. As a snowstorm rages outside (to the tune of the second movement of Suppés *Poet and Peasant*), the millionaire sits by his cozy fire, wearing a quilted smoking jacket and slippers, swirling brandy, puffing a cigar. Meanwhile, the pauper claws at his door begging to be let in. When we were kids, the gag used to crack me up.

Lloyd shows me around his house, each room a museum display with the velvet ropes down. Art-pottery vases and Eastlake frames; wallpapers by Charles Renee Macintosh; beaded curtains strung with tourmaline, amber, and hornblende (the replacement white wool threads stained with used tea bags to match the weathered originals); mosaic tables; tapestries; and stenciling everywhere. My brother's home is a meticulous study of Victorian clutter: no displaced books or strewn magazines or empty coffee cups or other signs of human habitation. The wicker wastepaper baskets yawn empty. An ornate coffin with coffered ceilings and central air conditioning. "Nice," I say.

My brother points to a pair of paintings over one of his three working fireplaces, both minor Hudson River School artists, asks me what I think of them. Lloyd owns two of my paintings, one of a fruit stand, the other of the Henry Hudson Bridge. They hang in his downstairs bathroom.

"Hungry?" he says, opening a bottle of wine in his kitchen. "I've made reservations at an Italian restaurant nearby. You may want to dress up a bit." He nods at my attire: a pair of cargo pants and an army green T-shirt.

In the garret guest room I put on new jeans, a clean pullover, and black sneakers. My best pair.

"Those are your dress clothes?" says Lloyd when I return. He sips wine, shakes his head. "Grab something from my closet, why don't you?"

My brother's closet, a room larger than the bathroom in my apartment: shelves lined with shirts, trousers, sweaters, all organized by season and color. Silks and linens of every conceivable hue, spread out like the colors on my palette. I choose a vermilion and gold striped shirt with cuffed sleeves and navy linen pants — both loose on me.

"Here," says Lloyd, handing me a pair of cuff links inscribed with his initials. "And please try not to spill anything on that shirt. It's raw silk. I got it in Hong Kong. It's expensive." He takes a pair of shoes out from his closet rack, hands them to me. I'm about to ask him if he wants to talk about things when he squints at me and asks, "Did you shave this morning?"

In Lloyd's bathroom, using his gold safety razor, I shave. While doing so, in the steamy mirror, I see not myself but my twin. It's Lloyd who looks back at me from the thin coating of mercury, Lloyd who cuts himself behind the ear, Lloyd who, while shaving, sips a glass of Pinot Noir in the kitchen and waits for himself impatiently there.

I apply the styptic pencil, slap my cheeks with Lloyd's cologne. I slap them again, hard.

By foot, the restaurant is ten minutes away. We walk past an old Coca-Cola bottling plant, recently converted to condominiums.

Lloyd points out more improvements to the neighborhood. "So Lloyd," I interject more than once, or try, but Lloyd just plows ahead, telling me what this or that piece of property sold for whenever and what it's worth now. When we get to the restaurant (Il Pappagallo), the proprietor, Maurizio, who wears a double-breasted suit and stinks of cologne, greets me and my brother expansively and says, in Neapolitan Italian, how he can truly see that we are twins.

"Effettivamente non e vero," Lloyd contradicts him. "I've never seen the motherless lush in my life."

Maurizio gestures with his fingers in his mouth, Italian sign language for "feed me more of your bullshit." He and my brother laugh. Then he escorts us to Lloyd's favorite table, a well-lit one to the rear of the restaurant, far from the bar and the piano. It is understood that my brother, who makes eight times what I do, will treat, and so he commandeers the wine list, running down the selections, all red, of which I know absolutely nothing. Yet for appearance' sake I venture opinions. For my brother it comes down to the Barbera or the Barbaresco, but I hold out for the Ecco Domani Sangiovese — the cheapest wine on the list, it so happens.

"I'm treating," says Lloyd.

"I know," I say. "It's just that I happen to like humble wines."

"Humble?" says Lloyd. "And Barbera is arrogant?"

"I prefer something simple, that's all," I say.

"What do you mean by simple? You mean void of character?"

"I mean simple. Honest and simple."

"The Sangiovese is shit," says Lloyd. "There's no comparison. If you're going to go for something basic, get the Chianti."

"I prefer Sangiovese."

"Shit," says Lloyd.

"Why don't we order by the glass?" I suggest. "That way we can both get what we want."

With a grimace Lloyd summons the waiter.

"The Barbera's fine," I say, seeing I've gone too far. "Let's get a bottle."

"You want your own glass, you'll get your own glass."

The waiter arrives. Lloyd orders a glass of the Sangiovese for me, a bottle of Barbera for himself. I'm not even sure he's supposed to be drinking. Did they give him pills, medication? Just what did they do with him in that hospital for ten days besides pump his stomach? Read nursery rhymes? Flirt? Maybe with a glass or two of good wine in his pumped belly he'll finally get around to talking about it. Meanwhile, we have the menu to contend with. To make up for the wine I follow Lloyd's recommendations slavishly, ordering the fish stew although I like neither stew nor fish.

From there things don't go too badly. I'd even go as far as to say that things proceed cordially, with Lloyd sharing his wine after I've drained my glass dry, and the subject turning — for no good reason — to Paris, a place I've been to once, when I was eighteen, and about which I remember only sleeping in a railroad station and stealing uneaten croissants from café tables. "There's this wonderful two-star hotel near the Place des Vosges," Lloyd tells me, "the most charming little hotel. Room no. 25, on the top floor. You can put two chairs out and sit on the balcony. That's where you should stay," he says, tapping the tablecloth for emphasis, though I've no plans to go to Paris anytime soon. So far this year I've had three group shows and sold one painting. If I make my rent, I'll be thrilled.

Lloyd is telling me the story of some woman he met in Paris, when he was on a Fulbright there, with whom he had a fling, about how comparatively natural Parisian women's attitudes toward casual sex are. "There it's considered a common courtesy," he says, "you know, like offering a glass of water to someone who's thirsty." He has just made this pronouncement when I notice him looking with horror toward the far end of the restaurant and turn to look that way myself. At the entrance a woman has just hung her coat on the rack. A well-built woman with an oval face and long, red hair.

"That's her," says Lloyd, and I know who it is: the assistant professor with whom my brother allegedly misconducted himself. She came to his office in tears, overwhelmed. My brother assured her too demonstratively — a hug, so he describes it. The next day she filed charges of sexual harassment. The campus newspaper got hold of the story and published their two photographs, his with a one-word caption, "Accused." The local *Herald* picked up and ran its own significantly different version, which Lisa read and gave credence to, prompting her to move into the neighbor's house. Days later my brother swallowed a dozen diazepam tablets with his favorite table wine.

She takes a seat at the bar.

"Why did she have to come here?" says Lloyd. "She knows I like to eat here. She's doing it on purpose. I know she is." His face is red.

"Relax," I say.

"I'm not supposed to be anywhere near her. I'm not supposed

to look at her. She'll say I'm harassing her. It'll cost me my job. Which is just what she wants. Bitch."

"You were here first," I say.

"It doesn't matter. The burden is all on me. She can do whatever the hell she wants. I had to sign a gag order. I can't even defend myself. That's how the system's designed, for her 'protection.' It means she can smear my name across the face of the moon, and I can't say a thing since that would be 'retaliation.' Nice, huh?"

"It's a tough spot to be in," I say, thinking maybe *now* we'll talk. But Lloyd just sits there simmering, his face as ruddy as his wine. "Come on," I say pointing to his entrée. "Don't let it ruin everything. Ignore her."

"My dinner's already ruined," says Lloyd tossing his napkin on his plate. "I can't eat with her here. Let's go."

We hurry past the bar and out the door. The woman doesn't see us.

I go to sleep drunk and hungry.

In sixth grade my brother and I pulled the ol' switcheroo. Mr. Barnes, my regular teacher, was sick that day, and we had a new substitute. Due to overcrowding, class was held in a so-called portable unit, one of a dozen one-room buildings erected in the parking lot. As the substitute took roll, Lloyd sat at my desk. When my name was called, he got up, went to the window, opened it, and jumped out. The substitute was still recovering from this act of gross impertinence when she heard a knocking coming from the supply closet. She opened the door and I calmly stepped out. She ran off to get Mr. Cleary, the vice principal. We never saw her again.

This story represents one of the few moments when, instead of fighting each other, Lloyd and I pooled our resources to triumph over the outside world. Otherwise we were by no means the Doublemint twins. We did not walk around in matching sweaters with matching tennis rackets slung blithely over our shoulders. As far back as I can remember, we were adversaries, even in our mother's womb, where we fought for the oxygen and other nutrients in our briefly shared blood — a fight I lost, born second and anemic, the runt of the litter. From there my memories grow bleaker, like that of wrestling each other in Coach O'Leary's gym class, with everyone gathered around the mat to watch us go at it like trained cocks. I still have nightmares — terrible ones — with me looking up from the ground where I sit covered in blood and dirt at a ring of faces looking down, laughing and nodding, having just witnessed one of our Spartacus-like spectacles. My brother is nowhere in the dream; I'm alone under all those faces. The person I've beaten up is myself.

I smell bacon frying. Lloyd has cooked breakfast for us. Wearing a pair of his pajamas, I descend the spiral staircase woozily. He hands me a bowl of oatmeal: hand-ground, organic, the best oatmeal in the world, cooked in the microwave and served with a splash of milk and maple syrup. I hate oatmeal but force myself to eat it anyway. While I do, Lloyd adjusts the seat on one of his two bicycles. The kitchen table is strewn with bike parts: gears, seats, seat poles, derailleurs, spread out like surgical or torture implements, those gears especially, with their shiny, sharp teeth. That table is the one messy area of my brother's tidy home, the one area given over to a passion stronger than his obsession with domestic pomp and order.

Today we are to go riding together. I am not looking forward to it, am dreading it, in fact. He bangs at a lug nut. I ask him what he's doing.

"I'm adjusting this seat for you."

"We're the same height," I remind him.

He shakes his head. "Cycling stretches your legs. Since I've been cycling and you haven't, I'm probably a half inch taller than you."

"We're the same height," I repeat.

"Trust me," says Lloyd.

After breakfast I walk through some brambles into the neighbor's yard. The neighbor: Polly, who makes costume jewelry and runs a little store in town. It is with her that Lisa, my brother's wife, has taken refuge. Unlike Lloyd's yard, Polly's is weed and dandelion strewn. My guess is she hasn't done a thing to it in years. The house fares no better. A Gothic Victorian similar to Lloyd's, it looks more like the house on *Green Acres*, with missing shutters, a sagging porch, rusting tin roof, and paint that looks like it's been blowtorched. Bird feeders everywhere. A motorcycle leans against the back porch. I am to speak to Lisa, convince her that my brother is a good egg, to come back home. Another unpleasant task my mother has put me up to. Wind chimes dangle limply by the door. There's no bell. I knock.

Polly, tattooed and smoking, answers.

"She doesn't want to see you."

"You're mistaken," I say.

"I'm not mistaken. She doesn't want to see you, Lloyd. You *know* that."

"I'm not Lloyd, I'm his brother."

"Oh, come on."

"Would you please tell Lisa that Edward is here?"

"It's not working, Lloyd. I'm not falling for it."

"Just tell her, okay?"

She gives me a "whatever" look, mashes the cigarette under a slipper. "Wait," she says and goes back inside. A minute later Lisa, wearing a robe and a blank expression, takes her place. She has classically Waspy features: fair hair, freckles, a small nose with microscopic nostrils. She is usually soft-spoken and agreeable, meaning that she can't stand to argue and would just as soon tell you what you want to hear.

"Hi, Edward," she says.

"May I come in?"

We sit in the breakfast nook having coffee while Polly bangs things around. The table is scattered with Lisa's vitae and job applications. She's got her degree in political science and has been trying to get a job with the state government. Her small eyes are thick with mascara. Sunlight swims in through the window, highlighting Lisa's already highlighted hair. The highlights flash around her head like a school of minnows. The robe parts delicately, revealing a splash of freckles between her breasts. She sits with both hands wrapped round her coffee mug, waiting.

"I'll give you three chances to guess why I'm here," I say.

"I'm not going back," she says.

"You're sure?"

"It's not as simple as it seems," she says.

"What *is*?"

"He's in love with her."

"Who?"

"Clarisse Dorfman." The woman who has brought charges against him. "He denies it, but I know."

"Anyone can have a crush," I say, stupidly.

"Lloyd can't take no for an answer. You know that." The way she says it implies that *I* can indeed take no for an answer. Lisa assumes I'm not like my brother, and she's right. I like to think that she would have preferred to marry me, except for my income. For the record, she's not my type.

"It seems more like he hates her," I say. Lisa says nothing. "Think about it, Lisa. My brother's made a mistake, and I'm sure he knows it. You both love each other. And you've got a lovely home."

"It's his home," she says with a sigh. "He picked out every last piece of furniture, every vase and pillow. He doesn't even let me put my books on the shelves. My paperbacks. He says they don't fit in. I have to keep them on my own shelf in the guest bedroom."

To which I can only shrug.

"He's not like you," says Lisa. "You're much more . . . gentle." A word chosen with utmost care in place of "wimpy." I have always let others push me around, always. "Anyway," she goes on, "I don't think our marriage would have worked even if that woman hadn't come into the picture. Lloyd and I haven't — " She is about to say that she and my brother have not had sex in (fill in the blank) months. She needn't; I can see it in her eyes. She does not love him, that much is clear. I doubt she ever really loved my brother. She married him because he is dean of the School of Liberal Arts and Sciences and because they both love antiques. But what do I know about love? My last girlfriend said I need to see a shrink, that I have a "commitment disorder." I'm not even sure that there is such a thing and yet am prepared to believe it. But for me a psychologist is out of the question, and has been ever since two of them threatened me with my own suicide. The first said I wouldn't see thirty-five; the second said forty. I am now forty-two and believe that I owe my survival to spiting the nasty fuckers.

"It was nice of you to come down here," she says. "You're a good brother, Edward. I'm sorry he did what he did."

"I'll survive, somehow," I say, and realize too late that she probably meant that she was sorry for Lloyd, not for me. Whatever, I have stood up; I am leaving. I have fulfilled my brotherly obligations, more or less. Lloyd is a selfish bully, and Lisa is a poster child for passive-aggression. They're better off without each other. I kiss her on both freckled cheeks and let myself out into the scorching day to find Lloyd in his gravel driveway, mounting the two bicycles on the back of his Jeep Cherokee.

The last time I rode a bicycle was eight years ago, my last visit here, and then I swore I'd never, ever do it again. Lloyd fixes me up with a bright-colored jersey, cleated riding shoes, cap, fingerless gloves with Velcro straps. He gives me a special lineament to rub in the crotch padding of my riding breeches, says it helps prevent chafing. He pumps air into all four tires, then mounts his bike, four thousand bucks worth of brakes, gears, and other components made by Italian companies with three-syllable names ending in the letter *i*. In the parking lot of a Baptist church, as recorded bells spill their notes into the sky, he has me practice my dismount. "Twist your heel out, like this!" he shouts, showing me. "And always be pedaling when you change gears."

He hands me my helmet and sunglasses. "You look good. Just try to keep your arms bent and your elbows down. And don't hold the handlebars like this," he says demonstrating. "If you hold them like that, I'll have to ditch you out of embarrassment."

"Don't," I say.

"I'm *kidding*."

"I mean it."

"Jesus, Edward, when did you become so humorless?"

"Just don't ditch me," I say.

We ride out of the parking lot. While leaving I note the name of the church, just in case. Lloyd rides behind me to check my form and see when I shift gears. "Great," he says. "That was a perfect gear change you made just then. You're a natural cyclist."

"Twenty miles, you said."

"Something like that."

"You said twenty."

"It's about twenty, give or take."

The last twenty-mile ride we took turned out to be forty miles, after twenty of which he ditched me, leaving me to find the very longest way home. I was sore for a week. I couldn't sit and could barely walk.

"Just stay with me, okay?" I tell him.

Lloyd shakes his head. "Jesus, Edward, you want me to put it in writing? You want me to swear an oath?"

We've gone four miles when my ass starts to hurt. I can never get used to bicycle seats. As far as I'm concerned they are designed to cause maximum pain. The saddle grinds into my anus, mashing my prostate. I wave for Lloyd to pull alongside me. When he does, I tell him my butt is already sore and say I doubt I'll make ten miles, let alone twenty.

"Try," he says.

"I am trying," I say. "This is the result." I point to my ass.

"It'll pass. Keep going."

With that he pulls ahead of me. Under his black tights Lloyd's calf muscles are enormous, like a pair of boxing gloves, I think. Under his lime green jersey his distended belly hangs like a hammock. I watch him shift into high gear and pull far ahead. "Hey!" I yell. For the next three miles or so I manage to keep him in sight despite my asshole feeling as if it's going to burst into flames at any moment. My shoulders and back are sore, too, as are my arms and hands from gripping the handlebars. I keep shifting positions, trying different configurations, standing off the seat when I coast downhill, sitting sidesaddle, or something like it, though this saddle is so slim it doesn't have any sides. Hot air whistles in and out of the helmet, while high overhead white clouds float uselessly in the sky. I pass a trailer park where a lady hangs wash. I want to pull into her yard, invite myself over for lunch, romance and marry her, sire her children, anything to get off this fucking bicycle. Another long hill, this one shooting straight up like a tsunami. Halfway up I've got to pedal standing, which I don't mind since it gives my crotch a rest. But soon my legs start to give out, and I'm wobbling all over the place until all forward motion ceases and I forget I'm wearing cleats and the bike goes down and me with it, crying out as the side of my leg and my elbow break the fall.

"Goddammit!" I shout.

My leg is all scraped and filigreed with blood. My elbow is a mess, too. My body holds so many pains I can't distinguish one from the other; they all blend together along with a massive dose of adrenaline. Lloyd is nowhere in sight. To my left a man-made pond with a dock and an aluminum rowboat, to my right a stand of sickly, scruffy trees. I have no idea where on earth I am. Oh, right. Alabama. A trailer truck passes, swirling grit into my eyes. I finish the climb by foot, then hop back on the bike and start pedaling again when I realize that the liquid drooling from my eyes is not sweat but tears. My brother has ditched me again, but that is not why I'm crying. I'm crying because he almost ditched me for good this last time. How could he do it? How could he go to sleep in that bed with his stomach full of wine and pills, knowing he might never wake up? Did he not think of me, his brother? Did he not see that it was my stomach, too, that he filled with poison? That his eternal darkness would be every bit as much mine, forever? Then to act as though nothing had happened. That's the worst part of it: that he can pretend it was nothing, that it means so little to him; that *I* mean so little. Jesus Christ, Lloyd, I want to scream, shout up at the useless clouds. You've killed me; you've killed me; you've *always* killed me. You're killing me now. You've been killing me for years. Since I was born, you've been killing me. Stop killing me, Lloyd. Please. Stop killing me. Stop killing me. Stop killing me.

A black man with a pickup truck gives me a lift into town. He drops me off near the Baptist church, and from there I pedal slowly to my brother's house. It is dusk. I've never known such exhaustion. There is something exquisite about it. I walk the last dozen yards up my brother's driveway. His Cherokee is there; a cognac-colored light burns in the snifter of his study. I walk around and let myself in through the back door. "Edward?" I hear him say. He appears then, greeting me in a sky blue kimono, his head slicked back from the shower, grinning. "What happened?"

I walk straight past him and up the spiral staircase, steadying myself.

"Edward?" he says. "Hey, come on!" His voice climbs the stairs. "I thought you were behind me."

In the upstairs bathroom I swallow two Advil. It occurs to me as I do so that in my medicine kit I myself have a prescription for diazepam. Among other things, Lloyd and I share insomnia, and we've both found that no other drug works as well. There are, it turns out, exactly twelve pills left in the vial. I take one, and then another. To take all twelve at once suddenly seems like not such a bad idea.

Then I think of those two psychiatrists, and of my mother, and even of Lloyd, and finally, somewhere down the line, of myself. I put the pills away.

Monday. My plane leaves at noon. Lloyd has to go to work. He asks me to come with him. He wants to show me his office. All morning I've been girding myself. I've had enough of Lloyd's bullying. At last I am going to tell him off. I'll tell him, in no uncertain terms, what a selfish bastard he's been, that I've made this visit only at our mother's request and under great duress and that I never want to see him again, ever. Kill yourself as many times as you like. Unless you look in the mirror, you won't see my face again.

We walk to campus. I am wearing Lloyd's raw-silk shirt and linen trousers: he wants me to keep them. He knows I'm angry with him; that's why he's so quiet. For once, he feels himself in the wrong, but it's too late. I've made up my mind; I am determined. As we cross the quadrangle (still mostly deserted at this hour of morning), I'm reminded of another campus and another visit with my brother, twenty-five years ago, when he was a graduate student and I had already quit school to become a full-time bohemian. It was summer, and I had decided to hitchhike cross-country. The campus was in Illinois, but it looked just like this one. Without asking I borrowed a pen, one of a dozen old fountain pens my brother kept in his desk drawer, my nineteen-cent Bic having sprung a leak. When he found out, Lloyd called me a "moocher" and a "libertine." I called him a "greedy capitalist pig." He told me to hit the road. It was near midnight. I crossed the dark and empty campus, headed for the highway with tears blurring my eyes, not sure which of us I hated or pitied more.

In his office Lloyd shows me his computer, the stacks of journals where he's published most recently, the photos in thin diploma frames capturing his meetings with important men. I wait for a lull, for a patch of calm water in his white river of self-aggrandizement; then I will strike: I will unleash the full force of my fury.

But the moment passes, or never comes. It's a quarter to ten. I need to be at the airport by eleven. My bags are in the rental car.

"I have to go," I say.

He throws his arms around me as I stand there with my own arms hanging, not knowing what to do with them. As he holds me that way, I find myself thinking, Aw, he's not such a bad guy, while every sore muscle in my body clenches in opposition to this sentiment. He is a bad guy; he's a terrible guy; he is the worst brother in the world. I hate him, I hate him, I hate him.

"It's been great having you," he says. "I missed you."

I nod. "I have to go," I say.

As I'm recrossing the campus, I see her. Clarisse Dorfman. She's headed straight for me across the sunny quadrangle, a defiant look on her oval face, her long red hair barely swaying, her eyes fixed on a point somewhere behind me and to my right. Then it dawns on me: she thinks I'm Lloyd. As she's about to walk past me, a huge, highly scented lotuslike flower blooms under my solar plexus. I turn, smile widely, and say,

"Hey!"

She walks right past me.

"Hey! *Hey!*"

She walks faster. As she does, with a smile on my face and an élan vital greater than any I would have thought myself capable of, I yell:

"I love you, I love you, I love you!"

THE SINKING SHIP MAN

MY NAME IS Mabeline Noonday Sanford Thurston (not my real name, but it will have to do), and my family tree is so old it has vines growing up it. But we're not here to talk about my family tree, ripe with the fruits of slavery and suffering though it surely is. Though the particular fruit that's me rolled far away when it fell, north to New York City, where it became a different kind of slave-fruit, the slave-fruit of a sinking ship man.

But I'm not about to discuss me. Nossir. Never talk about yourself if you don't have to, my mother always said. And I don't have to. I'm here to talk about Mr. Bishop, my employer, my master (he likes that word: like the master of a ship at sea). The Sinking Ship Man, that's what I call him and how people think of him, though they don't say it ever to his face.

No, Mr. Bishop's not his real name, any more than Mabel is mine. But if I was to do that, if I was to give you his real name, you'd be calling him like everyone else, inviting him here and there and all over the place to talk about a sunken ship.

Tea and cookies, they say, or wine and cheese, or cocktails and hors d'oeuvres. When what they're really serving up is questions. Was the ship really going faster than it should have been? Were there really not enough lifeboats? Did the band really play while the ship sank? What did the band play? Was it this song or that song? Did Captain Whatshisface really shoot himself with a revolver before going down? Questions like that that should've gone down to the bottom and rusted along with the rest of—

No: you won't get me to say the name of the ship, the T-word, a word that won't break the seal of these lips, not if ever I can help it.

"So it's cocktails at five, Mabel?"

No, it's tea at three. But what difference does it make? The Sinking Ship Man's memory is sinking along with the rest of him, and I'm sick and tired of correcting it for him. Let him think cocktails when it's tea, and tea when it's cocktails. Who cares? Long as I get him there.

"This is delightful," he says as I squeeze him into his old suit.

"My pen," he says. "Mabel, have you seen my pen?"

I say April is the cruelest month. I say it because that's when I spend the most time carting poor Mr. Bishop around in his wheelchair in all kinds of weather, be it rain or snow or icy winds that blow and keep on blowing. And poor Mr. Bishop so skinny in his wheelchair, the wind flapping against his toothpicky legs, blowing out whispery-thin strands of his white hair, making him rattle and tremble and shiver on top of his shaking, which he does, since he's got Parkinson's. I get him in and out of the taxi, in and out of his wheelchair, shove him back and forth and up and down sidewalks and stairs and into and out of elevators and up and down hallways . . . in and out, up and down, you name it, I've pushed him there.

He was four years old when a steward handed him to his mother in a lifeboat. He remembers big funnels, the sound of the big horn, white-gloved waiters, bouillon, shuffleboard, and seagulls. He lost his father, but he never talks about that. Three years ago, when the other last survivor, a woman of ninety-five, passed away, he mutated into a celebrity. Now he's The Sinking Ship Man. All through April the phone keeps ringing; the letters keep pouring in. "Dear Mr. Bishop (not his real name): We of the (Name of Sunken Ship) Historical Society do Humbly Request Your Honorable Présence for the Such-and-Such Anniversary Commemorative Banquet Blah de Blah Yours Truly Mr. and Mrs. Pain-in-the-Rear-End Chairperson Please R.S.V.P. A.S.A.P. . . . p.p.s.: Could you prepare a short speech?"

I tell him, "But Mr. Bishop, it's so far away." "But Mr. Bishop, it's a five-story walk-up." "But Mr. Bishop, you've got six invitations already this week." "But Mr. Bishop — " "But Mr. Bishop — "

"Mabel," he says, "why are you always trying to stop me from going places?"

What can I say? Because you're an old man; because you're more tired than you know; because your heart's weak and your memory is bad and your shaking is getting worse so you can't eat and drink without spilling, making a mess of yourself . . .

"It's raining awfully hard," I say.

"They've asked so nicely," says he.

Like they're doing him a big favor.

"They always ask so nicely," I wish I could say, "but they are not nice. They are *mean*. Dragging an old man out of bed to talk about a sunken ship. And what about me?" I'd like to say also. "I'm not getting any younger. I can't push you so good anymore, can't do stairs like I used to. Some of those ramps they have for crippled persons, they're like climbing Gibraltar. Don't you see: I can't go on mountain climbing for you."

But I keep my mouth shut. That's how I was brought up by the fruit of that vine-choked tree. To be silent, to bear witness, to obey, but not to say.

So up I get him out of bed and out of his pajamas (which are full of graham-cracker crumbs: how often do I tell him not to eat his graham crackers in bed?), slide his toothpicky legs into stockings, put on his shirt, button his collar, tie up his tie with the shrimp cocktail sauce stain on it, get him into his one and only suit, comb his whispery hair, brush his tiny teeth all stained sepia (the color of memories). All the while he's trembling like a leaf. It's the Parkinson's disease, but it's something else too. It's joy, because he's happy. Everyone's asking for him, wanting him. From now till mid-May he'll be a hero, Mr. Big Shot. Then he'll be alone again, lying in bed, eating graham crackers and Social Tea dunking biscuits.

I roll the Remington Microblade Shaver across his livery-spotted face.

Out on the street, in front of our tenement on East Eighty-fifth, we wait for a cab. It's freezing cold rain, and the taxis whoosh by, on-duty lights glowing. They hate stopping for a wheelchair man, means they've got to get out of their nice warm cabs and help fold up the chair, help put it in their trunk. So we wait in the icy rain, chunks of dead winter floating like icebergs down flooded gutters. Already it's half past two; The Sinking Ship Man hates to be late. He doesn't think of it as a party he's going to. To him it's a transatlantic crossing. His wheelchair, that's the ship. And out there somewhere, on Fifth or Park or Madison or Broadway, is an ice patch, or a slippery curb, or a crazed taxi driver, or a pizza delivery boy on a bicycle with no brakes . . . waiting, just waiting for disaster.

Four, five, six cabs whoosh by, like full lifeboats.

"No taxis," I say. "Let's call it quits."

The Sinking Ship Man shakes his shaky head.

"Giving up so easy, Lightoller?" he says.

Finally, out of desperation I almost jump out in front of a speeding empty cab, waving my arms like a mad lady.

"You're a fine first officer," he tells me as I help get him in.

Yeah, I think to myself, of a sinking ship.

In The Sinking Ship Man's study there's an old photograph that he keeps and makes copies of and sends to folks as a thank-you card. A picture of him in kneesocks and an old-fashioned hat standing with a lady on the deck of a ship. "Two more passengers for T——'s list, April 10, 1912," he always writes on the back of the card.

The lady: his mama.

Now I'm his mama, or close to.

"What time is it, Lightoller?"

He calls me Lightoller sometimes. Name of the first officer of the T—— (you won't get me to say it, uh-uh, no way). I guess it's a compliment, since Lightoller saved a lot of people that night. I tamp the rain off his face. The party's on East Sixty-eighth, an elevator building (thank God). The Upper East Side Anglophile Society, something like that. Overstuffed chairs and people; tuna and egg sandwiches cut into triangle-shaped wedges; black women like myself bending over with white gloves and silver trays; farty folks having tea, pretending to be like English people.

"Who are these people we're going to see, Lightoller?"

"The Camerons." I name our hosts for the fiftieth time.

"That's right: the Camerons for cocktails."

"It's a tea party."

"Tea is always nice," says The Sinking Ship Man. "Did you remember to bring my pen?"

He always wants his fountain pen so he can sign autographs with it, even though now his hand shakes so bad you can hardly read what he signs. Still, I bring it. Always.

"Now don't you eat too many sweets," I tell him.

"You look out for me, Lightoller," he says. "You always do."

They said it was an elevator building, but I know better. They say, "No steps," but there are always steps in this world. I get him off the chair and hold him and feel him trembling up against me and put one foot at a time, right foot first, and leave him holding up against something while I go and get the chair, then I push him up the ramp to the elevator, and it's a steep ramp (it's always a steep ramp), and then it's wait for the elevator and up one, two, three stories to these people who don't have any clue what I've got to deal with just because they want to have tea with Mr. Bishop and ask him all kinds of stupid questions about a ship that sunk so long ago who cares? When it sunk they weren't even born, most of these people: even *I* wasn't born. Still, they want to know. So I sit listening to the same questions over and over, so oftentimes my life feels like a broken record of a band playing on a sinking ship that keeps on sinking and they just keep on playing and never, ever stop.

We reach the third floor.

Oh, I know what to expect. First of all, there'll be a big lifesaver done up with the T-word hanging up on the door (never fails). Inside, a string band or, if they can't afford a band, a solo cello, will be playing old-fashioned music — waltzes, ragtime, and everyone's favorite, "Nearer My God to Thee." There'll be what they call a keynote speaker, author of the latest book on the T-ship, as if there weren't already enough books. Then, to great fanfare, the host or hostess introduces my boss, The Sinking Ship Man.

"Oh, Mr. Bishop, so nice of you to come!"

"Oh, Mr. Bishop, so glad you could join us!"

"Oh, Mr. Bishop, we're so honored to have you!"

"Oh, Mr. Bishop! Oh, Mr. Bishop!"

You'd think he was a movie star or something. They shake his trembly hand, kiss his livery-spotted cheeks, hug his thin, brittle bones, stroke his whispery hair, congratulate him. What on earth are you all congratulating him for? I want to say, yell. For being on a sinking ship when he was too young to know any better? For having survived, like it was anything other than sheer luck and the fact that he was a baby? Like we all in this world haven't survived disaster? For having lived to be a whispery old man, like *that's* anything other than sheer luck, and maybe bad luck at that? How about getting here today, in this freezing rain? Maybe that's what they're congratulating him for, in which case, ladies and gentlemen, I'm afraid it's me you ought to be congratulating, since I'm the one who got him here, since I'm the one who survived that particular disaster. How about offering me some white-gloved tea and little funny-shaped sandwiches?

I wonder sometimes: am I jealous of The Sinking Ship Man? Have I sunk that low? Everyone knows Lightoller was the hero, not the captain. The captain — he just went down with the ship, like he was supposed to. He would have been a coward to do anything else. Lightoller — he saved all those people. So what am I doing — standing here with my mouth shut acting invisible? Don't I deserve to be noticed? Do I always have to blend into the shadows like my mama taught me? Would it be nice to be a big shot — just for once?

And it's not like I don't care, either, because I do. I've been caring hard for these last fifteen years. Look at him, I want to say, will you just please look at him. For a split second stop thinking about a sunken ship and look at this man with his trembly hands and livery spots and toothpicky legs and whispery white hair. Stop thinking about that pile of rust under the bottom of the ocean and take one good, close look at this sunken wreck of a person, this tragic, old, salvaged ruin you have dredged out of warm sleep. Shake hands with him, ask for his autograph, tear off a few rusty bits of his hull, why don't you, or haul up some coal from his bunkers. You want trivia? He's a fountain: drink him dry. Memories? He's giving them all away, along with his bones and his teeth. You'll kill him soon enough, like you killed all the other survivors, sucked them dry of their memories till they shriveled up and blew away. That's what they want to do to you, Mr. Bishop, I want to say. They want to suck you dry and leave nothing and I let them; I have to let them. It's my *job*.

But I don't have to like it.

"Mr. Bishop, blow out your candles on your cake!"

The cake: shaped like the ship, black frosting for the hull, red frosting for the funnels, blue for the sea, white for the iceberg. When he blows, I'm afraid he'll go in his pants or worse, have a heart attack, die on the spot with his livery-spotted head in the cake, in the ship that refuses to stay sunken, that keeps rising back out of the ocean like a bad dream.

"Look, Mr. Bishop, a piece of coal!"

Look, Mr. Bishop, a shoe, a saucer, a spoon! Won't you please touch it, please feel it, please caress it, please bless it?

"More tea, Mr. Bishop?"

"More tea, Mr. Bishop?"

"More tea, Mr. Bishop?"

I wipe crumbs off his lap.

"Time to go now," I whisper in his ear.

Only I don't have to whisper it. Just the touch of my skin being tickled by the long hairs growing from his ears and he knows, he knows.

Evening. I tuck him in.

"Goodnight, Lightoller."

"Goodnight, Mr. Bishop."

I know he dreams, know his shivering in his sleep is more than just a disease at work. He dreams of a ship on a cold April night, himself high, high up in the crow's nest, the freezing wind tousling his whispery hair, peering through thick fog, seeing something like blue knuckles on the horizon, growing bigger and bigger until it's as big as the fist of God. "Iceberg, dead ahead!" he cries in his sleep. Then he's the second officer saying, "Hard astarboard!" Then he's the helmsman, turning the wheel. The iceberg glides by, like a mountain. Next he's the wireless man sending SOS. Then he's the steward knocking on cabin doors. Then he's a rich man being helped by his valet into his life vest . . . Somewhere on that sinking ship there's a scared little boy who's about to lose his daddy, who he never dreams about. He's too busy being all those other people, and the captain, shouting, "Women and children first!"

I look down at him sleeping, shake my head. He knows his ship is doomed. Don't we all know it? Still, he won't abandon her. Nossir. He'll go right down to the bottom with her. And me, whatever my real name is, I'm going right down with him; I always have; I always will.

I stand watching him dream. I've done all I can. I've passed him into the lifeboat of his medical bed. I'll spend a few minutes standing there watching him toss, turn, and shiver in his sleep, his boat-bed sliding down a set of long ropes, slapping at dark waves, the other passengers rowing him off into his sinking-ship dreams. I watch him, thinking we've done it; we've made it through another blessed day, and there's nothing more left for me to do but go off and sleep somewhere myself and pray he'll still be here tomorrow, that I'll still have a job, oh, dear God, I solemnly do pray.

I stand there watching him, shaking my head, hopeless.

After a few moments I give myself the order:

Abandon ship.

MY SEARCH FOR RED AND GRAY WIDE-STRIPED PAJAMAS

SINCE COMING TO New York two years ago, I've suffered from fainting spells. I'll be standing somewhere, doing nothing, *minding my own business* — at a street crossing or an intersection, somewhere where a decision has to be made. The first time it happened, I froze at the corner of Fifth and Forty-second, near the public library. I must have been blocking the crosswalk. People kept jostling me, cursing under their breaths. My back broke into a sweat. The moisture crept down my spine to gather at the waistband of my undershorts. My white shirt, the only dress shirt in my wardrobe, clung to my skin in ruddy patches as I stood in demented sunlight, paralyzed. Everything seemed to rush out of me then until nothing remained but a cold, clammy sense of my own uniqueness and a sound like a projector reeling. Then my knees went out from under me, and I toppled.

Strange, goggle-eyed faces lowered cell phones and peered down.

You okay, mister?

Mister, you okay?

Someone handed me a copy of the *News of the World*. "I believe you dropped this," the good Samaritan said.

At first I thought the fainting spells had something to do with my father, who'd died a few years before, since his face would always appear fleetingly among those looking down at me. My aunt and uncle took me to three doctors, one a specialist in inner-ear disorders, each of whom drew blood and reached no conclusions. Uncle Nick thinks I'm neurotic, that I should drink more ouzo and otherwise fortify myself. "You don't eat enough lamb shank; you don't eat enough spanakopita," he tells me, tugging down the lower lids of my eyes to see how anemic I am. "That or you need a kick in the ass," he says.

The evening after my first fainting incident, riding the subway train home with the *News of the World* spread open before me, I read, *"A passenger from the Titanic wreck has been discovered frozen solid inside an iceberg. Scientists and archaeologists are debating whether to thaw him."*

I thought of my dead father: to thaw or not to thaw?

I turned a page, read on.

"A Haitian voodoo priestess claims that Hitler has been resurrected as a zombie and is raising an army of the undead to invade the United States. One eyewitness has reportedly spotted the Führer, a known vegetarian, sitting on a campstool in a graveyard, chewing on raw chicken livers."

"A *purpose*!" says my uncle, slamming his fist down hard on the dining-room table — hard enough to rattle the plates in the china cabinet behind him. He knocks back a glass of ouzo. "That's what all humanity is after. To struggle for something well within your grasp — that's *wisdom*!"

Uncle Nick sits at the head of the long dining-room table, holding forth, as he himself would describe it. "To quote the great man Epictetus, *whosoever longs for or dreads things outside his control can be neither faithful nor free.*" Aunt Ourania, Nick's dark little ball of a Greek wife, watches in jittery silence as he chews, swallows, sips, considers. Nick fancies himself likewise Greek, though like my father he's only third generation. Ourania, my aunt, he met at a motivational forum that he presided over, this one for the Greek Restaurant Association of New York — one of dozens of such forums conducted by him each year in gray and mauve conference rooms across America.

Meanwhile my cousin, Marcia, his twenty-two-year-old daughter, eyes me with sullen contempt from the far side of a sage-encrusted lamb shank. Is she contemplating her lost virginity? She is; I smile. From the depths of one of Dante's lower regions, she repackages my smile into a sneer and ships it back to me.

"Am I right, Nephew?"

I'm getting that floating feeling again, like I'm in one of those sensory-deprivation chambers. The dining-room table, the floral wallpaper, the empty ouzo bottles lined up like infantry before the fireplace, Uncle Nick's lamb-and-ouzo-scented words — they all close in on me. Sundays are cruel.

"Am I *right*?"

Uncle Nick swats the back of my head, taps my untouched ouzo glass. "I don't drink," I explain to him for the hundredth time — as if it matters, as if anything matters to Uncle Nick but what *he* thinks.

He carves lamb, forks meat onto my plate. "I don't care if you're fat or thin, rich or poor, dumb or smart," he says. "It makes no earthly difference." The combined smells of lamb and anisette increase my Sunday nausea. "No difference whatsoever."

I await the aphorism, the one that invariably ties the knot on my uncle's dinner speeches. Uncle Nick has made a modest living, not to mention a name for himself, churning out aphorisms. He's written over two dozen — I hesitate to call them books — pamphlets? monographs? all with chrome yellow dust jackets and titles like *How to Lick This Old World and Everyone in It.* The pamphlets are packed with tidy Ben Franklinesque sayings. *"A penny saved is a penny scorned." "If you can't stand the heat, buy an air conditioner." "A fish out of water can't do much with a bicycle."* A person could spend many hours trying to decipher some of Uncle Nick's more elaborate aphorisms. Still, they've earned him a decent living, not to mention all those plaques and photographs lining the walls of his wood-paneled Astoria den: him shaking hands with the president and CEO of Marcal Toilet Tissue Corporation, for example.

"A man without a purpose," Nick proclaims, *"is a chameleon on a scotch plaid."*

By George, he's done it! Satisfied with this conclusion, Nick rewards himself with another glass of ouzo, places the empty in line with four others ranged before the fire grate next to his snakeskin cowboy boots. *"Stinyássas!"* He drains his glass, then eyes my full one with a brave man's disdain for cowards. "Got that, loverboy?"

Does my uncle know I've bedded his daughter? A prickle runs up my spine. Ever since I arrived in New York, Uncle Nick has been pimping his daughter to me as if I'm the last man on earth, and maybe I am. Or maybe he just wants to get rid of her, marry her off. Or maybe he sincerely thinks we'd be good for each other — incest and other small matters aside. Or maybe, just maybe, he just wants us to be *friends*.

Uncle Nick has my father's eyes, but none of my father's warm-heartedness. His daughter has the same eyes. When she and I make love, I close the blinds.

My search for red and gray wide-striped pajamas began this past Christmas and has since taken me from the disheveled, multicolored plastic bins of K-Mart, at Astor Place, to the vinegar-and-soap-scented oak cabinets of Brooks Brothers, at Madison and Forty-fourth. Uptown by subway, downtown by bus, crosstown on swollen, blistered, sweaty feet. Three months into my search I'm bruised but not beaten, tired yet hopeful, drawn but not defeated. Even, for brief shining moments, faintly optimistic.

Saturday — a day of dull, drizzly rain. I ride the no. 7 train from Sunnyside, where, in the graveyard-encrusted, working-class muddle of Queens (zone of bars and cemeteries: a turf war between drunks and the dead), I rent a nine-by-ten room from a retired church organist named Filbert, who keeps a pipe organ in his vestibule and plays Bach to raise the dead.

But about Filbert I'll say as little as possible, having more important things on my mind, like the men's clothing store on Greenwich Avenue, in the Village. It came to me in a dream this morning, while dozing between snooze alarms.

"May I help you?" the clerk in the dream — his face its own caricature, poorly drawn — asked me.

"Yes," I answered. "I'm looking for a pair of red and gray wide-striped pajamas."

"Red and gray *wide* stripes?" said the clerk, raising his thin eyebrows, squeezing into the word "wide" a whole eastern city full of snideness.

"That's right," I said, slowly. "Red and gray wide stripes."

"Wait here," said the clerk.

And that's when I woke up.

I've seen paisleys, plaids, checkers, swirls; I've seen abstracts, geometrics, diagonals; I've seen winged horses, flying fish, golf clubs, chili peppers, hummingbirds, sunflowers, and tennis balls; I've seen bacon and eggs, doughnuts, coffee cups, stars and stripes, exotic fish and birds of paradise, trains, cars, ships, planes. I've seen smoking pipes, playing cards, woodwind and brass instruments, violas and violins, waterfowl, rainbows, puffy clouds. I've seen mandalas, spirals, stars, polka dots. I've seen pajamas of every color, every style, every pattern. I've even seen stripes: pink stripes, green stripes, red, white, and blue stripes, wide stripes and pinstripes — even red and gray stripes. But never, *ever* red and gray wide stripes.

The search goes on.

They're what he wore. My father. He wore them ragged, as a matter of fact, so ragged you could see the skin of his knees. Rayon? Silk? Plain cotton? I don't remember. But I do remember the faint smell of bourbon and unwashed vegetable bins burrowed deep into their fibers, musty and ripe. Though he died just over five years ago, it seems like so much longer, long before Astoria and Uncle Nick; long before Sunnyside and Filbert and his organ. Long before my obsession with red and gray wide-striped pajamas took hold of me and made me its crusader-slave.

Something about the combination of those colors both grounds and disorients me, throws my world off balance while anchoring me to it.

They say that boredom arises from one's sense of detachment from all things, in which case a pair of red and gray wide-striped pajamas has become the least boring thing in the world, for me. For me those colors conjure a privileged, happy childhood. How many boys grow up with their very own private trolley car? My father built it from scratch in his spare time in our garage. Yellow with red pinstripes and varnished cane seats that flipped back and forth depending on which way it was going. The trolley ran on twin lawn-mower engines and had a brass bell I'd ring as we clacked along. We rode it up and down the wooded hill overlooking the brass-fastener and hat factories that dotted the landscape. My father wore his red and gray wide-striped pajamas. They were the closest thing he had to a conductor's uniform.

My father and I would watch the hat factories burn down. Some people wondered how he always knew when there'd be a fire; one man, a fellow employee at the Christmas-bulb-socket factory where he worked, even went as far as to accuse Dad of being an arsonist. But the fact is that when it came to predicting hat-factory infernos my father was possessed of a Promethean foresight. And insurance fraud was rampant.

We'd find the best vantage point up on our hill, then sit next to each other on trolley seats with dampened rags covering our mouths — since the hat-factory smoke carried noxious fumes from the mercury salts used as a block lubricant. More than once, the evening before the factories went up, he'd build a campfire, a tiny blaze to mirror the larger one at the bottom of the hill.

Then, armed with marshmallows en brochette, as quiet as monks, we'd wait.

The factories burned gloriously, with marmalade flames augmenting the dusk, spitting sparks where they licked utility wires. Once, when the wind blew the right way, burning hats flew through the air. One nearly landed on my head. "Now *that's* something!" my father said.

Another time, just a few weeks before he died, for the very first time my father gave me some advice. "Son," he said while bobbing two marshmallows on a twig. "I've got two pieces of advice for you." He kept his bourbon bottle handy always and drank from it now. "Fifty-eight years alive on this earth, and I've only got two bits of advice to give to you, my son. The first bit is: *want everything, need nothing.* That may not sound like anything useful, but believe me, it's *very* important. The second piece of advice is . . ." He chewed his lip, looked around. "The second bit of advice . . ." His eyes went blurry and lost their focus; he scratched the short, rough hairs behind his neck. "Son," he said, "I'm sorry, but I forget what the second bit of advice was."

By way of consolation he handed me the bourbon bottle. For the first time I tasted, along with his tobacco-flavored saliva, the burning amber fluid that was as much a part of my father as his skin, and which tasted to me like the hat-factory fire. The whisky carved its own path through my lungs, into my stomach. With metal-stained fingers he pried a braised marshmallow — its formerly white flesh caramelized to a perfectly even ocher — from the end of his twig and fed it to my open mouth. We went on watching flames — those of the campfire and of the factory blazing — letting their tongues do our talking for us. When two firemen arrived to ask us what the hell we thought we were doing, my father smiled, slapped them on their sooty backs, and offered them marshmallows and bourbon.

I was sixteen when he died in the bathroom, straining and coughing on the bowl. He'd smoked like a burning hat factory all his life, until his pulmonary cells mutinied. I found him slumped against the cool tiles, blood drops flecking the front of the red and gray wide-striped pajamas, which hung from his shoulders as if from a wire hanger, he'd grown so thin. I sat on the floor near him, listening to the last chains rattle through his sacked lungs, then he was gone. I held him, the fingers of his hand in mine stained with powdered metal and nicotine. I smelled his earth-soaked mustiness, the tobacco of his hugs and kisses, the unwashed, vegetable-bin/bourbon odor of his flesh. His cancer soaked into my skin.

The trolley went up on cinder blocks in our swampy backyard. For a while I sanded and varnished the cane seats, polished the bell with Brasso, smeared moving parts with white grease, freshened yellow paint and red pinstripes. But the bell tarnished. Rust froze the driveshafts in their bearings; vines crept over the seats, strangling and finally splitting them apart. Two years ago, the day of my nineteenth birthday, carrying my father's ashes in a gray plastic box with a number on it, I arrived here, in New York, at the front door of my uncle's Astoria home.

Midafternoon. Greenwich Village. November. The air heavy under gray-bellied clouds. A sweet smell of honey-glazed peanuts tugs at my heart like leaf smoke. For a moment I'm at a loss: one of those moments when all existence slips out from under your shoes, when you forget to breathe, and heartbeats turn voluntary.

Then I remember my mission.

From outside the store looks pretty much as it did in my dream, but smaller, warmer, and infinitely sadder. The blue and white sign says "Minsky's Men's World." I peer through plate glass. Slowly a precognition grows, swells, and settles in the spongy mass of my lungs. I feel outlandishly small: a barnacle on the back of a sperm whale. Suddenly the plate glass freezes into an iceberg, my body frozen inside it like a fly in amber. My heart decelerates. I can't breathe; I need to lie down. My father's whisky-moistened eyes shine through the frozen glass. I faint.

I know what Uncle Nick means when he says I need a kick in the ass. But it's not a kick in the ass that I need. It's what some people call ambition, and others call motivation, and others call God. Whatever — they're lucky to have a built-in "kicking machine" they can rely on, whereas people like me, we have to kick ourselves, or be kicked. When I hear the word "potential," my first impulse is to lie down somewhere soft and go to sleep. And though potential may *seem* like a fine thing, stored up for too long it eats away at the soul. You go through life thinking there are other choices, and so all days are rented and not wholly owned. Like buying subway tokens one at a time, or hiring a hotel room by the hour, hour after hour, day by day, year after year.

And as for commitment, to me commitment is a burning hat factory you can never escape alive. Nor does my uncle understand that during my worst periods of floating, fainting is all that tethers me to this world. It has *nothing* to do with ouzo or spinach pie. It's just me and this whole red and gray wide-striped dream that some people call life.

I look up, see faces looking down, their eyeballs swollen with concern.

You okay, mister?

(A fainting perk: they call you "mister.")

Fine, fine, thank you.

But I'm still floating, swimming in inner space. The lifeline has been cut, and I'm drifting free of the space capsule, which grows smaller. Now they've got me sitting up on the sidewalk against the window display of Minsky's Men's World. I turn, look inside, my eyes dead level with a silk plaid bathrobe. I think: *I'm the chameleon.*

"May I help you?"

The real salesclerk at Minsky's wasn't at all like the one in my dream. He had a soft, neatly feminine face, a *kind* face — nothing pointed or severe — almost listless in its lack of distinct features.

"Pajamas," I said, still woozy from my faint.

"We don't carry many," he said with a sorry look. "I'll show you what we've got."

He showed me the so-called pajama section, and right away my heart sank. There were no more than a dozen pair. All solids, no stripes. Not even piping.

"That's *all?*"

The salesclerk shrugged. He looked sincerely sorry.

But this is no time for hopelessness. Ahab had his whale, Shackleton his South Pole, Jason his Golden Fleece, the crusaders their Holy Grail. Off I march to Barney's, to Loehmann's, to Macy's, to Bloomingdale's, Saks, Lord & Taylor, Paul Stuart . . . Like a pig rooting truffles, I snort quickly through the discounted bins at Filene's, then head uptown, to jaunt along Madison Avenue in the sixties, among fur-coated, imperially slim housewives with tucked chins and powdered noses, and gather in the thrilling bad taste of the rich.

Sunday, that most tyrannical of days, a day dedicated to dates with my cousin Marcia, my beloved, Uncle Nick's sullen little lamb. For almost a year Uncle Nick has been bribing me to take her out with me, slipping me crisp twenties in the shadowy recesses of his plaque-lined den, whispering to me, "Show her a good time, eh, loverboy?" And I try, honest, I really try. But Marcia has no manners. She's constantly sulking, telling me off with that soggy face of hers. She knows what her father's up to: she's no Einstein, but she's not stupid either.

Alas, I have no folding money. Three evenings a week I wash dishes at one of several Greek restaurants owned by *her* uncle, my uncle's brother-in-law. I make barely enough to pay my bills. And so every Sunday, after lunch, Uncle Nick presses a fresh twenty into my reluctant palm.

But I refuse to spend his money on her. I keep all Uncle Nick's twenties neatly stacked on my dresser top, weighted down by the plastic urn holding my father's ashes, and treat my cousin as I see fit, with pocket change. At first I tried taking her with me on my pajama search, but Marcia would have none of it. "What the hell do you need pajamas for? Sleep in the raw!" She thinks the whole "quest thing" is loony. And maybe she's right. But I'll be damned if I'm going to stop on her account.

It's raining. We ride the no. 1 local downtown. I love riding the subway; I love the element of surprise each passenger brings into the car, like guests on a variety show, or show-and-tell. You can *smell* the damaged souls as they enter — a sharp, electronic odor of massed negative ions, a smell of anxiety and defeat. The lady seated across from us says over and over to herself, desperately, *"He was all I had!"* I hear my father's whiskey-logged voice, *"Want everything; need nothing,"* and want to correct her. I've no business giving people advice — I'm not sure anyone does. Still, I can't resist. And as I lean forward, Marcia's head, which she's been resting on my shoulder, stirs in protest. She opens her mouth to try to stop me, aware of my habit of confronting troubled strangers in public places. But this time Marcia is too late.

"No, ma'am, he *wasn't*," I say, reaching forward to grasp the subway soliloquist's hand.

The lady, whose cheeks are like powdered dough, looks surprised but doesn't pull away. "How do you know?" she asks.

"Because — I *know*." Marcia elbows me; I elbow her back. My cousin has deep brows and silky black hair and is exotic looking, for an Astoria girl.

"Who the fuck are *you*?" the lady wants to know.

"Steven — mind your own *bus*iness!"

"My name is Steven Papadapoulis. This is my cousin, Marcia." She elbows me again. "I'm taking her sightseeing." I elbow *her* again.

The woman stares at me. I raise her hand to my lips and kiss it, then fold it gently back into her lap, where I pat it like a small creature.

"What is *wrong* with you?" says Marcia as we climb out of the subway at South Ferry. Then, realizing where we're headed, she cries, *"Not the Staten Island Ferry again!"*

"What's the matter, don't you like the ferry?"

"Fuck you!"

"Tsk! Language."

"Can't we at least go to the Statue of Liberty?" she whines.

"What, and get trapped with all those tourists?"

She stops dead, gives me a devilish look, hand on out-thrust hip. "Or else take me to your place," she says. Her lips part hormonally; spermatozoa swim in her eyes.

Patience, I tell her with my flattened palm. Soon I'm marching three steps ahead of her into the crowded waiting room, an echoing cavern of spent faces. On the wall a lighted sign tells when the next ferry departs. The place smells of crowds and sticky orangeade. It's our third date here. Marcia grabs the tail of my windbreaker.

"Come on," I say. "Be a sport."

"You really, really hate me, don't you?" she sniffs. Our family runs to long, narrow heads, and she's got one.

"Hate you? What makes you think I hate you?"

The truth is, I like Marcia — more than I should. She's quite wonderful in bed and can be funny. I just don't want her getting wrong *ideas* about me, such as that I'm the type of guy who takes a girl out to dinner and the movies.

"It may surprise you to learn," I say, seating her on a long, chewing-gum-barnacled wooden bench beside me, "that there are in this world women who would all but die for a chance to ride the Staten Island Ferry in the rain with the likes of yours truly."

"You're right — it *would* surprise me," she says.

"You're sullen."

"And you're a creep."

"I'm also your cousin, and I have deep feelings for you."

"What the fuck is *that* supposed to mean?"

"It means — "

A bell rings. Grappled to each other by DNA, we shuffle up the gangplank.

"You were saying, creep?"

"Blood is thicker than water. Didn't your dad ever teach you that?"

"My father thinks I'm still a virgin."

"That makes two of us."

At seventy-five cents a round trip the Staten Island Ferry is still one of the best deals in town. And for one fare you can ride forever. Having grown up landlocked, with the hot breath of hat-factory smokestacks breathing down on me, I love everything to do with the ocean, including scavenger birds and iron corroded by salt. My father found his ocean in bottles and *drank* it. I won't make that mistake. Far better to be corroded from without, more natural. I watch the dirty waves slosh up against the pier coming and going. The *galumphs* of water against black pylons waterlog me with joy. Salt air inflates my lungs.

"Isn't it great?"

"You make me puke."

I plan our dates for late in the afternoon, in time to watch the sun spatter downtown with gold dust. Smoke-colored gulls follow orange and black tugs. The towers of downtown Manhattan pockmarked with twenty-four-karat gold. It's strange seeing the city looming so giant and silent, the towers like stalagmites and the sky a Hollywood rear-screen projector fake. So much removed beauty, silent, majestic, while at our feet banana peels and scum float in brown, murky waves, and in the waiting room behind us people swallow their daily dose of shouting headlines (I swear, some people live for gray suits and newsprint). Only the tourists pretend to see the skyline.

As for my cousin, she doesn't give a fig about this display. She huddles inside with the rest of the drained newspaper faces, her hands folded in her pugnacious lap, hating my guts while dreaming of the warmth between my sheets. I lean on the rail, feel the salted breeze in my hair, toss bits of pretzel to raucous gulls, glance at my cousin through rain-beaded glass, knock on it, point out the Statue of Liberty. Her sulk is as fixed as the skyline. I go to the concession stand, buy two oranges for fifty cents, toss her one.

"Eat up!"

"Up yours."

I sit beside her, peel my orange. "You know," I say, "it bothers me that you think I hate you. I think you have lots of good qualities." She gives me a fish eye. "Really. You're honest, fair . . . a bit on the flip side, but fair. You have a sense of humor, and integrity — a rare quality these days, or so I'm told. Plus you've got a very nice figure."

"I'm fat."

She's not; she's pudgy. But I like a little flesh. "The point, Marcia, is I think we have lots in common. I just wish you could understand just what these ferry rides mean to me; then you'd realize I'm trying to share something very important with you."

"Why does everything you say sound like a rehearsed piece of shit?"

I clutch myself, wounded. "What I'm trying to say, Marcia, is that . . . well . . . it's very possible that *I'm in love with you*." Do I mean this? Could I mean it? Honestly I don't know. As if to plug up the hole from which that statement leaked, I plop an orange section into my mouth. Marcia looks at me. Her orange has fallen with a thud to the steel deck; I hand it to her. She beats her skull with it. I go back outside and finish peeling my orange in the drizzle. The peel floats out to sea. Then she's next to me.

"*What* did you say?"

She bends way over the rail to catch my eye. I face the water, take in flotsam and jetsam, finish segmenting my orange. The faint, oily smell of the bay corrupts its flavor.

"If you love me so fucking much, why don't you take me someplace decent — like the Rainbow Room?"

"This is fun," I say quietly.

"It was fun the *first* time."

"The first two times it was the *Samuel I. Newhouse*. This is the *American Legion*. It's a whole new ball game." I'm still not looking at her.

"It's *boring*! And *my ass is frozen*!" Boredom: when people refer to it, do most of them really have any idea what they're talking about, one of the most complicated emotions — a heady mixture of fear, loathing, and dread — a silent, poker-faced form of sheer terror?

She leans her plump breast into my arm. I feed her the last piece of orange, put an arm around her. She bites her lip. She has her father's eyes, my uncle's eyes, my father's eyes. The sunset turns bloody red against ash gray towers. My pulse stumbles, dies.

"Oh, God, Steven, no — *please don't faint*!"

From where I live, in Sunnyside, you can see the spire of the Empire State Building, but it may as well be on Jupiter. When not otherwise engaged, I'm here, in my rented room, with its foam mattress and metal trash pail stinking of yesterday's banana peel. Every so often, on weekdays when I'm not getting fed at Uncle Nick's or at the restaurant, I go out for dinner and to escape the funereal vibrations of my landlord's organ. There's a Chinese place a few blocks from here, where the boyish waiter always seats me facing the boulevard, where, under the elevated's girders clawing up into darkness, a red neon sign flashes

STEVEN'S

with the T and V in "STEVEN" turning blue every other flash. For the price of an order of chow mein, I can sit there all night watching my namesake flash in neon.

There's something very cosmic about eating alone in a Chinese restaurant in Sunnyside on a cold night. But mostly I stay holed up in my room in Filbert's apartment, at the mercy of a boredom so intense it turns the fruits in a bowl on his dining-room table gray as if seen through color-blind eyes. Thus I avoid the banality of having to go anywhere. It seems to me, has seemed to me for a while now, that many if not all of the ills of this world would be solved if only people could learn to sit quietly in their rooms. Where's there to go, anyway? What's to be done? Why all this hunger for activity? The earth spins: isn't that activity enough? Not that I mean to hold myself up as an example. It's just something that's occurred to me, as it occurs to me that my Christian name, punctured by a period, turns me into a saint of uniform disposition, an angel in equilibrium.

Lives are so disposable, moments like after-dinner mints melting in our mouths. It isn't so much a feeling that things don't matter, but rather a feeling that what we choose to *make* matter is arbitrary: a bright, vertiginous feeling, like sunstroke shining through gloom. This remarkable yet perturbing sense of arbitrariness goes everywhere with me, carrying with it the seeds of both possibility and impossibility, the need to do so many things, and likewise the urge to do nothing.

I bungle along Queens streets, dark with newspapers blowing. The lights of Manhattan shine upward, painting a fake aurora borealis in the night sky. A drunken sailor — or someone wearing what looks like a sailor suit — stumbles along ahead of me, clanging a section of metal pipe against the cast-iron fence that separates us both, at least for the time being, from the dead. My breath fogs the air. Within a block of my building it starts to rain; I hold my collar close. The wind makes a sound rushing through alleys, a drawn-out moan, a dreary sound. It seems to be telling me something, to want to grab me by the shoulders and shake me, as if I'm dreaming and it wants me to wake up, to snatch me from oblivion and call me a fool as the subway rattles off into darkness overhead.

Then I realize it's not the wind at all. It's Filbert's organ wafting down into the street.

Sunday morning, before lunch, Marcia and I make love on my foam mattress. We do it to the vibrations of Bach's Toccata and Fugue in D minor; we do it to the Tune of Conspiracy, to the Beat of Betrayal, to the Melody of Mutiny. Above the urn containing my father's ashes, Uncle Nick peers down at us, sipping ouzo from a glass as he watches the slow dance of his daughter's unvagination unfold under goose-pimpled flesh. Like the explosion that ten billion years ago sent all the stars and planets hurtling into space, our lovemaking is cataclysmic and chaotic, as if a critical mass had been reached, a density beyond that of all existing stars. In my fervor I forget about such things as guilt and where my skin ends and how long it takes Marcia's inverted nipples to pop. One of us is the chameleon, the other the scotch plaid. We disappear each in each.

"More ouzo, loverboy?"

We're woefully late for dinner. Uncle Nick keeps shedding his eye on me, a different look this time, like this time he knows for certain that I've deflowered his daughter, but whether this means victory to him or defeat I can't say for sure. Ourania seems to know it, too, but she merely looks thoughtful and sad. But then she looks that way always.

"You kids had a nice time last Sunday?" Uncle Nick asks.

"Oh, yes, very nice," I say.

"We rode the ferry," says Marcia through a lamb-stuffed smile.

"Again the ferry?"

"The *American Legion*," says Marcia.

Uncle Nick leans close and whispers, ouzo-breathed. "I give you good money and you take her on the *ferry*?"

"Next week we go to the Transit Museum," Marcia blurts. "Right, Steven?"

I smile.

Passing by Rockefeller Center. The heaven-topping tree is up. A crowd watches the colored lights as golden Prometheus burns, his torch shooting colored sparks that scurry up the dark facade of the RCA tower. I think of my father, who stole fire not from heaven but from burning hat factories. How I long to curl up in red and gray stripes, to sleep tucked into their ripe smell.

Snow falls as I cross Fifty-seventh. A cold gust blows. I fold up the collar of my windbreaker, wait for the ache to pass. The sky thickens to darkness.

"I'm looking for pajamas," I tell the salesclerk at Bergdorf's, a man with a nervous twitch to his upper lip and thick lines shooting up the middle of his forehead.

"What size?" He seems completely uninterested.

"My size. But it's the pattern and colors that concern me."

I follow the salesclerk's dispassionate back to a display case bursting with pajamas — diamonds, shields, polka dots — and, yes, stripes.

"Any wide ones?"

"Wide?"

"I'm looking for wide stripes. Red and gray, preferably."

With a desultory air the salesman opens drawers. From one he withdraws a stack of striped pajamas. Second from the bottom, I see them: a pair with red and gray wide stripes.

"It's a medium," says the clerk, unfolding them. "They run a bit large. These should fit you just fine."

I nod thoughtfully into my index finger, which I've pressed against my lips as if to suppress a painful outburst — something between a groan and the mewl of a cornered, pocket-sized creature — then take a step back, and then another, as the clerk, a toreador dangling a red and gray striped cape, fixes me with questioning eyes and the department store walls (decorated in wide vertical red and gray stripes) close in on me like the bars of a colorful jail cell. Question: how did they kill him? Answer: they gave him everything he wanted. *(He was all I had. No — not exactly.)* I think I'm going to die; I *know* I'm going to faint. Minutes later I'm sitting with a Dixie cup of cool water to my lips, surrounded by concerned faces, including that of the desultory clerk, who asks me do I still want the pajamas? should he ring them up for me? My mouth goes dry. I stammer.

"Well . . . actually . . . I really wanted . . . pink and blue," I say, merely to extricate myself. "You haven't got pink and blue, have you, by any chance?"

Spring. Together with my cousin I watched the magnolias in Central Park blow out again, flinging their snowy branches to snare the sky. The daffodils the gardeners had planted bloomed in sudden affray. By May's end I'd never felt better, only lighter, as if my bones had hollowed, like the bones of birds. I no longer floated; my lightness attached itself to earth. When the magnolia blossoms shivered, I shivered with them; when fat raindrops dimpled the glassy surface of the rowboat pond, my skin took their imprint, too. There was no obvious joy in any of this, mind you, only a great substantive indifference, as if the long, nearly total vacuity of the past year — my year of searching for red and gray wide-striped pajamas — had served its purpose, had scooped my longing for old comforts out like so much melon meat, had emptied me of something I didn't need *or* really want, and by emptying me had freed me — or at least delivered me from department stores.

I no longer suffer from fainting spells.

Standing on the stern of the *American Legion*, sifting my father's ashes into its wake, I watch the wind whip them into gray smears. I toss the plastic urn in; it bobs, floats. *O sweet gray banality of life! O bloody shank of day's end! O bourbon-and-ouzo-scented breath of night!* Under a red bay of sky Marcia wraps her plump arms around me.

Uncle Nick has asked me to go to work for him, setting up

his symposiums, peddling his chrome yellow manifestos. A man needs a purpose, after all. *A man without a purpose is a chameleon on a scotch plaid.* In celebration we locked arms across his dining-room table, drained each other's ouzo glasses, then hurled them synchronously into the fire grate, where they shattered like snowballs. *Stinyássas!*

So I shall live on, lightening and lightening, until my body cells quaver in frequencies of every wavelength and spectrums of every hue.

Speaking of spectrums: next Sunday I've promised to take my cousin to the Rainbow Room.

Uncle Nick is pleased.

ACKNOWLEDGMENTS

Swimming: *Literary Review* 46, no. 4 (Summer 2003)

The Wolf House: *Missouri Review* 26, no. 2 (2003)

Color of the Sea: *Missouri Review* 27, no. 3 (Winter 2004)

Driving Picasso: *Boulevard* 22, no. 1 (Fall 2006)

Sawdust: *The Sun*, no. 352 (Winter 2005)

Our Cups Are Bottomless: *Alaska Quarterly Review* 23, nos. 3–4 (Fall and Winter 2006)

The Girl in the Story: *Wisconsin Review* 38 (Fall 2003)

The Sea Cure: *Carve Magazine* (Fall 2005)

Wednesday at the Bagel Shop: *Oasis* 6, no. 3 (Winter 1998)

El Malecón: *South Dakota Review* 32, no. 4 (Winter 1994)

Boy B: *Global City Review* (Winter 2005)

The Sinking Ship Man: *Like Water Burning* (Summer 2005)

My Search for Red and Gray Wide-Striped Pajamas: *Glimmer Train Stories* 52 (Fall 2003)